TOUCH

TOUCH

NATALIA JASTER

Books by Natalia Jaster

FOOLISH KINGDOMS SERIES

Trick (Book 1)

Dare (Book 2)

Lie (Book 3)

Dream (Book 4)

SELFISH MYTHS SERIES

Touch (Book 1)

Torn (Book 2)

Tempt (Book 3)

Transcend (Book 4)

Cover by Mirela Barbu, https://99designs.com/profiles/1328241

Interior typesetting by Roman Jaster

Set in Odile, Trajan, and Melany Lane Ornaments

For my brother, the first storyteller I ever met

PROLOGUE

Now she knows what heartbreak feels like.

His fever gets worse. There's not much time left, but he's stuck with her, a girl from an otherworldly place, a sad someone with no clue how to save him. Or how to lose him.

Even if she were to brush her knuckles across his cheek, he would still be dying. She finally understands—a touch between them isn't enough to fix this.

He's fading because of her, and she will miss the chance to say she's sorry. Sorry for this end. Sorry for betraying him in the first place.

She will miss everything: the inquisitive slant of his head, his storyteller's voice, and the way his hand would stubbornly try to reach for hers. She will miss those tireless questions skipping from his lips. Especially the question he asked back when he discovered what she was.

Who takes care of you?

Silly human. For a little while, *he* did. But he shouldn't have. Oh, he shouldn't have.

1

Love's arrow strikes the boy first. It punctures his heart, turning it into a flashbulb within the shadowed halls of his body. The impact causes him to grunt and stumble backward into his dresser. Triumphant, the light disappears with a wink.

The girl is next, the jolt of Love's weapon shoving her onto the boy's unmade tornado of a bed. The lovers' gazes collide. Mouths slacken, eyes glaze over, and hearts arc straight from admiration to adoration. The girl opens her arms, inviting the boy in, and he leaps toward her with such clumsy enthusiasm that they almost topple off the squeaky mattress, the sound of which matches their own squeaky noises—*ouches* and *oohs*.

Love stands in the corner and smirks, watching the couple neglect their textbooks to ride the whirlwind of first love. Hands pull on curtains of hair. Nails scratch and excavate moans. The boy's lanky form balances on the girl's buxom curves as they try to coordinate the rest of the act.

So clumsy. So mortally predictable.

But so intimate.

The thought tugs down the corners of Love's lips, pinching her chest with longing. For all that she can sense human emotions, taste and smell their awe, hear the eagerness brimming inside their bodies, she still wonders what it's like to touch—and to be touched—like that.

Being around mortal youth always does this to her, spirits away her reason and makes her yearn for foolish things. Maybe it's because they're only seventeen and, well, for a goddess, she's just as young as them.

But that hardly means she can identify with these lovers, or that she should hope to. They're human. She isn't. She's here to create love for others, not to want it for herself.

The boy and girl fumble around in the sheets. They'll figure out the rest eventually.

Love does a plume count to make sure the two spent arrows have reappeared in her quiver, then leaves the couple to their pleasure. The tricky part is sneaking through the first-floor window without alarming them. It was open before, but the boy closed it to block out the supposed chill. It's tempting to thrust open the pane without a care, like some naughty spirit, and laugh at the couple's bafflement. A window can't open by itself, they would think.

That's the way it goes when she's in the mood to play. Like now. Like always. But she forces herself to behave. After all the work it took to get this pair into a bedroom, she's not about to ruin the moment.

Bracing her hand on the window, Love eases it upward, and the partition gives a slight screech as it rides up the frame. She stops and glances over her shoulder. The lovers are busy with buttons and zippers. Good.

She ducks under the pane and hops outside, then closes the window and waves good-bye to the pair. Strapping her longbow to her back, she sucks in a breath. It's winter. The sky is a gradient of white and gray, with an occasional tease of blue. Ice covers every frostbitten porch along the residential lane while thickets of snow, potholed with footprints, conceal the sidewalks.

Beside the boy's home, decorative, plastic snowflakes dangle from a tree. As the breeze swirls, one of the ornaments falls off a branch and lands near the toe of Love's boot. She tips her head to the side. The ornament isn't fancy, but it's flawless. She snatches it off the ground and tucks it into her quiver.

The woodland town of Ever is shaped like the stolen snowflake she's carrying. The lacy star of streets meets in the center, where a gazebo holds everything in place. On her way down the road, she spots a middle-aged woman climbing out of a car while balancing a tower of books. The woman looks like she was pulled from an archive, with her vintage trousers and a pencil jammed behind her ear.

Impulsively, Love twirls right through the lady, who gasps and nearly drops the books.

As Love keeps going, she passes familiar faces. Boyfriends and girlfriends. Husbands and wives. People with crushes and grudges. People with amorous hopes. Many are matches she's created in the last three months, since the Fates assigned her here.

I brought those two together. And those two.

Oh, they were difficult. The old ones are stubborn.

At the metropolis called Ever High School, the nasal drone of a central buzzer blasts through campus. The rebellious pair she left behind in the bedroom defied the attendance rule today, but their peers are just getting out of class now.

Love stands on tiptoe and peeks over the gate. She has lost count of how many times she's come here to watch the students, savoring these jaunts into their scholarly world, this little oasis of activity during the quiet season. She likes slipping into the cafeteria and eavesdropping. And it flatters her quiver, as the

Fates say, to perch queen-like on the teachers' desks while the students hunch forward in their seats during lectures.

At other times, the sting of being insignificant and unseen is overwhelming. When it gets bad, she comes close to throwing things.

It's like matchmaking. Her work is fun—and funny, ridiculously funny. And so much more that it often leaves her amused yet achy.

Students pour from the main doors, either speaking in loud voices or plugging their ears with tiny speakers that emit thumping music. One by one, the multitude of emotions breeding within them begins to froth on Love's tongue. She tastes sadness, delight, bitterness, fear, desire ... The list of feelings is as long as the horizon. It brews with a peculiar restlessness inside her, causing her to squeeze the fence, amazed by how wholly and completely they all *feel*—even more so than their elders.

It's different back in the Peaks. Young deities aren't as primitive or vulnerable. At least the majority of them aren't.

The bitter taste of a quarrel gathers in Love's mouth, and she follows that taste, locating a couple grumbling at each other.

"Can I talk?"

"Can I finish?"

"Can you stop?"

"Can you listen?"

She rolls her eyes. Watching the pathetic display, she's reminded of what happens when her arrows aren't involved. Without her intervention, the fight will escalate, resentment will build, and things won't end well. An imperfect match.

But even when couples argue like this, life seems less ... vacant. There's still room for a joke and a laugh, or a pure, untainted touch. That must be nice.

Nice. It's all Love can do not to swat her arrow at a nearby lamppost.

I'm an outsider. That's how it's meant to be. That's the price of being a myth.

At least she hasn't done something futile like get attached to one of them.

Love stomps off. She keeps to the edge of the teenaged crowd, steering herself away whenever she gets too close.

On the border of Ever, her forest awaits with its surplus of pinecones and fir. She hops over a mountain of snow, the hem of her white dress sneaking up her thighs and scarcely covering the hills of her bare backside.

The forest is seasonally calm. Time to change that.

Reaching the first suitable tree, she scales the trunk and springs from branch to branch, burrowing into the snowy woods while knocking nature out of her way. Twigs. Critters. The wind itself.

Her favorite tree appears. Love vaults, arms extended above her head, and catches one of its higher branches, lifting herself onto it. Once settled, she retrieves the plastic snowflake from her quiver and hangs it on the bough above her. There. Now she has an ornament, too.

Keeping a single arrow on hand, she stashes her bow and quiver in a gap in the tree trunk, then reclines. The bark's rough texture scrubs her spine, her legs hang off the sides, and her feet swing like a pair of bells. She picks her teeth carefully with the arrowhead's tip. For the thousandth time, she envisions the mind-warped spectacle she'd become if she accidentally sliced herself with her weapon. When fired from her bow, an arrow will fly seamlessly into a person's body, without drawing blood. If wielded otherwise, the weapon will cut skin—never to a deadly extent, but it would take a mere slit to render the target love struck.

And the Fates constantly remind Love of the great irony, as if she'd ever forget: Deities are not immune to their own powers.

Compared to mortals, how quickly would the cut affect her?

Love stops prodding her incisors. As daring and stubborn—and oh, yes, mischievous—as her people accuse her of being, she doesn't want to find out. She's not *that* curious.

There are other things to be more curious about. Sweeping her fingers over her lips, she imagines what it feels like to kiss just as that couple did in the boy's room, with smooth, open mouths. To share a touch of affection, a loving touch.

Gah. What a lightarrow she is, wanting what humans have. She's been working this world for a century and a half, yet time hasn't snuffed her obsession. Deities embrace out of camaraderie, respect, lust. That's all. It's not natural for a goddess to have urges beyond that.

Obviously, this is why she has no friends back home. In the Peaks, she's ridiculed for her delusions about tenderness and poignancy. Most of her fellow archers look at her like she's weird, but Envy, Sorrow, and Anger are the harshest. Wonder is the only one who's kind to Love, but the girl has her own reasons for that.

Who needs friends anyway?

The sun begins to set. She stores the arrow in her quiver and then settles back down, closing her eyes to rest.

A breeze tickles her ears and brings with it the sounds of snow crunching beneath shoes. Her lids flip open, eyes focusing on the powdered branches above her, as a distinct scent cartwheels through the forest. It's young but masculine—and close.

Alert, Love jerks upright and slips sideways off her perch. Lashing out, she hooks her fingers into the bark and dangles.

Almost. She almost fell. That would have been irritating.

If people could see her, if they knew who she was, they'd be confused. Their first questions would be "Where are your wings?" and "Why can't you fly?"

The next question would be "Isn't Eros a man?"

Eros. Ah, mortals and their fanciful beliefs and misplaced facts.

She hoists herself back onto the branch, crouches, and waits. And sees.

A boy.

A teenaged boy.

A teenaged boy with a hiccup in his stride.

As he limps through the forest, the spiky layers of his white-blond hair materialize below. The color is striking on him, and it makes Love reach for her black locks. She envisions how the two of them would look side by side, all lightness and darkness.

She detects another scent coming from the boy, a minty one. The feelings that swirl in his body hint at a certain temperament: peacefulness.

He lumbers toward a tree and then digs through his backpack, the contents rattling as he produces a thermos. Zipping the bag up, he shrugs it back over his shoulder and gets comfortable—and what an odd place for him to do so, with all the snow—slouching against the trunk and unscrewing the thermos cap. He sips and stares into the distance, lost in an abyss of thought.

Love grins. *Well, what have we here?*

She leaps off the branch, drops twenty feet, and lands behind him with a resounding thud that causes the ground to ripple. She intends to jab at his backpack and knock it off his shoulder. For disturbing her rest, this boy deserves a good scare, and she's keen to give him one.

However, she is not prepared for him to dart around. And to lock eyes with her.

2

They jump back at the same time. Love's body hits the tree. The boy stumbles and fights to regain his balance, his backpack and thermos landing on the ground.

"Holy shit!" he yelps.

It can't be, she thinks. It can't. How can he see her? How?

"Holy shit!" the boy repeats, his breath punching the air. He scuttles a few feet away, then stops. Blinks. Takes a good look at her.

Love does the same. Their heads tilt, mirroring each other.

She feels the atmosphere change. Pine needles shiver, as if waking from hibernation, and stretch toward what's left of the muted sun. She and the boy study each other openly, from their contrasting hair colors to the shells of their shoes, intrigue trumping their fear.

His gaze affects her in an unfamiliar way. Deities might be immortal, but they need air as much as humans do, and yet it feels like her breath has gotten tangled up in her lungs and won't come out. It makes her feel powerless. And worse, self-conscious.

Her. A goddess.

The boy's fitted coat hints at a strong physique, though he's not very big, and based on his slender fingers he's probably more bookish than athletic. Snowflakes dapple his lashes, surrounding irises the color of pewter. He's the most infinite thing she has ever seen.

"What the hell? Where did you come from?" he snaps.

Though he's not the most eloquent. His question is brazen, thrust out there just like that, like that's the customary way of asking something in his world.

Those winter irises glint. "Are you lost?"

She feels her expression tighten. *Do I look helpless to him?*

Her mind whirls and destroys everything in its path. He's the one who ventured into the woods without a practical purpose, not her. He's the one who invaded her turf, not the other way around.

He steps toward her. His gait is lopsided yet so confident that, try as she might, she can't move. She's riveted, bound to the cliffhanger of what will happen next.

His attention travels downward, registering her short dress, the thin material wrapped around the crescent of her waist. She realizes what he must see: a girl in the middle of the forest, who dropped to the ground from a very high branch and landed on her feet while wearing nothing but a tiny garment and lace-up boots.

The boy pulls off his coat. She'd been right about his build. His shoulders are marvelous, living, breathing cliffs beneath his sweater.

He holds the coat out to her. "Here. Take it. Jesus."

Love ignores the coat. He can't be human. Humans can't see deities.

Is he an immortal like her? She's heard of gods and goddesses who were dumb enough to get themselves banished from the Peaks over the ages. He could be one of them.

She narrows her gaze. Just in case ... The boy gasps when her hand reaches out and swims through his.

All right, so he's not an exiled god. Then is he some sort of creature? Nonsense. There are no creatures roaming this world.

Love slaps the coat from his hand. It goes flying and lands in the snow. She swipes a hefty branch off the ground, rams it into his chest, and hammers him into the nearest tree. She stops when her chest is inches from diving through his. He doesn't resist. He's too startled, his eyes wide and bright.

"What do you want?" he asks.

I want you to be quiet, boy.

His voice is an orchestra, bursting into that place humans call the heart but deities merely consider an organ. A bumpy sort of rhythm quickens there, throbbing inside her. She may as well have swallowed a drum. Is this what it's like to really feel her pulse?

She smells the earth on him. He is not her kind. Her kind wouldn't be flustered. Her kind would fight back. Her kind would have expected an attack.

And of course, it's not exactly common for her kind to have a limp. How had she forgotten that?

He's nothing but a mortal.

The fingers of her free hand begin to trace him. They *attempt* to trace him, from his forehead, to his nose, to his chin. Surprise slackens his face. Love's hand has barely begun to skate along his jaw when she jolts back, dropping the branch and releasing the boy so swiftly that he has to grip the tree.

She clutches her fist. It's like bubbles are popping beneath her skin. This reaction to a lowly mortal isn't normal, is it?

"Wait!" he shouts as she scales the tree like a bug.

She tastes-smells-hears the proof of his shock on her way up, but it's not due to her speed—she isn't moving as fast as she could. It's because he's seen underneath her dress, seen the evidence that deities don't bother with undergarments. Why should they? Nudity isn't sacred in her realm.

Love hides on her branch. It's a novel exercise that causes her face to do things it isn't used to, like squint. Woefully embarrassed, she yanks on the dress's hem to cover herself.

His voice echoes through the woods. "Hey! Commando Girl."

She stops tugging on the dress, detecting the sarcasm in his words. Commando Girl? That's one she hasn't heard before, not even in the high school where words are constantly, confusingly reinvented and in flux.

Maybe she fell asleep on the branch, and this is a dream. Or perhaps her isolation has outdone her, and this boy is a figment of her solitary imagination.

He rounds the tree, forcing her to hop from bough to bough while wrestling with her dress. This game of chase is a nettling chore. She doesn't like it one bit, not when she's the target.

She listens to him swear under his breath. He must not like the game, either.

"Who are you?" she shouts.

"Who are *you*?" he throws back.

Never mind. This was a grave mistake. What has she done revealing her existence to him? What has she done displaying her strength and short skirt? What has she *done*?

She would be lucky if this boy were an illusion. Otherwise, she's in big trouble and could very well receive an immortal spanking from her elders.

"Hello?" he asks.

"Do you hear me?" he asks.

"Are you deaf now?" he asks.

This is not a dream. His voice cracks too much for it to be a fantasy, and she wouldn't have conjured up a flawed boy, certainly not one with a disfigurement.

The sun is almost down. Exasperated, she slaps the tree trunk. He needs to go away.

"Go away!" she pipes.

He hesitates. She catches the fresh scent of his concern wafting from below.

"Go away, dammit!" she repeats.

"Fine." He swipes his coat off the ground, muttering that he must be going nuts, then curses as he gathers his thermos and wet backpack. He takes a few hobbling steps to leave. Then he stops.

Love's nails stab the bark as she peeks around the tree. The boy braces his foot on a fallen log. He digs through his bag and pulls out a pen and notebook, thumbing through it until he reaches a blank page. She watches his head bow in thought before he begins to write, his knuckles flexing, the ink of his pen bleeding onto the paper.

Minutes later, he's finished. He folds the note, places it in his coat pocket, and sets the coat on the log. "Freeze or don't freeze. It's all the same to me," he lies, because she knows when mortals are lying. In her early years, before she ever set foot in this realm, she overheard Pride and Guilt venting about human liars: the reluctant snatch or quick rise of their voices, their defensive postures, their flitting gazes.

Over the decades, Love has observed it, sensed it, for herself. Either pride, or guilt, or both, fester inside mortals who conceal the truth, and she's familiar with the tangy taste and bumpy texture of those emotions.

The boy slumps away as if she's forced him to sacrifice his only source of warmth. His limp leaves behind a trail of slanted, dragging footprints in the snow, beside a set of normal footprints from his good leg. The mismatched tracks wind through the trees like an awkward kind of signature—his signature.

Love grits her teeth and creeps down to the coat. Digging through the pocket, she finds the paper and smoothes it out. As she reads, her eyebrows furrow.

Cat's legs. Raven's hair. Swan's dress. Fox's attitude.

A climber. Watchful eyes. Violent hands that cannot touch me.

It's some sort of queer list about her. She peers around to make sure he hasn't returned, then reads the next line.

Who is this girl?

And the last line.

P.S. My name is Andrew.

In a daze, she crawls back up her tree with his coat. Ensconced on her branch, she snuggles into the garment, slipping her arms through the oversized sleeves, then holds the note up with one hand, twirling one of her arrows like a baton with the other. He got a brief look at her, yet he made her sound wild, graceful, and sly.

Love wouldn't want to be friends with the girl he described, though she respects the note's directness. He hadn't been trying to polish the truth about her.

"Andrew," she says. It's a name that opens the mouth wide and then puckers the lips.

She recalls his handicap and imagines her hand riding his waist, feeling his pace and the disjointed revolution of his hips, while he walks beside her. She presses the paper to her nostrils and inhales his fingerprints. It's a mixture of tartness and sweetness, the emotions of a troubled life, without self-pity, with nothing to hide and everything to give. The signs of selflessness.

She jolts up and snaps her fingers.

Oh, Fates! *That's* why he can see her.

3

Only a truly selfless human can see deities. That's what the magical doctrine says.

This boy is a novelty. He's remarkable. And just her luck.

Love falls backward on the branch, slapping her forehead repeatedly. Where have her wits gone? How could she let this skip her mind for more than an instant?

Pure selflessness. A perfect virtue that's a curse to her world for some mysterious reason.

It is said that if a mortal looks upon a deity, it's a death sentence for the Fates. Invisibility is her people's lifeline. Provided that what she's been taught is right, this boy will weaken and eventually kill her like a virus—and everyone else from her world. Such a virus will spread from one immortal soul to the next, starting with the first deity reflected within that mortal's eyes: Love. She will fade first. And every deity she has ever crossed paths with—in other words, all of them—will follow.

The mist becomes thick enough to swallow. The trees march and close in on Love. She has to tell the Court about this boy. What's she waiting for?

If I tell my people, they will destroy Andrew.

That's the problem. Annihilating him would work like an antidote and fix this, but the very thought takes a bite out of her.

Not that she's worried about him in particular. She's merely *in the zone* of worry. He means nothing to Love personally, but humans are considered sacred. She has to be sure before she opens her big mouth. She can't be rash about this. Because maybe . . . Maybe there's another explanation for him.

Why was he even in the woods today? In the wintertime?

She should seek him out and learn more, determine for certain what she's dealing with. Assuming there is no other explanation for Andrew, being near him doesn't make a difference. He's already seen her. Her existence is sealed in his memory, so the damage is done.

Love gulps down her fear, reminding herself that this isn't the end. The Fate Court can wipe out Andrew in a millisecond and cure her.

Still, she broods until morning, at which point she grows cranky. She requires half the sleep that humans do, and she doesn't get hungry as often, but she didn't get the smallest wink, and her stomach is hollow. If she weren't such a dimwit, she would have thought of retiring to her glass cottage last night, to eat and rest. Deeper into the woods, there's a small dwelling, invisible to mortals, where she's meant to spend her days while in this town. Every archer gets a new home wherever they're assigned, but she doesn't spend many hours there. Although tailored to suit her basic needs, the cottage isn't truly hers. Everything within its translucent walls was created by the Fates, not by Love. She likes this tree better, this place of her own choosing, with its little ornament hanging above her.

Morning turns into midday. Time to manage this nuisance of a boy.

It's a Saturday. He should be home.

Draped in his coat, with the note in her pocket, she descends the tree—he's not a love target, so there's no need to bring her weapons along—and journeys back into the world of pens and paper. She tries to navigate the residential streets, but she has no clue where to find Andrew. She needs to get closer in order to sniff him out.

Love passes rusty mailboxes with enamel handles. Frustrated, she slaps down their metal mouths, leaving them hanging open while her boots mow through slush.

And then, amidst the charred odor of stress and the floral scent of melancholy drifting out from the homes, she catches the current of Andrew's minty boy-woven smell. She follows it and finds him. He's tying a scarf around his neck, his backpack looped over his shoulder as he clumps down the walkway of a paint-chipped house.

Covert observation is best. Love hides behind a giant family car parked on the sidewalk.

A man sticks his leathery face out the front door of Andrew's house. She guesses he's the father, but she thinks again. That can't be right, for this man doesn't possess Andrew's gray irises or impressive shoulders. This man has black marble eyes, muddy brown curls, and a neck as long as a beanstalk.

She recognizes the sour taste and grating sound of rancor. She doesn't approve of Andrew living here. Knowing that he does gives her a bad feeling, which is comical. Love has no business feeling protective of him.

"Don't you walk away without answering me," the man barks. "I said, what happened to that coat of yours?"

Love draws the coat closer to her body while surveying Andrew's meager replacement. It's a threadbare jacket, hardly like the woolen options people wear in town and at school. He sacrificed his comfort for her, unaware that she doesn't need it.

Cold and heat are enigmas to deities.

Pausing on the sidewalk, Andrew turns toward the man. "Gave it away."

"You dumbass. There's a fine line between charity and stupidity."

Indignant, Love releases her hold on the coat. Charity?

"Can't do anything right." The man thrusts out his hand as though to say, *Good riddance*. Love sees the residue of bitterness on his fingers. It occurs to her that he could be the one responsible for Andrew's limp.

She curls her mouth as she fantasizes about ways to repay the man, but abusing power is a despicable act, one the Fate Court doesn't take lightly. It's judged and punished more harshly than, say, impishness.

The front door slams again. Andrew waits, watches the house cautiously—for what? For the man to come back out?

When the moment has passed, Andrew sets down his backpack, gathers snow, and forms it into a ball. One long look at it, and then he's hurling it at one of the windows. The snowball throttles the partition hard enough to make it rattle.

Loves wishes that he'd aimed the snowball at the man's head. She would have clapped.

Andrew slumps. He grabs his bag and ambles away. She follows him as he tramps through town, hands tunneled into his pockets. She can't see his face, but if the distance bothers his leg, his senses don't give him away.

He stops once. A complete stop. An attentive stop, as if struck by something.

Love takes cover in the arms of a bush. Instead of turning around to see if he's being followed, he cocks his head in the direction of the woods, to where evergreens spear the sky. The fascinated look rolling down his profile as he regards the trees chases away her concentration. Could he be thinking of her?

Inexplicably, there's a slight and sudden fogginess to his emotions. She's unable to grasp what he's feeling, for his senses flicker on and off. Unusual ... Or not.

Andrew turns away from the forest and keeps going. She pursues him as he crosses into the square, then ascends the stoop of a house located off the main thoroughfare. The house has been converted into a bookstore, and the swinging sign by the steps says, *Ever Stories, Rare and Used.*

Love considers flipping the *Open* sign to *Closed* for immortal kicks. In her last domain, she liked to remove parking tickets from the windshields of cars. In another region, she pranced after her targets, monitoring their courtship in a grocery store while placing random items into people's shopping carts. Humans are entertaining creatures when they're inconvenienced.

Andrew practically skips up the steps. His healthy pace signals he's relieved to be here.

She leaves the sign alone.

He wipes snow off his shoulders and disappears into the yoke of light oozing through the entrance. Love peeps into the window before slinking past the front door.

She hasn't set foot in here before. The place is small and old-fashioned, with wood paneling and decorative props scattered around. There's a typewriter, compact and made of navy-blue metal, on a table displaying poetry collections. A box radio with embedded speakers and round knobs sits on the floor. A nonworking wood stove occupies the main room, which connects to other rooms shelved with books.

A jazz tune bustles out from overhead speakers, brass instruments skipping across the shop. A scratchy voice sings about *his baby, his lady, his gal.*

The doorway to her right leads to the children's section and the register where a woman sits at a counter. She looks to be in her mid-forties, but there's a nostalgic side to her wardrobe, and she pulls it off well. Not many human women can make a brooch look chic. Actually, her face and vintage men's trousers are familiar.

When Love notices the pencil wedged above the woman's ear, she remembers. Ha! This is the mortal she'd walked through the day before, right after she matched that teenage couple. The woman who was carrying all those books.

She must be the shopkeeper. She's perched on a barstool, scanning the pages of a book. Love steps behind her and is about to read along, but without warning the woman stiffens and spins in her chair. Her eyes probe the space between them, bemused and searching. Love inhales sharply. The moment lasts a second, but it's enough to leave her shaken after the woman glides back around, rubbing the back of her neck.

Certain humans display a sixth sense about deities, especially when Love struts through their bodies or hovers behind them. This usually diverts her.

Today, it's bad timing. Love's too skittish to enjoy it.

An adjacent door opens. At the flash of white hair, she twirls away and makes an elegant—she flatters herself—flying leap around the corner. Landing on the other side, she peeks as best as she can. Scarfless and jacketless now, Andrew emerges from what appears to be a stock closet.

"Morning, boss," he announces.

"Morning, kiddo," the shopkeeper answers, poking his side with her pencil eraser. "You keeping out of trouble?"

He smirks to himself. "Unless *trouble* finds *me*."

The shopkeeper peers at him. "You've met a girl."

Love balks at her observation, then fears Andrew might tell the woman about their encounter yesterday, then reminds herself that he has the opportunity to meet lots of girls. This might not be about Love at all.

Andrew scoffs in response. "What have you been reading?"

"Kiddo, I have magic eyes. I notice everything. Besides that, you're flushed. You're never flushed. Looks to me like trouble is a girl." She fans herself with dramatic pride. "I'll tell you what, I've been waiting for this day."

"Magic eyes? You need to cut back on the fantasy paperbacks."

"Then stop recommending them to me," the woman remarks, losing some of her humor.

"You okay, boss?" Andrew asks.

"Is there a window open? I feel a pocket of cold air hovering around. Felt it yesterday, too, just like a ghost blasted through me."

Love braces herself, gripping the corner of the wall.

A frown gathers on Andrew's face, but he shrugs. "Ghosts happen. I hear people become more sensitive to paranormal stuff as they age. As the *people* age, not the ghosts."

The woman laughs and shoos him away. "Oh, go be an employee if you're not going to humor me."

"I haven't met a girl."

"You lie. Dust some nonfiction while you're at it. It'll serve you right."

The workday commences. As the hours pass, the woman rings up customers—balding men, and mothers with wind-up toys for children who sprint around the place saying, *no no no no no no*—Andrew mends tattered books and stocks new ones. Love moves soundlessly and swiftly on her feet, dropping and hopping and springing out of the way whenever he approaches.

It's a boon that he moves slowly, hindered by his leg and engrossed in the books. One notable shelf catches his attention. His eyes narrow as he scans the titles, then he makes his selection and flips through the pages as he saunters away. She can't get close enough to see the text, so Love checks out the shelf.

A Guide to Ghosts and Spirits of the Real World, Volume III.

When the Sun Goes Down: Neighborhood Faeries, or Tricksters with Teeth.

Beyond the Myths: An Annotated Journey.

Coincidence after meeting her? Doubtful.

He studies a particular passage while rounding corner and collides with a girl, knocking her armful of purchases to the floor. From a clandestine spot behind him, Love watches the pair. The creased paperbacks, as well as the phone the girl had been whispering into, litter the ground by their feet.

"Oh!" the girl says.

"Shit. Sorry, I—," he sputters.

The girl is his age. She's attractive, with a waterfall of honey-colored hair cascading down the back of her fur-lined jacket. Her upper lip arches toward her nose, revealing a slight wall of teeth.

A guy's voice peels through her phone. She swipes it off the floor and says, "Gotta go," and then, "No one" before hanging up.

Andrew kneels to help collect the books. "I didn't mean to—"

"No, no, it's fine," she insists, batting him away from the novels, pink racing across her cheeks. The covers of the paperbacks exhibit half-naked bodies in hyperbolic embraces. Other covers show teen couples mooning at each other and holding hands.

"Seriously, it's fine," the girl protests again, swinging her arm out and gathering the novels in one industrious move. She stands, clutching the books to her chest, and takes inventory of his features as he staggers to his feet. "Oh, hey. Um, Andrew, right?" Her confidence grows back like a plant. "I'm Holly. Wow. This is, like, déjà vu. Are we destined to do this a lot?" she asks in amusement, her berry scent hinting at a tendency toward friendliness.

She's easy to read. But for the second time today, Love fails to comprehend Andrew's emotions.

Not good.

From what the girl said, it seems these two mortals share a memory. Yet Andrew doesn't say anything. Why is he looking at the girl like she's made of sugar?

"Hey, it was no big deal," she assures him. "I mean, the last time. My ankle's fine."

Again, no response. Her eyes dart off to the side, her mouth quirking the way mortal mouths do when confronted with a sufficiently weird reaction.

"Okayyy," Holly draws out. "Well, see you around school, I guess."

She prances toward the register while Andrew shuffles in place. He retrieves his book on paranormal phenomena off the floor, but he doesn't open it again. Eventually, he puts it back on the shelf.

The shopkeeper pokes her head into the room and gives him a knowing look. Her expression asks, *Was that the girl?*

Andrew rolls his eyes, color riding up his neck. "Cut it out."

The woman disappears with a chuckle, but Love doesn't see what's so funny. That girl knew Andrew's name, and he acted mesmerized by this fact. Replaying the whole scene bothers Love. Inexplicably, she feels a spark of rivalry toward that girl. That Holly.

She investigates the romance section where Holly came

from and plucks a novel off the shelf, then pauses, thinking of the beautiful girl holding all those paperbacks.

With a huff, Love thrusts the book back into its slot and starts to walk away.

Damn. She flips back around, grabs the book again, and dumps it into her coat pocket.

By then, it's time for Andrew to go home. As he wrestles into his pathetic jacket, the shopkeeper watches him out of the corner of her eye. "Need a ride, kiddo?"

"Nah. I'm fine," he replies.

"It's getting dark. Slippery streets."

"It's not like I live far."

"In this town, who the hell lives far?"

Love bites her lip to quell her grin. She likes this woman, despite her disquieting reaction to Love's proximity and the way she teased Andrew about Holly.

The woman points her pencil at him. "Breezes and ghosts, remember? They could be out there. I'm a believer. I can't help worrying about what's following you." When Andrew refuses a second offer of a ride home, she grunts. "At least tell me you're keeping warm in that getup."

"No."

"Well, tell your father to do something about that."

Andrew offers her a weary salute. "Stepfather," he corrects, and then leaves.

Love trails him home, recapping the day's biggest clues. Andrew is possibly researching her, which will get him nowhere since he's limited to mortal texts. It's not much, but it's worth keeping track of.

More important, her sensory connection to him is waning. Not to anyone else, just him.

Wait. What are those smells? Emotions colliding, but eliciting what?

Competitiveness. That's what.

She realizes that Andrew has taken a different route, perhaps a shortcut, through a park. He passes a pair of boys his age, who stop talking when they see him, enticed by his unexpected presence. The larger of the two has bulky arms that shift beneath his athletic jacket, and his brutal expression makes him look beastly. His eyes prowl Andrew while his troll of a friend snickers.

Andrew's limp gets worse. He keeps his head down as if he doesn't see them, but he knows. Love knows that he knows.

The landscape is so fraught with cold that there's no one around except Andrew.

And these boys, who begin to follow him.

4

Boys are stupid. That's all there is to it.

It happens at the edge of the park, near an empty playground and a rusted swing set. So many sensations assault Love at once that it's hard to sift through them. The leftover candied taste of joy from a seesaw. The stench of someone's inclination toward territoriality.

Behind Andrew's back, the beastly boy pauses beneath the glare of a streetlamp. Love narrows her eyes. *Contain yourself, beastly boy.*

The troll at his side is a nonentity until she considers his wicked leer and paddle-sized hands, which are out of proportion to the rest of him.

With the sky getting darker, the atmosphere shrugs off its wintry calm and puts up its fists. The beastly boy treks toward his prey, with his troll marching beside him.

They flank Andrew quickly. Humans can be mighty fast when they want something.

"What's up, Andy?" the beast says while the troll flicks his cigarette at Andrew's feet.

Love wrinkles her nose in disgust. Nicknames. If they're not meant to be sappy, they're meant to belittle.

Andrew looks everywhere but at his predators. Love has

learned from her people the importance of eye contact. She would lecture Andrew about it if she weren't busy picking a rock off the ground and squeezing it in her hand, just to have something to do.

"Not trying to run?" the beastly boy asks. "That's brave."

Andrew shoots him a sidelong glare that appears to say, *Yeah, it is.*

She closes her eyes, scavenging for emotional signs from him, but again she finds none. She does, however, locate his pulse. His heartbeat falters, a tender heartbeat that drives Love crazy during the split second that she hears it. The rock shatters in her grip and powders to the ground.

They will not touch him.

Yes, they will if they want. It's against the rules for her to interfere with mortal dealings unless it has to do with matchmaking. Taming beasts is Anger's job. Not that Ever is his jurisdiction. He's stationed in one of those cities known for having lots of traffic, where he's trying to pacify the hysterical tailgaters of this country.

"Got nothing to say?" the beastly boy asks. "I thought we could be buddies, but see, I don't understand some stuff. Like why you got a problem with my girl. Thanks for twisting her ankle in front of everybody at the rally. She was pretty embarrassed about it."

Ah. In the bookstore, beautiful Holly mentioned something about an earlier incident between her and Andrew, something about her ankle. Is she the one this beastly boy is talking about?

Andrew grimaces but stays quiet. Wise move, Love thinks. It's better not to contradict his adversary. It would only sharpen the beast's incisors, and it wouldn't change a thing.

"He shows up wherever Holly is," the troll remarks.

The beast spreads his arms. "We've talked about this, haven't we? Haven't we had nice talks?"

"Nice?" Andrew repeats.

"You don't think I know how to be nice?"

"I didn't even know you could pronounce it."

Love drops her head into her hands. Brainless, blasted boy!

The beast's jaw clenches. "What's not nice is getting in my girl's way all the time. I was on the phone with her not too long ago, and whadda you know, you two bumped into each other again."

Love recalls Holly talking on the phone in the bookshop. She's indeed the girl in question.

"She hung up on me, then called back and said you rammed into her in some store."

"I work there," Andrew points out.

"And you work real hard to get in her way. You hear me, *cripple*?" The boy punctuates the last word by shoving Andrew, and he doesn't stop. "You need to watch where you're *going*. Were you trying to get her *attention*? You want my *girl*?"

Shove. Shove. Shove.

"Like you have a chance with her," the boy hoots. "What a waste you are. From what I hear, your old man thinks so, too."

Andrew shoves back, plowing the beastly boy into his friend. They stumble, but Andrew isn't fast enough to dodge the beast's answering blow. It cracks into the side of Andrew's face. He manages to duck the next punch and backhand his opponent, busting the guy's lip, but then the troll takes Andrew and his backpack down by sweeping under his bad leg.

Love seethes, forcing herself to be still, reminding herself that she cannot intervene. She simply cannot!

The beast kicks Andrew in the stomach, making him keel

over and cough into the snow. Love rips a metal bar off a bike stand. She lunges, strikes, and twists away so fast the boys barely see the object flying toward them, but oh, do they feel its impact. The bar flips and pivots. It pitches the beast sideways, sending him spinning into the snow, and before he's landed, she wheels and stabs the makeshift weapon into the troll's ribcage. He hunches over with a grunt. She lashes at the backs of his knees, sending him on top of his friend.

She falls into a crouch, blocking the boys from Andrew. They belt out a string of curses, the beastly boy spitting the word *loser* as they flee the playground.

Love whips her head over her shoulder to see if Andrew's all right. He's on his back, braced up on his forearms and gaping at her in disbelief—or maybe revulsion. Maybe he thinks she's no better than those boys. Maybe she isn't.

They stare at each other, clouds of frost popping from their mouths as winter returns to its normal, silent self. He's looking at her intently, consuming the details that don't belong in this world. She's caught in the net of his gaze like an animal. It's her own fault. She brought this on herself.

She drops the bar, surges to her feet, and runs, feeling her heels kick up snow as she bolts into the forest. She scrambles up a tree near a bridge that arcs over a dry brook. Shielded from view, she counts to ten.

He's there by the time she finishes. His breathing sounds as though his mouth has been plugged for centuries until now. He's clutching his stomach, hurting but relentless.

Love growls. She should have outrun him, but she wasn't fast enough—same as when she'd climbed the tree in front of him the day before. Her powers are intact with everyone but Andrew. Perhaps this is the unpleasant beginning of her end.

He halts at the threshold of the bridge, his eyes tracing the branches, his silence a pesky thing that can't be deciphered. To human psychology, emotions and feelings are different.

But the Fates determine what's what, not humans.

To the Fates, emotions and feelings, body and mind, are the same thing. Deities have the power to sense them in mortals, and for that reason, Love is also skilled at interpreting mood. Yet without emotional cues, she is lost. And she is not a mind reader, dammit!

"Why do you pull this crap and then jet on me?" Andrew shouts. When she makes no reply, he turns to leave. "Whatever. Thanks for the help, but I didn't need it."

"Yes, you fool. You did!"

He wheels around. "She speaks."

Love blinks, realizing he baited her on purpose. "He tricks."

"He does," Andrew answers. "He also has questions. Lots of them."

"She isn't going to answer."

"Her core yearns for him. A feral desire races from her toes to her tongue."

What is this now? What nonsense is he blabbering? It doesn't sound like him. It sounds recited. It sounds like . . . She peeks down at the paperback he's wiggling at her. The one she took from the store.

"Muahahaha," he says sarcastically. "You drop this?"

Oh, that she could throttle him with her bare hands! The book must have fallen from her coat. She wants to scream that he'd better give it back.

"I'm not afraid to keep reading," he projects.

He's doing this to goad me, she tells herself. Who cares? It's nothing but a measly story. She's not a divine sissy, but there's no way she'll give him the satisfaction of responding.

But if he continues, she will be annoyed. Very annoyed.

"She knows what she wants, and she wants it multiple times, and she wants it now. In a heartbeat, she's flat on her back and clawing at his skin in ecstasy. By God, she's a greedy little nymph in her indecent, white dress—"

Love lands on the bridge, her boots smacking the wood planks a few feet from Andrew. He sucks in a mouthful of air. The dusky sky highlights the architecture of his shoulders and the slope of his nose.

He slaps the book closed with one hand. "I may have embellished a little."

"Well done," she concedes.

The book falls to his side. "Why are you half-dressed like that?"

Her plans for retaliation are forgotten. "Like what?"

"Like a sex goddess."

The strum in his voice caresses her ego. Perhaps she doesn't have to be coy about her dress after all. She lets the coat fly open and flap in the breeze. Keeping her eyes on him, it takes her a moment to locate her hips and prop her hands there. "Maybe I am one."

"Maybe you're trying too hard."

She pouts, pulls the coat closed, pulls herself together. "Maybe you're blind."

He gazes at her, unflinching. "Maybe I'm a challenge. Maybe you have no idea how difficult I can be."

"Did you hurt that girl on purpose?"

"Huh?"

"The big one's girlfriend. The one he was talking about."

"Holly? I didn't do anything to her, but good luck explaining that to Griffin McAsshole." Andrew pumps his thumb back toward the park. "Once that dipshit gets an idea into his head, there's no stopping him. He was chasing her around at the rally when she ran into me by accident, and my leg got in the way, and she tripped, and he blames me. That's the deal. That's all."

That's not all. In the bookshop, the girl managed to leave Andrew speechless just by standing there.

"Do you like her?"

"You mean the way I like gum?"

She snaps, "I said, do you like her?"

He snaps back, "Are you serious?"

His question is loaded with incredulity. He just saw her unleash with inhuman speed on two boys. True, his crushes aren't important at the moment, but she doesn't have to explain herself to a mortal.

He crosses over to her, approaching with measured steps. While he scrutinizes her from head to toe, Love does her best to maintain her dignity. Deities aren't self-conscious. There's no reason to be.

"It was like they couldn't see you. You moved too quick," Andrew says.

Not too quick, if he was still able to catch up to her here.

"You're not . . . real, are you?" he asks.

Love frets. She's broken a rule by protecting this boy and shouldn't be entertaining him. She shouldn't be moving toward him, but she is.

Closer now, she raises her hand, her palm up. Without hesitation, he lifts his own palm and attempts to press it against hers, but he gasps when his fingers slip through. In her weakest moments, she has thrown tantrums wanting to connect with students at Ever High School, but at no time has she mourned the vapor her body becomes around humans more than now.

"I can't touch or be touched by you," she says. "So no, I'm not real. Not in that way."

His frown is too cute for his own good. "You held that branch yesterday. In the park, that metal bar—"

She grabs the book with her other hand, mimicking his earlier action and wiggling it in front of him. "It's different with objects of your world. They're fair game," she explains, sliding the book into her pocket.

"How did you know where I was?" he asks. "Were you following me?"

Love nods.

"Why?"

"Because you're the only one who can see me."

"Why?"

"Because no one else has the power."

"Why?"

"Because no one else is . . . special."

"That's lame."

"What?" she demands.

"Come on. No one else is special? That's unfair, not to mention untrue. What's that even supposed to mean?"

She makes the mistake of glancing at his handicap, which earns her a prickly scowl. His hand tenses even though he keeps it poised in the air with hers.

"Are you freaking saying it's because of my—"

"Oh, please. Your leg doesn't make you special. It's as irrelevant to me as your teeth."

Out of nowhere, he chuckles. "Okay. Cool, then."

"Cool," she repeats, the mortal word dancing on her tongue.

They stay with their palms floating against one another.

34

Andrew of the pewter-gray eyes stares at their hands, his face lit with fascination.

Her mouth has a will of its own. "Thank you for the note."

His lips twitch upward. A purple bruise, courtesy of the beastly boy—Griffin McAsshole—stains his cheek like a watercolor. "What about the question I wrote? Who are you?" he whispers.

The glossy darkness surrounds them, snow collects on their shoulders, and the far-from-innocent question hangs by a thread in the air.

Don't tell him, she warns herself. Then she does the opposite.

Pulling her hand away from his, she gives a mocking bow and flashes a devious grin. "My name is Love."

"Really?"

She straightens and glowers. "You have a problem with that?"

"Nope. It's pretty."

She bets he likes the name Holly better. It's a flowering plant. She wants to tell him it's also poisonous.

A dash of skepticism lurks in his voice. "Spit it out. Am I going insane?"

"If you think so, it's fine. It will pass," she answers.

"If I am, I don't mind. There are worse versions of insane." His gaze fastens onto her. "What's your story?"

Love retreats a step. His presence has bedazzled her, managed to coax out the truth in droplets, and now he's looking at her expectantly, waiting for more.

"This is dangerous," she warns. "Pretend you never saw me."

Andrew shakes his head. "But I did see you. I don't pretend things."

She supposes it's an understandable reaction from somebody encountering a mystical being in a forest. "I should never have preyed on you to begin with."

"Preyed?" he echoes. "As in, I was your next meal?"

"Don't be ridiculous. I wanted to toy with you, not eat you."

"Okay, now that we have that out of the way, enlighten me, if you're so dangerous. Blow my mind more than you already have. What are you?"

"Nothing."

"Where do you come from?"

"Nowhere."

"Nothing. Nowhere," he imitates in a singsong voice. "Not good enough."

Lovely. He's as obstinate as she is.

To Love's dismay, she still can't tell what he's feeling, but his expression speaks volumes. It brightens with impulsiveness as some pebble of an idea forms in his mind. "I'll make you a deal. It's only around five-thirty, I'll be bored at home, but *you're* definitely not boring."

"I should say not," she declares.

"You're unsafe to be around, so you say, yet I don't have to worry about being gobbled up. Am I right?"

"It's more complicated than that."

"No offense, but I'd like to decide for myself. I could be making a huge mistake here, but I'm not scared of you, even if you're some kind of forest sprite or town spook. No, the dummy in me is intrigued and likes what he sees, sort of trusts what he sees, and wants more time to soak up what he sees before he lets it go." He crosses his arms. "You want me to pretend I never saw you? I'd be willing change my attitude about that—later."

"Meaning?" she asks, dubious.

"Meaning, take a walk with me. Hang out with me. Tonight."

5

Tonight. This boy wants to spend time with her tonight.

Of all the reactions she could have, Love shouts with laughter. A visceral, derisive laugh of absurdity, of outright refusal that ripples through evergreen needles and bare branches alike.

"Wow," Andrew remarks. "I never thought rejection would sound so pretty."

In an instant, Love gulps down her mirth. "I'm not going anywhere with you."

"You got plans to prey on someone else?"

"No."

"Well, that's a relief," he quips. "After all, you said I was special. I'd like this danger thing to be exclusive."

A dead vine is tangled around a portion of the bridge's railing. She yanks a twig from the vine and points it at him like a scepter. "You take this situation far too lightly, mortal."

"That's for sure, but calling me a mortal confirms you're anything but that."

"You might say I'm a myth. Leave it at that."

"A myth, huh?" He tips his head to the side. "Yeah, that sums you up. Laughter that sounds like a wind chime, perfect features, apparent superpowers, etcetera, etcetera. If you wanted to harm me, you would have done it by now. You would have let Griffin kick my ass in the park."

"Consorting with me is perilous in other ways."

"Even for just an hour or two?"

"I cannot promise anything."

"When you think about it, nobody can really promise anything."

Love flips the twig between her fingers, considering. Andrew has already poisoned her, and the effects will get worse no matter what, so spending an evening with him won't matter. But what if a deity turns up here and sees them together?

Then again, what are the chances of that? And this morning, she'd decided to find out more regarding this boy before warning the Court about his existence. This could be a fine opportunity.

She glances at the cloak of sky. The sun sets early in the winter, wiping the landscape of energy, yet the crystalline light is mystic and soothing. Rustling from overhead causes something tiny, most likely a stone, to skitter from the treetop. The arched bridge creaks beneath their boots, the noise seeming playful rather than fatigued.

If a small part of Love tingles at the prospect of indulging Andrew, she ignores it. She flings the twig to the ground and begins to shuffle out of his coat. "You will freeze in that pitiful jacket."

"No," he insists with an ill-timed sniffle. "I'll be all right. You keep the coat."

"I don't need it."

"I don't care. Keep it. It'll weird me out and give me constant guilt trips seeing you in nothing but a dress in this weather. Besides, the coat suits you. I like seeing you wear it."

Treacherous pleasure fizzes in her chest. "You're a foolish creature."

"If it bothers you that much, I know a warm place, via a scenic detour through my neighborhood." He jerks his head toward the lights of Ever. "Wanna be foolish with me?"

She huffs. "If this is will convince you to stay away later, I suppose one evening won't kill either of us."

For the first time, Andrew looks slightly troubled. "What exactly would kill me? I kind of have a right to know that."

"Coincidence," she replies, opting to be vague. "Poor timing. Irony."

That's what would have to occur for another deity to show up here and spot them, and as she pictures it, she realizes how improbable that is. Perhaps her concern has less to do with her people and more to do with how easily Andrew tempts her to go against her baser instincts, leading her astray like this.

"In other words, you're operating on a hunch," he surmises. "There's no guarantee this could lead to trouble."

"You'll simply have to trust me. No questions asked."

"I can live with that, temporarily. But just to make absolutely sure, tell me: Are you a dream?"

Oh, that she were, fleeting and inconsequential and safe within a pool of unconsciousness. "No," Love answers.

"Okay. Now that that's out of the way, can I call you Love?"

"You asked who I was, and I told you, which counts as permission. Or would you prefer Lily?"

A smile tugs at the margins of his lips. "It's just that Love sounds, I don't know, like a private name."

"Ha. It's the least private name in history."

"This coming from an invisible girl." He swings his arm in the town's direction. "Ready whenever you are, Love."

They return to the park, where he left his backpack. Bending over to pick it up off the ground causes Andrew to grimace and clasp his stomach, reminding Love of how hard Griffin had kicked him. She wants to rub that wound and then trace the watercolor bruise on his cheek. If she could explore and heal his injuries with her fingers, it would be another type of magic, her skin making contact with his. She imagines the texture of him, pliant but solid like cotton over bone. Her hands would learn how to make him sigh with relief: how much pressure to use, and in what direction to sweep her fingers, to make him feel better.

Putting her mind to it, Love would become familiar with his body. She would know him from top to bottom, from beginning to end.

Touching this boy would be the death, and life, of her.

She finds herself staring too long at his cheek, then finds herself the center of his attention as he watches her. She's gone and let her mind wander again, and he looks tickled pink at the prospect, as if he knows what she was thinking.

With a glower, Love flounces off ahead of him, not having a clue where he plans to take her, or if she's going the right way. With a laugh, he catches up.

The early evening puts Ever to rest quickly. Doors have closed. Shops have closed. People have disappeared from the sidewalks, so Andrew takes advantage. As they stroll through the main square, he points out landmarks and supplies Love with local trivia. Despite having such a pronounced limp, he's sprightly, particularly in the vocal sense. He speaks with an unbridled enthusiasm that strikes her, because he didn't give this same vibrant impression when she first met him, or whenever she's seen him interact with others.

Andrew knows how to tell a story. She likes listening to him.

She recognizes each corner they turn, but she's never thought of this hamlet, or any place she's lived in, as having its own soul.

They pass the gazebo where, according to Andrew, the man who constructed it for his beloved died of a broken heart after the woman rejected his grand gesture of affection. There's the teahouse, run by a pair of spinster sisters for the last forty years. On another street is an old jailhouse that a failed poet converted into a record store.

Further up a hill, a church bell tower tapers into the darkness. The bell has the nerve to ring every night at midnight. Oftentimes, Love hears the sound from her perch in the forest.

She inhales roasted chestnuts and tranquility. With the snow piled on the rooftops, and the bell tower, and the gleam of the streetlamps, she's hyperaware of how mortals would view this atmosphere as romantic. Andrew's presence makes the scenery pleasant, less stale than usual.

Love's been mute this whole time, but it hasn't seemed to bother him. His words peter out, leaving a comfortable silence, thick as sap, in their wake. How unexpected, to be walking with a mortal—and to behave herself while doing it. Not once has she considered teasing him, or ridiculing him, or judging him. Or changing her mind, turning around, and leaving him behind.

At a bungalow house on a residential lane, Andrew stops. A blush steals up his neck, the ripe color contrasting with his unruly, white hair. "Am I boring you?"

"If you were, I would say so," Love assures him.

"I got carried away," he admits. "I went off on a tangent and assumed you were new to town. For all I know, you've been scoping out the premises for a while now. At least tell me where you live."

"It varies. As we speak, I live nearby."

"That's all I get after the riveting tour I just gave you for free?"

Damn this boy and his alluring sense of humor. She mashes her lips together to keep from chortling. "I take up residence in the forest."

He exhales, his breath a veil of frost. "I was afraid you'd say that."

"Don't get any ideas of visiting me."

"Don't flatter yourself," he counters with a shivering grin.

"Your teeth are chattering," she complains.

"Relax. We've reached our destination."

Andrew knocks his head toward the bungalow house. Love follows his gaze, suspicion rippling up her arms. It's a confection of place, painted a vivacious violet candy tint. It has a porch, a pitched roof, and a dormant garden of what might be wildflowers come spring.

The lights are out in the windows. No one appears to be home.

Andrew pulls out a set of keys, dangling them in front of her nose. "My boss won't mind."

The woman at the bookshop? This is her house? They must have a kinship if Andrew owns a key to her private sanctuary.

"She likes to go to this music joint after work on Saturdays," Andrew explains, leading Love to the front door and sliding the key into the lock. "Then she has another date with the bookstore. It's inventory night. She hired a couple of college girls to help, but it'll still take a while. We have the run of the mill." The lock clicks. He smiles. "I think you'll like this."

As they step inside, her reluctance washes away for good, replaced by anticipation and the usual effervescent zeal of exploring a mortal's home without their knowledge. If the shopkeeper decorated this house, she's talented. It contains a cluster of mismatched furnishings that harmonize well, inviting a person to either kick up their heels or nose around.

In the kitchen, Andrew opens the freezer and pulls out an ice pack, presumably for his cheek, to keep the bruise from swelling like a hot air balloon.

Maybe Love has been waiting, or hoping, for a chance like this. "Wait," she says, edging in front of him. "Let me."

She steals the pack from his hand, her pinkie sailing through his wrist, and presses it to the watercolor. They pause, the shadows dappling their skin. Andrew's pulse visibly quickens in the nook beneath his jaw. He nudges his face further into the ice pack, his pupils a set of flashing sparklers.

Restless, she pulls back. She wiggles her digits, determined not to miss the moment, here and gone in a blink. "And how are your ribs?"

"Still there." Taking the pack from her and nursing his cheek, he retreats down the hall. "Um, this way."

This way leads her to the second floor and up a third set of steps, into an attic of dust and moonlight that spills in from a pair of skylights. The space is big enough to walk around and tall enough to stand upright in, except for the sides where the roof slopes downward.

It's all Love can do not to rub her palms together with glee. She's inside a human treasure chest. There's a changing screen, an antique writing desk with a dozen slots for letters and envelopes, a double arm chaise lounge, and a flea market's worth of mementoes.

Andrew idles in the center, awaiting her verdict. His expression straddles the line between pride and insecurity, it could go either way. He was right, because she does like it here, and she tells him as much.

He beams. Somehow, seeing him like that makes Love feels as if she has won something, too.

While propping the ice pack against his face, he spreads out his free arm. "Have at it."

If there's one thing she is not, it's shy. She accepts with gusto his invitation to snoop, discovering a music box, a set of encyclopedias, old board games, a child's sled, and a steam trunk filled with playbills and costume jewelry.

The telescope is her favorite. It's brass and cherry wood, positioned beneath the east skylight. Love adjusts the lens and locates an ocean of stars.

Hello, there!

She fiddles with the telescope and listens to Andrew shuffle about, opening and closing things, picking them up and putting them down. She peeks at him over her shoulder and catches him standing beside the writing desk, holding an empty glass jar in his hand, a private smile on his face that sends a tremor though her.

Love returns her attention to the telescope. She reckons it was a good choice coming here, surrounding them with distractions, buffers to put them at ease.

"I've never seen a person so fixated on something," Andrew remarks. "Do you have a thing for the stars?"

She straightens and turns, pondering how to express what the stars mean to her, to the Fates, without it sounding like gibberish to him. "No matter how much you make sense of them, they stay transcendent. We should be used to them because they're always around, like the sea and the soil, but . . ." She treads carefully. "But they constantly astound me. They are— they *seem*—capable of grand things, and people think of them in grand ways, even though they've been given all the rational,

44

technical explanations."

Andrew sets down the glass jar. "I get that. They're scientific and mysterious at the same time. That's nature in general, especially space—solar systems, planets, constellations—since we can't see all of it. It's the great unknown."

"Yes, but I hate comets. Either they go in useless circles for eternity, or they get knocked out of their orbits and destroy things. There's no magic in that."

"Who has time to actually dislike a comet? Like, who has room in their head for that?"

She does. She has plenty of time to collect likes and dislikes.

The thought would normally weigh on her, but coming from Andrew, she chuckles at herself. "In my defense," she argues, pointing at him, "disliking comets is more prudent than wasting time disliking someone for voicing their opinion. From what I've seen in your world, people do that far too often. And too eagerly. And prematurely. And dramatically."

"That's a leap, jumping from comets to social melodrama. But if I get more creative, I can almost see your point."

"Let me know when you do." Love settles onto the chaise. "In the meantime, I take it this attic is a retreat of yours."

He sets the ice pack on the ground and drops onto the opposite end of the chaise, resting his back against the arm. "It used to be when I was a kid."

Well, that explains why he has a key to this house. In some way, the shopkeeper has been a part of Andrew's life since his childhood, with her bookshop and attic of keepsakes.

"There's a lot of cool stuff," he says. "It was easy to get lost in everything for hours. I haven't been up here in a long time, but I could seriously set up camp for the night and still like it. I don't think anyone's too old or too young for attics. It's a good spot to let your mind drift, remember or reinvent, get inspired."

"What did you used to do up here?"

"I'd rather talk about you, anything about you, anything you're willing to tell."

"I might oblige if you go first."

"I'm counting on it."

Andrew drifts into the past, telling her about being a kid and playing in the attic. He reminisces about a spring day when he made a mountain out of the boxes and pretended to conquer it, then fashioned a tent out of a patchwork bedsheet and slept in it with a flashlight. There were summer days when it got so hot—"that kind of mean, aggressive, unapologetic hot," he says, though Love doesn't know any kind of hot—that all he could do was lie on a picnic blanket and flip through picture books about knights storming fortresses, occasionally dozing off to the whir of the fan propped beside his small head, then later to the strum of crickets in the evenings. One autumn afternoon, he painted leaves the colors of spices on the floor, then hid the evidence by dragging the steam trunk on top of them. On the cusp of winter, he practiced for the first snowfall, making a ramp out of a folding ladder and catapulting down its frame on his sled.

When it's Loves turn to speak, Andrew listens without interrupting. She omits the part about being a goddess, about training for that role from the day she could walk, and the magic of her own big, bad celestial world, the greater details that Andrew would have to see in order to believe. She plucks safer memories from her mind like flowers. She talks about growing up in nature, climbing, swimming, navigating caves, bonding with the stars.

It's clear from the slants and twitches of his mouth that he's holding himself back, hankering to ask her for more, a million questions crowding his face. It's magnificent and terrible to behold.

In the midst of her words, they pause and stare at the ceiling, the floor, their hands. It's a soft, easy pause that she could get used to.

Love doesn't realize how much time has passed until a metallic noise swells to a crescendo, tolling through the streets and into the attic. The church bell. It's nearly midnight.

"We better go," Andrew mumbles.

"Yes," she agrees, but also disagrees, because she doesn't want to go. No, she wants to stay and do more of this talking, this simple, meandering act that leads to nowhere, but turns this spot, on these cushions, beneath this roof, into everywhere. A place where nothing is asked or expected of her, where she only needs to be one thing: young. Just like Andrew.

⁓

He walks her back to the forest, near the park. They dally at the edge of the woods, bookended by trees on one side, Ever on the other.

"Well, that wasn't so bad," he concludes. "We went into overtime."

"That's because I was in a generous mood," Love jests.

"I had fun."

Me, too.

And it's over. And she feels bereft, cheated, newly afraid. What is she going to do about this viral human who's killing her? She has no right to have fun with him.

Something beeps into the space between them, the sound feeble yet demanding his attention. The intrusive noise comes from the phone that he retrieves from his jacket pocket. It's a crude model compared to what she's seen most people using.

Flipping it open, Andrew checks the screen. "It's late. My stepdad monitors my ass. He's going to be pissed." He glances at the woods, doubtful. "Will you be okay out here?"

Love points in the direction they came from, the world of backpacks and beautiful girls with actual names. "Will you be okay out *there*?"

"I have been before. It's just, having a friend is better, right?"

"I don't know," she says. Why is he asking her that?

Andrew shakes his head. "Look, I want to see you again."

This is why she should have kept their evening short, like they agreed to. He lured her with a telescope, a chaise lounge, and all that talking. Yet going into overtime still wasn't enough to get the novelty of her out of his system.

She refuses. "It would be dangerous to make a habit of this."

He gives her a mournful look, having hoped for the opposite response. She has disappointed him. Well, it's better this way.

"Can't blame me for trying," he says. "If you change your mind, you can always find me at the bookstore. I'm there all the time, when I'm not at school or home."

"Or when you're not lurking around the forest."

A fleet of clouds gathers in his eyes. Instead of acknowledging that comment, he just says, "I guess this is good-bye. I'd shake hands with you, but you're invisible."

Love grins in spite of herself. "Thank you for the tour."

"I'd do it again."

As would I, if you weren't such a deadly creature.

After another long, unreadable look at her, he tramps back through the woods. It makes no sense, but she pursues him as if it's the right thing to do. Or the greedy thing. At one point, he turns his head over his shoulder to look behind, and she jumps out of sight.

After a few more steps, he peeks back at her a second time. She ducks, then catches the amused grin in his profile. If they were the same type of beings, she wagers they would do this a lot, frolic the way they did tonight. She would enjoy that very much. She spent the evening with a boy who's slowly destroying her, yet it was the nicest night she's ever had.

Letting him go, Love stashes herself behind a wall of lifeless brambles and smiles, then frowns as Holly comes rushing across the playground.

"Andrew," she sighs, stupefying him by touching his shoulder the instant she closes the distance. "I just talked to Griffin. He was supposed to come over my house tonight, but he never showed up, so I left him a message, and then it took him hours to call me back, and he said he wasn't feeling well and had to go to the hospital, but he wouldn't tell me why. I had to wrestle the truth of him, and then he finally told me what happened."

Andrew obviously isn't used to conversing with her this much. "I ..."

"I wasn't sure if you'd be in the park anymore," she babbles, "but I was worried since he just left you here. I thought you might be really hurt, or freezing to death or something. My parents aren't home, so I didn't have the car, so I ran here, but I live only a few blocks away on Mayfair Court, and—anyway, never mind. Are you all right?"

"I ..."

"My ankle really wasn't that bad. And I didn't say you *rammed* into me today. I swear, I have the most irrational boyfriend. Griffin misinterprets everything. He totally shouldn't have started—God, your face." She runs her fingers over the purple watercolor.

49

An emotional landslide pours through Love. She fumes, then whimpers when the mortals' hearts begin to sparkle like fireworks raining down on the world. Andrew and Holly can't see it, but Love can. She hasn't beheld such a marvel before—this is different from the lights of her arrows, which flare rather than glisten—but she understands the signal.

Her head pitches toward the sky. As the two hearts on earth glint, a pair of stars twinkle like mad above.

Do you have a thing for the stars?

When Andrew asked her that in the attic, she'd longed to be honest. To be real with him.

In either dimension, here or there, the stars are many things to the Fates: vessels of immortal life, keepers of wishes, and tellers of fortunes, prophecies, and truths. And messengers, funnels that deities use to contact each other. Whatever the message's meaning, it can be sensed by the recipient.

Love knows this message is for her. And that it's a command.

The freedom to decide her matches is a pleasure. Not once has the Fate Court, who trusts their archers' judgment, demanded a specific pairing from her. Yet it's the Court's right to do so. It's been their right for eternity—and they've just exercised it.

It hits Love. Besides Andrew's death, there is another way to save everyone. It will protect her kind and spare him. This is the answer. This is what she'd want. She should be relieved.

Andrew and Holly. They're her next match.

"No," Love whispers.

6

Dawn has arrived. Love's back on her favorite branch, prepared to spend this misty morning sulking, but she cannot find a comfortable position, much less a dry spot. The bark is damp from the snow, and the sleeve cuffs of Andrew's coat emit the scent of wet wool.

Hoping to lose herself for a bit, Love prowls through the romance paperback. The story is heavy in her hands, split open like legs, the letters very small in spite of describing such a big moment. The heroine has just realized the hero she loves is also her enemy. Love rages at this shocking literary twist. A few days ago, she would have wondered what the fuss was. Now her powers get a sensory kick. She feels the rawness of their pain.

The apocalypse builds in her toes, up into her torso, and wages emotional war across her face. She feels the ugliness of her wrinkled chin.

Gah. This is not helping.

"Why do you insist on trees instead of your actual home?" a male voice drawls.

She slams the book closed. Of course they'd show up now. Their ability to travel between realms and territories instantaneously helps with that.

Love glances to the right where Envy drapes himself across

a parallel bough. Clad in a modern pin-striped suit, he rests his back against the trunk, one leg bent, his wrist balanced roguishly on his knee. Love doubts that anyone has mastered posture as he has.

Envy's dark skin blends into the bark. His broad features are as timeless as a tree, as though he requires little beyond sunlight and water to thrive.

She doesn't answer his question right away. Instead, she reacquaints herself with the sight of the other deities surrounding her. Wonder swings upside down, her legs hooked over a branch, and her off-the-shoulder blouse tucked into a pair of harem pants.

Wonder gets to wear pants. It's not fair.

Her curvy figure is admirably plump, and she has bottomless dimples to match. But for all her physical appeal, scars distort the tops of her hands: raised slashes that intersect and resemble exploding stars.

On the branch above her is Sorrow, scrutinizing Love through half-moon eyes. She's outfitted in a black skirt shredded into different lengths and saggy black boots, and there's a stitching needle pinned to her vest collar like a badge. Her short purple hair matches the purple tracks up her arms, elegant cuts made by a razor to symbolize suffering.

In the tree to Love's left, standing upright and drumming his fingers against the trunk, is Anger. He's as tall as a fortress, his fingerless gloves are stretched over the fitted sleeves of his tunic, and a single stud flashes in his left ear.

And oh, there's more. Immortal weapons are intricate treasures, crafted and designed by their owners, and forged from whatever source they choose. Envy carries arrows made of glass. Sorrow, ice. Wonder, quartz.

Anger's choice endlessly irritates Love. The component of their weapons is the same—iron—as though the emotions are somehow synonymous.

The five of them make up the Fates' most prominent class of archers. Too bad this fact has never sparked any kind of bond between them. Her peers are notorious for flouting Love's impish ways and grousing about her misdeeds—except Wonder, who's not entirely innocent herself.

"Enlighten us," Envy asks. "When did you decide to shack up with the squirrels? Good grief, you have a fetching glass cottage a stone's throw from here, but you prefer this." He waves at the forest in disapproval.

"I like being in the air more than on the ground," Love responds.

He nods. If there's anything her people understand, it's the desire to remain above mortals, in a literal as well as figurative manner.

The god doesn't dwell on it for long. The paperback grabs his attention, specifically the cover with its surplus of naked limbs, swollen lips, and thrashing heads. "What's that?" he purrs.

Showing embarrassment will do nothing but tickle his funny bone. Love protects the book against her stomach and mumbles, "Nothing."

"That nothing looks like fun."

"It was until you barged in. I was getting to the good part."

"The sex you've never had?"

Words like *why* and *me* tempt Love to resort to brutal measures. Forget his looks. That his rakish behavior is seen as sexy in their world is a testimony to the flaws of every goddess who desires him.

"Leave her alone," Anger says, which stuns everyone. As an

53

afterthought, he adds, "We're wasting time."

Grimness eclipses sarcasm. Clearly, they haven't gathered here for a humorous powwow, to poke fun at her and watch her squirm. They last saw each other a year ago, in the Peaks for a brief period of rest. It's impossibly early for a reunion, so there's only one explanation why her classmates would abandon their assigned territories at once: to warn her.

Envy wags his finger at Love. "Bad goddess."

"What have I done now?"

"Take your pick," Wonder hints like it's a game.

Anger can be counted on to get to the point. "What the Fates is wrong with you?" he snaps. "Beating those humans to a pulp. It's my job to deal with that stuff."

Envy inflates his chest, doubling his size in the process. "And it's my turn to suggest we cut the little goddess some slack. This mountain hamlet isn't your sector, and that human may be killing her, but she's bewitched. According to what we've been told, she's no longer acting like a prude. In fact, I'd bet my quiver that she's been a walking puddle since they met."

"Leave the yuck out of this, if you don't mind," Sorrow nags. "I'm rapidly getting a mortal idea of what it means to be sick."

"Can't help it, my nymph," Envy says to Love. "The signs are all over you. It's obvious."

Love doesn't want it to be obvious. She doesn't want the signs all over her. She definitely doesn't want these idiots to see them.

"I'm nobody's nymph," she grumbles.

"Not yet, but you're on the cusp. So wound up, you don't know what to do with yourself. It's unfathomable how you can be in charge of matchmaking and not have been plucked by now," Envy laments. "Look at you. You're red as a pomegranate and still a virgin."

Even though she cannot feel heat, her body still produces it, insisting on giving her feelings away. She fights the urge to cover her cheeks and fantasizes about ways to make Envy's anguish a reality. A permanent drooling problem. Eternal impotency.

His remark has been an ongoing point of contention since the beginning. The Fates have tolerated Love's chaste status for a century and a half, however patience from their dimension will wane eventually. She's a love goddess and needs to act like one.

She's been taught the mechanics of intimacy, yet in no way has she experienced it, nixing the offers she's received to rollick and raise legs with the gods, to ride and be ridden. Her excuses are plentiful, if not profound in their eyes. She may be needled for it, but sex with her people is meaningless compared to the way humans let their hands roam tenderly.

"I could help you with your quandary, you know," Envy coos.

A familiar tune from him. In his inflated head, it makes the utmost sense to think with his prick in times of crises.

Love's not a fraction of the prude he fancies her to be. She has cravings like the rest of them. While it was fine in her early years, being dormant has wreaked havoc on her body lately, the past few decades testing her hunger for a swift, rough fix.

She has come close to surrendering to anyone who happened to be in grasping distance. Very close. Many times.

Soon enough, she will burst. She might have already by now if not for one fact: She's Love. Either it's a miracle or it's her very nature that she's been able to hold out for a special first time. In essence, a pipe dream.

Until then, she takes care of herself. And yes, she enjoys it. Frequently.

"Let it go, Envy. We have bigger problems," Anger interjects, then scowls at Love. "The Court knows the boy can see you."

Love crosses her arms. "Impressive considering they weren't here to witness a thing. Might they teach me that trick?"

It's not as though the Fates have a crystal ball to gawk into. It's an archer's job to keep watch on the mortal world, so the Court couldn't know about Andrew and the fight in the park unless they were in the neighborhood.

Were they in the neighborhood? Love feels a spike of dread. Last night, she had feared that a deity would catch her with Andrew, but she disregarded the possibility. In any case, she'd been fretting over an archer turning up, or one of the Guides, not a member of the Court. That would have seemed too outrageous.

"The point is, they do know," Anger says. "They sent us here to tighten your bowstring."

Of course. Every class is responsible for its members. Through the stars, the Court could have told her all she needed to know, but for something this delicate, sending the archers is the Court's regal way of making extra sure she understands what to do.

"And?" she asks, feigning innocence and naivety, purely because it's fun to vex Anger.

"And the boy's cataclysmic!" he fumes.

Envy flicks his wrist into the air. "Please, Anger. Hyperbole is tacky."

Anger's not listening. "Your powers are fading around him, Love. That will get worse. Need I say, it's a preview of what will happen to the rest of us?"

Love knocks the back of her head against the tree trunk. "Certainly not."

"At last, a sound answer," he jeers. "Good. So long as you're strong enough, your weapon is strong enough. Strike him and his intended down, bring them together, and everything will be back to normal. He won't be able to see deities anymore. He'll forget that anything beyond humanity exists. He'll forget you."

She wants to bark at him for rehashing what she, and every immortal in the cosmos, already knows. This impossible situation hasn't arisen before, but the wisdom of how to deal with it is another thing to thank the stars for. Archers' targets become so consumed by the arrow's magic that they go blind to magic itself.

"And if I don't listen?" she counters, which is the most visceral, most imbecilic, most illogical question.

Envy smirks. "You must truly want to get him naked."

"I didn't say that," she mutters, choking the paperback in her lap.

"You didn't have to. Ah, the irony."

If she denied it, he wouldn't believe her anyway. It *is* ironic. Finally someone lights the flame the Fates have been hoping to see in her, to make her the supple goddess she's supposed to be, and that person happens to be a human. A human whose heart she has to steer toward someone with bigger breasts.

"Looks like somebody's jealous," Envy sings, enjoying the gong of his voice. Deities can tap into human emotions, but not the emotions of other deities. This should protect her from his prying gaze, but with regard to jealousy, he dissects her expression way too easily.

"What happens if I don't do it?" Love repeats before she can stop herself.

"You tread a thin line voicing that query," Anger says, still drumming his fingers.

All right. Love wishes he would stop doing that. It's annoying.

"Just what do you *think* is going to happen?" Sorrow squawks.

"The Court will get rid of the boy themselves," Envy answers.

"They don't need you for that. However, this is your turf. Your arrows are a forgiving solution. Do the math."

"You want math? Killing the boy is faster and safer," Love says. "Matchmaking will take longer. I'll be dying the whole time, and so will you once the ailment gobbles me up. It's going to spread. Why take that risk for the sake of civility and mercy?"

"The stars advised them to," Envy clarifies.

She should have known. The stars are mysterious in their ways, but they serve the Fates. The Court listens to them, especially regarding humans.

"Don't get ahead of yourself," Sorrow says, gathering snow and forming it into a ball. "The stars urged us to try a love match first. They didn't suggest we pursue it until the bitter end. The Court will bury the boy if it comes down to our lives—if you don't do what you're told." She bobs the snowball in her cupped palm. "Think you can handle that?" she dares.

"Andrew's death is a last resort," Love translates.

In no way is she objecting to her task. She's merely harnessing the facts. Ordering her to match him, to erase his memory of her, is the kindly choice. It's the route she'd want to take. She just didn't expect the Court, or the stars, to be on her side.

"Ready for the best part?" Sorrow says. "If you say no, or if you flop at this, the Court won't be generous. They'll teach you a lesson, and they'll make sure we help with that. Lucky us, history gets to repeat itself."

Meaning Love will be tortured as punishment. Well, that's the least of what they could do. Any other goddess would be sentenced to execution or banishment. They won't go that far, though. She's too important to them.

But they will show her pain. Or make her watch Andrew's death. Or both.

As Sorrow said, their methods will involve her class. With that, a memory resurfaces and forms a ring around the archers. Wonder has been quietly musing to herself all this time, but they avoid glancing her way—except Love, who stares at the scars laced across the girl's hands. The only way for deities to scar like that, or to feel physical pain, is if it's self-inflicted, as is the case with Sorrow, or if it's caused by another deity, as is the case with Wonder. It does not occur naturally.

The same with death. They're immortal so long as they're not stabbed in the chest. They cannot deteriorate the way humans do from old age or illnesses.

Unless they're infected by a human who can see them.

In any case, when one is dishonorable, their class is ordered to carry out the punishment. Love is certain none of them will ever forget that day, what they were forced to do to Wonder because of her crime.

Envy tosses Wonder a wry grin that doesn't reach his eyes, that says, *No hard feelings*.

Love has done plenty to earn her fair share of retribution, but her greatest penalty so far, defending Wonder, was mild in comparison. Love withers at the thought of her class pushing her to the brink, their hands rising and cutting across the air to take her down, cracking open the great mystery that is suffering.

Envy hacks through the silence. "Do what you must, but be careful with that human. You're subject to his influence. None of us expected you to favor the blemished type. Anger got a peek at him and says he's rather askew."

Love glowers at Anger. Anger glowers at Envy.

Envy doesn't care. "Your contorted little mortal is—"

She swats him upside the head with the book. "Don't call him that!"

"Wow," Sorrow says. "You sound like a human. It's pathetic. It's depressing."

"You would know."

"Yeah, I would. Shut up about it."

Sorrow's purple hair makes Love think of the purple bruise on Andrew's cheek, the one he got because of Holly, the one Holly got to touch. The one he *let* her touch.

Love peels that rotten thought from her mind. "None of you think I have the stomach for this match."

Envy inclines his head. "If you want to see it that way."

"I do see it that way."

"You questioned the consequences twice within minutes of us arriving," Anger bites out.

"Do not accuse me of being spindly. I was not serious," Love grates.

"Like your sentimental tendencies aren't serious? Or your attraction to human touch?"

"Trifling details. I can't touch the boy, so he's hardly a temptation. He's useless to me."

"He's dangerous, yet you didn't reveal his existence to the Court!" he shouts. "One might think you were protecting him!"

"I needed to gather more information about him first. I wasn't about to dash off to the Peaks without knowing everything!"

"Yes. I sold the Court on that theory, thank you, but no thank you."

Love pops up. They bolt toward each other.

With a sigh, Envy lashes his arm out and rams it into Love's stomach, halting her. "Settle down, beauties. As much as I'd love to watch you slap one another around, the tension is enough to make me feel excluded and, ahem, envious."

Anger stops as well. It's a riot how determined he is to insult

Love. He can't stand her, and more than any other god, she can't stand him. Whenever they bump horns, she wagers somewhere in this world volcanoes erupt and storms whip houses from their roots.

Well, there have been kindly moments between them, too. Moments that glinted with empathy.

Anyway. Unimportant.

Envy returns to the subject at hand. "We don't need more renegade goddesses in this group. Want the dainty version? Get it done before our elders lose faith in your prowess and have us take a strap to your pretty skin. I'd like another chance to seduce the goddess of love while she's flawless, but you're stalling with this task. At this rate, you'll end up as blemished as Wonder and Sorrow."

Snowball still in her palm, Sorrow lobs it at Envy. He dodges it with a cackle.

"How long do I have?" Love asks.

"Around a fortnight before you deteriorate completely and we follow suit," Sorrow answers. "But the Court will give you ten days."

"I won't fail at this."

"We'd like to think so," Anger says without admiration.

Instead of simply vanishing, the archers depart on a less dramatic note. Envy jumps to the ground and struts into the forest. Sorrow lumbers behind him, her body leaning forward as though she's used to things being out of reach. Anger storms off in the opposite direction from them.

Still hanging upside down, Wonder maneuvers off her branch. She drops to Love's level, folds her hands pertly in her lap, and chirps, "You never cease to amaze me, Love. You don't change. Of all the people to antagonize, you have to pounce on

Anger when he's already in foul spirits."

Love was done thinking of Anger the moment he left the woods. "They should have let me choose," she mumbles to herself.

If they want her to do this her way, the Fate Court should have allowed Love to choose the girl for Andrew. How fine and dandy of them to pick Holly when they weren't here to scout all the candidates. Love guesses they called upon the nifty stars for that, too.

Wonder is a champion at understanding vague comments. She sees past them like no other goddess. "Oh, hush. Love, you've admitted before that you're picky. The Court didn't offer you the liberty because they wanted an immediate selection. They told the stars to find a girl that the boy's noticed before. Someone he's thought about. It's as plain as that."

Love nods. It's a sensible request if she can get past the knowledge that Andrew has thought about Holly. "We're greater than mortals, yet we serve them."

"Hmm. Most of us like to think we govern them."

Yes. The human world is fragile, which gives the Fates power over it.

Granted, humans touch beautifully. With all their romantic entanglements and complications, their hands accomplish the kind of ardor that Love dreams of.

To the contrary, they're awful at mastering the other acrobatics of courtship. They kiss the wrong people and disregard the right ones. Once the thrill of new beginnings has ebbed, their intimacy segues into shaky terrain. Disagreements. Misunderstandings. Blame. They break up, then suffer, becoming woeful or infuriated. Then irrationality sets in. They do pointless things like quarantine themselves inside their rooms until a soft layer of stink covers them, or they overdose on self-destruction. They feel sorry for themselves and cry a lot.

Some mortals indeed love well, but most don't. And none do it perfectly.

They need help from their betters, who can guide emotions and keep hearts intact, and Love does enjoy being better. She sweeps their past mistakes under the rug, and honors them with an impeccable life mate and an enduring bond.

She cleans up their world. This is her destiny.

Andrew is not. She doesn't know him, but she likes him. Her heart likes him very much, yet she has no choice. Matching him will be easier than condemning him. Notwithstanding her earlier rants, it will be easier to see him enamored than to see him die.

Wonder's voice is like a candle in the white woods. "Or . . . There is another way to fix this."

7

Love's head jolt up at Wonder's words. The other archers' idea of deity damage control was brusque. It is only Wonder who has remained behind. Wonder, whose bright gaze is a kaleidoscope, often urging people to shift closer, as Love does now.

Wonder presents a puckering white bloom from her pocket. The pale petals suit winter, though the flower isn't the kind that thrives in the frost. It must come from her newest domain. "A present from the soil," she says, then tucks it behind Love's ear. "Greenhouse soil, that is."

In light of what's happening, the goddess's voice is breezy. After nearly one hundred and fifty years, she has recovered from torture. Yet how she can admire pretty little things right now, turn them into an occasion to celebrate, is hard for Love to accept.

Wonder admires the forest while grooming her hip-length curls. "I like it here. I'm stuck in a windy, rainy city. Too much distraction makes my job harder, but this town is quiet. You get to concentrate."

"I'll trade you," Love replies.

"Would you? The snow is perfect."

"Perfectly dull."

Love prefers the thoughtful burgundy hues of fall, the flirty tones of spring, the bold tangerines of summer. She's not fond of the somber silver of winter, nor its eerie isolation. It figures that people need more love in places like this.

But would she honestly trade being here? Yes. No.

Love kicks the girl's calf. "Windy, rainy city, eh? Wonder, of all people, is actually complaining? You've been to worse regions."

"I suppose I take after you. *Perfectly dull snow*."

"Ha. You're not remotely akin to me. Nor are you Sorrow."

"Nor am I Joy."

"Thank the Fates for that!"

They laugh. Joy is the most nauseatingly cheerful being alive. She once advised Love to smile more often and tried to tickle her—at which point, Love gave her an appropriate scare, wielding an iron arrow and fake-scratching the girl, convincing her she was about to turn into a rabid, love-battered mess. It was a glorious two minutes.

Love's mirth ebbs. She adjusts her short dress while staring at Wonder's pants. She trusts that Wonder will get to the point. If not, Love can simply pull Wonder's hair.

She pulls Wonder's hair.

"Hey!" the goddess squeaks.

"Tell me or go away," Love says.

Wonder shakes her head and then glances around, presumably to make sure Envy, Sorrow, and Anger have really left. "The stars say if he can see you, he can kill you. But if he can see you, then he can also love you."

Love couldn't have heard her right. "What?"

"And if he can love you, you have the chance to become like him—a human."

"What?!"

"It's penned in the ancient narrative." Wonder licks her lips. "Long ago, the stars advised the Fate Court on the essentials of protecting their world. One of the essentials was a warning about mortals who can see gods and—"

"Do I look like I grew up in a mineral cave?" Love asks.

Wonder smiles. "No, you look like an ungrateful, ethereal brat."

It's just that everyone knows this story. The stars counseled the Court about truly selfless mortals and the crippling effects they would have on their kind, though the stars were not able to explain why. Even their knowledge has limits.

Chewing on one's fingernails is supposed to be a sign of nervousness. Love, on the other hand, gnaws on her thumbnail out of aggravation. Wonder leans forward and swats Love's hand from her mouth. "Before you interrupted me, I was going to say there's one essential we never knew, but each generation of Court members has. It's been hidden for ages in the Archives."

Love knows that the subterranean hall of records and manuscripts is Wonder's favorite place in the Peaks, and that when Wonder's an old deity, she wants to be Keeper of the Archives. It houses every bit of lore about their world, including scrolls documenting what the stars have shared with the Fates.

Hidden tidings from the stars? That's doubtful. The Fate Court sets truth on a gilded pedestal and keeps nothing from their people. Love quirks a brow, silently expressing as much.

"Well, not precisely *hidden*," Wonder concedes. "They stored it in the Hollow Chamber."

That, Love can believe. The Hollow Chamber is a place deep within the womb of the Archives where the Fates store volumes of little importance. Insight and history that has overstayed its welcome, outlived its value among gold-leaf titles, spools of paper, and dust. All the same, each member of the Court must study the Archives from top to bottom as part of their vow of service, even the contents of the Hollow Chamber.

Wonder lowers her voice, speaking behind a veil of secrecy. "I was down there, and I may have … discovered a scroll. The writing says the stars inferred to the Court that if a human and deity fall in love, they will be bound to each other, and that deity will become mortal, forsaking their previous existence."

Love surges to her feet. She leaps onto the branch where Envy had been sitting and prowls its length. Flummoxed doesn't begin to cover how she feels about this. For the next ten days, the Court will be bowing to the stars, although it puts their kind at risk, and tasking her with a boy who can change her? That makes the gamble worse. Of all the deities, she was the hardest emotion to create. She's the first love goddess ever conceived, thousands of years in the making, and therefore not easily replaced. Humans are sacred, but so is she.

"Then why would the stars advise that I match this boy?" she demands, hackles raised. "The Fate Court must have clamored."

"Oh, Love. You're more exhausting than Angst." Wonder peers around the snowy forest once more. "I'm sure it wasn't easy for them to give you this chore. As for the scroll, I said it was in the Hollow Chamber, didn't I? The Fate Court may have forgotten about it. It's been eons.

"My guess is, none of the Courts throughout history took the stars' guidance on that front seriously. It wasn't a prophecy. It was a precaution. Come now. An immortal and a human smooching? An immortal capable of love and who wants to become an aging, smelly human enough to pursue it? Possible in theory but perverse in reality. That's why the scroll must be in the Chamber. Are you still ungrateful?"

"More than anything."

Wonder grins at her. "You like him."

Love forces herself not to hiss at the accusation.

"We all saw it when we got here. Any time we mentioned him, it looked like you were about to float away or throw a colossal fit. That's a radiant start. Loving him back is the other half of the change. That cements it. Isn't it marvelous how answers to the greatest obstacles can be found right under our noses? It's ever so much fun."

"What if an immortal doesn't want to change?"

Wonder shrugs with pleasure. "I wouldn't know what to tell them."

Love drops back onto the branch. A chorus of brittle twigs cracks around her. "What were you doing in the Chamber, sneaky?"

"Nothing. I got lost."

Wonder's scarred hands are stuck in her lap now rather than brushing through her hair. She often gets lost when she's in a new human town, so Love has heard. Not in the Archives, though. That's Wonder's happy place.

No. She was down there for another reason. Was she looking for something else when the scroll ended up in her hands? Like the rest of their class, Wonder hasn't been to the Peaks in a year. How long has she known this?

Wonder casts her a sidelong glance. "You helped me once."

The memory between them grows thorns. So that's what this is about. Wonder feels like she owes Love this knowledge, after what Love did—*tried* to do—for Wonder on the day she was tortured.

Wonder adjusts the flower behind Love's ear. "I'm also telling you this because you're not like the rest of us, but I do like you. Who wouldn't like a love goddess? Other than Anger?" She bites her lower lip for a moment. "He's been watching you, you know."

Love bolts forward. Anger has been leaving his turf to spy on her? What for?

"He saw you and the boy meet," Wonder confides.

"That's how the Court knows about Andrew," Love growls. "Anger snitched on me."

"He followed the rules, for the sake of our people, because you were preoccupied. The Court convened with the stars, agreed to have you match the boy, then told Anger to round up our class and speak with you, though I'm sure he would have done that anyway. But before he came to us, Anger also saw the mortal fight you stopped. He saw you and the boy at the bridge. He watched you traverse through town together."

"Just how much did he see? We weren't outside the whole time," Love says.

"Oh yes, he mentioned that," Wonder acknowledges, as though entertained. "He kept vigil outside the mortal home you disappeared into."

Love resents him being there at all, that the archers know anything about last night. Though she's relieved he didn't ruin things by following her and Andrew into the house. Those hours were private. They were . . . meaningful to her.

What must the archers think, aware that she'd remained inside for so long, alone with Andrew, instead of rushing to the Court and warning them about him? She can't fully blame her peers for doubting her.

"And then Anger saw you whisper *no* to yourself in response to the Court's request," Wonder says. "They're going to want reports from him, but he's vowed to keep that verbal blunder of yours to himself, so retract your claws. Anger means well, whether or not you notice or appreciate it."

"What was he doing, sticking his nose in my business to begin with?" Love gripes.

Wonder hedges. "What you do reflects on the rest of us. Before you existed, the Fates had never had a love goddess to send to the mortal world. As leader of our class, I suppose Anger wanted to make sure your time went smoothly."

Except that Love has been matchmaking for well over a century. How much supervision does she still need?

"If there's another reason, take that up with him," Wonder professes.

That's the last thing Love plans to do.

"It was a risk telling me what you found," she says.

"It was."

She tries to say *thank you*, but the words turn into, "I don't like that boy."

"You want him more than you want my pants. That counts for something." Wonder taps her chin. "Flattering coat, by the way."

Love's grateful the girl can't see into her pockets, where Andrew's note rests.

"I won't endanger the Fates to be with him," she declares.

"For mercy's sake," Wonder sighs. "I wouldn't tell you this if I thought your success would endanger our people. According to the scroll, your union with the boy would alter things. You would lose your memory of deities and of being a goddess—let me finish," she says when Love is about to revolt.

"It's not instantaneous, but it would happen over time. Bonded with you, the boy would forget as well. Neither of you would know any better, yet your love would remain. And the Fates wouldn't be threatened anymore.

"Whatever you choose to do, be cautious. You don't want to make treachery obvious, especially if Anger turns up again. There's only so much he can keep from the Court to protect you.

Don't put him in that position."

Love dismisses that with a wave. "It won't be necessary."

Her infatuation with Andrew, a boy she only just met, is irrelevant. For mortality to happen, he would need to fall for her, and she would have to feel the same, and all of this would have to happen without them touching. And she would have to *want* this.

Wonder has it in her head that that's possible. How quaint, and queer, of her. She may be familiar with Love's curiosity about human touch, but that doesn't mean Love's willing to sacrifice this superior life for a paltry slice of lower-race affection.

Having the chance for a real embrace terrifies her. The bliss would pale in comparison to its price: her memory gone, her past erased, the loss of immortality, facing the unknown with its illness and death and imperfections and unpredictability. It's unthinkable.

So what if she likes Andrew? She doesn't like him as much as she likes living forever, or as much as the Peaks, the blossoming purple slopes that she loves to roll down, the noble cliffs she loves to scale. It's a beautiful dimension. It's home.

Nor will she leave her people. Her Guides, who've taught her, humored her, talked with her. With them, at least she knows where she belongs.

And she will never, never, never give up her bow. Matchmaking is her purpose. It's what she's good at.

Andrew was a distraction, but he is not meant for her. She has to pair him with Holly and skip on.

Love remembers her invisible palm blending with his, and how he didn't recoil.

I hate his fingers.

She checks the cloudy sky, split by occasional threads of blue.

I hate his coat.

The day is only beginning.

I hate him.

She has work to do.

And I'll prove it.

It's a fine time to sharpen her arrows.

8

Across the street from his house, Love crouches to the ground. Digging her toe into the earth, she taps the plume of her arrow against her chin. As much as she wants to strike Andrew and Holly immediately, she cannot. Matchmaking is a craft that requires an artistic sleight of hand. Each pair is a riddle. She can't breach the heart without maneuvering the lovers into position, steering them in the right direction first. Not only do the targets need to know each other beforehand, they need to reach a mutual state of genuine regard. Otherwise, they end up confused and anxious about why they love each other so much, when they don't even know each other. They make everyone around them, family and friends, confused and anxious, too. It's an eternally choppy bond.

She did a superb job preparing her weapons earlier this morning, after Wonder left, but now they must perch in her quiver like good children and wait to be used. Some myths claim that Eros carried two different arrows—one gold, one lead—for two different purposes, to incite love or extinguish it.

Wrong. Very wrong.

Iron is the only material for her. Although yes, her arrows either give love or take it away, depending on what's necessary—every deity's weapon either gives or takes.

In Love's quiver, there's also a third option: arrows that invoke lust. She created them at the Fate Court's urging, to help nudge targets along if things became tricky, yet Love prefers not to use these particular arrows. It feels like her talents are being cheapened by relying on them.

Her weapons all look alike, but she can tell them apart—can tell which type of magic they wield—simply by touching them, sensing their power like a life force.

The arrow she's presently holding induces love. She runs her thumb along its spine, inlaid with stars that match the ones sprinkled across her quiver. She learned how to hold her weapons before she learned how to use a knife and fork. They have grown as she has. They're part of her.

What would it be like to give them up? Would she miss the arrow's whistle as she lets it fly, the vibration of the bow, the flash of light?

Never mind. It's pointless to dwell. The first step is to explore Andrew's life, see what matters to him and how it might harmonize with Holly.

Beyond his bedroom window, his form moves around, getting ready for the day. Yawning, he scrubs his hair with a towel, then tosses it to the side. He migrates from one end of the room to the other, where he opens a dresser drawer.

And then he crosses his arms, grabs the hem of his shirt, and whips it off.

He's sculpted nicely, his abdomen tight, his upper arms and shoulders flexing. The sight robs her of breath, causes her mouth to fall open and dry up. It makes her wriggle the way she did reading the more *enthusiastic* scenes in that romance novel.

Love's fingers sneak up her thighs, higher and higher, until he drags a new shirt over his head, bringing her to her senses. With a growl, she springs to her feet and marches across the snow. She cannot think like this. She's a goddess.

The gray house has a bright blue door. Yellow blooms from within the ovals of fog outlining the windows. The square jaw of the porch wraps around the facade, laced with vines of frost. Icicles line the roof.

As she gets closer, she smells burnt toast, rubber boots, and the shampoo Andrew must have used to lather his wintry hair. She follows the thunk of his footsteps hiking down the stairs.

She rounds the corner to the back window of the house, which has a view of the kitchen. Andrew's presence clashes with the stench of his stepfather, who's hunkered over a table, slurping on his coffee. He's wearing a grease-stained jumpsuit the dispiriting color of mud, with a name tag sewn into the fabric, and his face is still leathery. His eyes narrow to slits as he scrutinizes Andrew, who burns his own toast, sits across from him, and eats.

Love gazes at the pumping column of Andrew's throat. A defiant noise of appreciation threatens to curl from between her lips. She puts a leash on it, tugs it back into her chest, and wills herself to focus. The interior is rustic but not entirely masculine. There's a device attached to the edge of the counter, meant for coring apples. Dusty wine glasses are displayed behind a clear cupboard. She sees a frayed woven basket and faded curtains.

The stepfather grabs a butter knife and scrapes it over his toast. Andrew's teeth rip off a corner of his own slice.

The stepfather sips. Andrew swallows. Love shuffles.

The coffee mug smacks the table. Love jumps. Andrew doesn't.

The tyrant aims a finger at the watercolor bruise floating across Andrew's cheek. "You ever gonna tell me where that came from?"

His words are measured and cold, like the question could turn into a demand at any moment. Andrew keeps his head down and says, "I woke up with it."

"Don't be a smartass. You've been walking around with your noggin in the freaking clouds, you let your coat get stolen or whatever, you made me wait up for you last night, and shittiest of all, you let somebody jump you. Looks like they won, too."

Love puffs herself up but frowns when Andrew keeps silent. What's the matter with him? Why isn't he defending himself? Griffin and his troll didn't win!

The stepfather drawls, "I got enough on my plate without you losing fights. If your nuts aren't big enough to stand a chance, don't bring the evidence home. I suppose I'm gonna have to keep you busier if you have bonus time to get your ass kicked. Do some laundry when you get home today, you hear me?"

Andrew nods. His stepfather pauses, then circles his thumb along the rim of his coffee mug. "All the crap I do around here, and you can't be trusted to take care of the rest."

It's official. Not only will her strength continue to ebb because of Andrew, but she can no longer grasp his emotions. That ability faded shortly after they met, shortly after his eyes landed upon her and sealed her fate.

However, it's only *his* emotions. Everyone else is still penetrable. Love hunts through the stepfather's senses to determine if he's concerned about who hurt Andrew. Unfortunately, the man's feelings, a whole jungle of them, are going berserk on her, fluctuating too fast to catch.

"Who was that girl?"

The man's question knocks Love's concentration off course. For a moment, she thinks he means her.

Andrew starts. "Girl?"

His stepfather sneers. "Last night, when you got home after hours. Who was the blond hussy walking with you?"

Holly. Love had just found out they were her next match, but she didn't stay behind to see what happened after the girl caught up to Andrew in the park. She must have accompanied him back to his house. A promising start for them.

Love's shoulders collapse beneath an unknown weight. If she had wings, she's certain they would sag and fold in on themselves.

Andrew's posture relaxes. "She's no one," he answers.

His stepfather snorts. "That 'no one' have anything to do with that shiner you got?"

"She just walked me home."

"Girls don't walk guys home."

Andrew tosses down the last of his toast.

"What happened? You tried to play the hero?"

Andrew shoves back his chair.

"Did she pity you for getting whupped?"

Andrew stands.

"Because the stupidest thing to get into a fight about is a girl."

Andrew heads to the sink.

His stepfather leans back, trapping his mug in a chokehold. Love grasps one lucid thing about him: resentment. It's webbed around him. It shudders through her and causes her quiver to knock against her tailbone. No matter what's about to happen, there's no guarantee the man will leave his fists out of it.

He says, "You're just about the biggest fool if you let a girl run you into the ground."

Andrew's dish clatters against the countertop. "You would know."

At his own words, he freezes.

Something acidic rains down Love's throat just as the step-father's chair skids across the floor. Before she knows it, the man is crushing Andrew's shirt collar and ramming him up against the fridge. "What'd you say? What!"

Her arrow catapults through the window. It punches a hole through the pane, whizzes passed the stepfather's head, and narrowly misses his face. The glass cupboard next to him shatters. Two of the wine glasses explode. The arrow sparks, disappears, and then reappears in her quiver.

Love gawks between her bow and the damage. What did she just do?

The stepfather releases Andrew. He strides toward the cabinet, his shoes crunching shards of glass on the floor.

Andrew whirls the other way, toward the point of entry, and there's an instant, a glimmer of recognition in his eyes. Love ducks, but it's no use. He saw her. She wasn't quick enough, again.

"Did you feel that?" she hears the stepfather say.

"See what?" Andrew blurts out.

"Not *see*. Feel. Like a . . . a kind of wind or something."

Sure footsteps pound toward the window, followed by the stepfather's leathery face mashed against the pane and glowering into the distance. Love's temper flares—at herself, at Andrew, at this man.

The stepfather growls, "So now you got people targeting you here?"

Andrew's bewildered voice drifts from behind. "People?"

"Hell, you couldn't even lose that fight right. Whoever decked you isn't satisfied and wants to throw shit through our window. What'd you do to piss them off?"

That does it! Love refuses to be likened to a second-rate antagonist like Griffin McAsshole. Teeth bared, she jumps up and aims another arrow at the slit of skin between the stepfather's nostrils.

Andrew bounds forward, halting behind his stepfather, his eyes drilling into hers. He looks livid as he raises his flat palm and makes a panicked cutting motion across his neck, indicating for her to stop.

This is what her destiny has come to. She is a wreck, taking orders from a mortal boy who possesses more dignity and mercy than she does. What the Fates!

Bristling at him, she lowers her bow. Andrew releases a breath that gets his stepfather to twist around. "You better have something to say for yourself."

"I didn't—"

"Did you even fight back?"

Yes, he did! Love wants to yell.

Andrew averts his gaze, eyes skipping to the window before focusing on the doorway to the kitchen. The man grunts, "Whatever, Lost Cause. There's a rock somewhere in here with your name on it. Find it quick and get your stuff. Five minutes or I'm taking off without you." He stomps off, his shoes rapping on the wooden floor as he thunders down the hall.

The instant a door slams, Andrew hoists the window open. "What the fuck are you doing?" he hisses. "How do you know where I live?"

A grisly protest roars up Love's throat. *Hey, listen, mortal—*

"And would you stop defending me? You're making me look like a total moron."

"He's a wicked man," she says, judges, insists.

Andrew does a double take. "You don't know him or me."

She gestures with her arrow in the direction the stepfather disappeared. "Oh, but you're doing such a marvelous job knowing each other," she declares.

He points to the watercolor on his face. "Well, he didn't do this."

"He could have."

"Excuse me? You were the one who was going to slice his face in half!"

Love rolls her eyes. "No, I wasn't."

Her weapons have been forged specifically for matchmaking. They have the capacity to cut a person if wielded by hand instead of by bow, but they won't have a fatal effect. A small wound can be inflicted, however the arrow would slip through a person's body if it were an attempted death blow.

Though if used incorrectly, other complications arise. Arrows that erase the feeling of love means that her target simply stops loving the person they're with. That's harmless. That is, unless she accidentally shoots a person who is not enamored in the first place, which would render them eternally incapable of feeling love—even she wouldn't be able to reverse that, once the person has been hit.

Arrows that produce raw lust can make humans aggressive, forceful even, if Love wishes them to be. She controls the intensity of the desire and must be careful not to overdo it.

And when struck by an arrow that incites love, the target's heart needs to be united with another. If not, the person will become consumed with madness. They'll wander around lovesick, desperate for affection, losing their mind if they don't find it.

This goes for deities, as well. They cannot feel love inherently, much less go crazy for it, but they *can* feel it through magic.

Such a catastrophe hasn't happened, yet it's possible. Being connected to her weapons, she knows what they're capable of. She's had nightmares about it. It was never her intention to give her arrows these handicaps when she forged them—the disadvantages sprouted naturally, as they do with all archers' weapons, as conditions to wielding power, because everything comes with conditions. So say the stars.

It's important to have perfect aim and reflexes, to hit the right target, to *not* miss and end up striking someone else instead. Love isn't the only deity who has this problem. Whereas she reigns over couples, her peers are assigned to individuals, but the archers must strike the right people, too. If Anger were to, say, deliver a healthy dose of wrath to someone who wasn't angry, that person would go equally as crazy, spoiling for fights with anyone who got in their way.

With the type of arrow she'd been aiming at Andrew's stepfather, she could have had the man stumbling around, heartsick for a mate until he went insane. Or until she took pity on him, found someone who wasn't allergic to his flaws, and matched them.

Love packs away the arrow. She wasn't going to slice his face in half. She simply wanted the satisfaction of pointing a sharp object at him.

"My weapons don't kill," she says.

Andrew studies the bow. It's the first time he's seen her with it. And next he'll want to know—

"What do they do?" he asks.

She steps back. No way is she going to explain.

Andrew braces both hands on either side of the window frame. "I bet that dress I can make you talk."

Huh. A challenge. "I wager you can't."

"Do you always wear the same thing?"

While she searches for clever response, his gaze travels across her figure. "You're in my coat again," he says, the incense of his breath rushing into the morning air.

Love swallows. His voice makes the intonations of everyone else seem mass produced, unvarying and unspectacular by comparison. She wants to store the sound of him in a jar and carry it everywhere she goes.

"You came to see me, after all?" he asks.

"I—"

"Does this mean you have a crush on me?"

She squares her shoulders. "Crushes are beneath my concern. We may have frolicked last night, but do not get the wrong impression. I'm here for practical reasons, not for pleasure."

"Oh." The delighted expression he'd been wearing a moment ago slips through her fingers. She didn't give it permission to disappear. She wants it back.

One thing at a time. "My arrows exist for a peaceful purpose."

"That's way too cryptic. You have to give me more."

"No, I don't."

"Well look, you've gotta stop sticking up for me."

"Agreed."

"Hey." The stepfather emerges from his dungeon, spinning a set of keys around his finger while stalking to the front door. "Let's go. You can clean this mess up later."

Andrew remains at the window. "I have to get to work," he says reluctantly after his stepfather has gone outside.

Love nods. "Very well. I'll come with you."

"On one condition." He reaches out and dares to rattle the arrows in her quiver. "Don't use these again, okay?"

"I won't," she lies.

9

The rusty truck smells of stale feelings and exhaust. It wheezes to life, then barrels into a chugga-chugga-chugga rhythm that causes Love to jam a finger in her ear. Humans have invented many impressive things, however it's a mystery why they don't stop to consider the way those things sound. It's an affront to the inventions themselves.

Andrew chuckles while watching her. The chime of his laughter, as wonderful as hearing the stars' laugh, eclipses the truck's drone. His features have relaxed since the short walk from his house to the driveway, and in the minutes spent waiting for the car to heat up.

Hearing Andrew's mirth, the stepfather pauses in the act of scraping frost off the windshield. He frowns across the gurgling hulk of metal, then purses his lips and climbs inside without a word.

The evil, noisy truck seats only two people. Love springs into the air, into the rear bed, and lands upright, the coat flapping around her legs and teasing her bootlaces. She adjusts the hem of her dress, which has ridden up her thighs.

Andrew's laughter stops. She glances sideways and finds him staring at her in a trance, blushing and thinking boy things.

"Are you going to get in or stand there like an idiot?" the

stepfather asks from inside, his words infesting the moment like fumes.

Andrew tears his gaze away from Love and stumbles into the truck. She bites her lip. He definitely didn't see anything this time, but she'll have to rectify the issue of undergarments soon. The last thing she needs is to give him a show.

As the truck putters onto the street, the wind tickles her cheeks, devoid of that thing called *cold*. She settles on the hood, her legs dangling over Andrew's side and purposefully blocking his view out the passenger window. She hears his fingers tap the glass by her heel and, feeling saucy, she taps back with her boot. They fall into a funny but tuneless percussion that eventually lures a smirk out of her.

They drive through the main square, past the gazebo. Many times, it's been a practical spot for matchmaking.

In front of the bookstore, the truck jolts to a stop. She eavesdrops as the stepfather complains, "What's with you lately? Wipe that shit-eating grin off your face and get out."

Get in. Get out.

Get in. Get out.

Andrew gets out. Love hops down at the same time, landing in front of him. The stepfather gives Andrew one more toxic look before driving off. It's a pity to waste rugged handsomeness on an undeserving soul. For a mortal, the man would be nice to look at if he weren't busy hating his stepson.

"He's not as bad as he seems," Andrew says, shoving his hands into the pockets of his thin jacket.

How irksome that he's determined to defend the man. An honest response from her would be unwelcome, so she restrains herself. Andrew leads her up the steps to the shop, swinging his head over his shoulder to see if she's following. He halts at the door and leans against the frame. "Before we go in, let's get down to business."

She glances around to check if anyone's watching him talk to himself. "Business is good," she concurs.

"I liked—what was the word you used back at my place? Frolicking? I liked 'frolicking' with you last night, but you said it was dangerous to hang out again. I'm all ears for whatever changed your mind."

Yesterday, she worried about another deity turning up and finding out about Andrew before she could investigate him thoroughly. Little had she known that Anger was there, following them, watching them the whole time.

It's not dangerous anymore. Having a connection will give her better access to Andrew's personality. The Fates know that she's doing what she must to match him, so they won't do anything harsh—yet.

Not that they'll appreciate her answering whatever questions Andrew has about her people. She'll have to flutter her fingers and deflect. Surely, that can't be hard.

"I was lying," she says. "I gave you one evening, and then I wanted you to leave me alone, but I've had time to think. I'm curious to know more about you. And I trust your inquisitiveness hasn't ebbed so soon. However, I warn you: I prefer to speak in riddles. I'm cautious that way, in case you haven't noticed."

He pounces. "Tell me what you are."

"I'm neither living nor dead."

"There's more."

"Probably."

"And I may as well be digging for fossils with a fork, for all the details you're going to spill." When she nods with mock regret, he sighs. "I suppose you want to see where the little people work."

"That would be nice."

He opens the door and steps aside to let her in first. The gesture amuses her.

Although she's been here before, Love notices for the first time how fiction has truly made a home in this shop. She imagines stories of secrets and lost dreams, betrayal and cautionary tales, and a myriad of emotions thriving inside the pages. Fear, pity, rapture.

Like yesterday, the shopkeeper sits on the barstool by the register. She's wearing a 1940s shirtdress, with her glossy hair pinned up into victory rolls to match—Love recalls the style well. The decade is impossible to forget. She was in Europe, as many of the archers were. The war kept Love, Anger, and Sorrow busy.

"Morning, kiddo," the woman greets Andrew.

Love remembers how the shopkeeper nearly sensed her presence the last time. She's prepared in case it happens again. Andrew, on the other hand, looks between the shopkeeper and Love as if expecting the woman to spot Love. His jittery behavior doesn't go unnoticed. The woman's forehead crinkles into an accordion.

Love elbows him. "Say something."

"Kiddo, are you all ri—"

"Hell no, but who cares?" He points toward one of the rooms. "The books still that way?"

"Unless the gods moved them around overnight."

Love snorts. *She* might do something like that, but the Fates have better things to do than ... oh. That was a joke.

Andrew gets to work. His first task is to reorganize the Mystery and Suspense sections. Love shadows him, content to watch his knuckles and knees bend, as well as his backside. Mostly his backside.

For a while, they don't speak, the intermission allowing him to get settled, though every so often he looks over at her.

Whenever he does, Love can't help smiling. *Yes, I'm still here.* And the corner of his mouth quirks, reminding her of a letter written in cursive.

He selects books with humorous titles and shows them to her. He finds thoughtful passages to share: confessions, revelations, awkward interactions, grand settings, unwelcome memories. Passion. Death. Friendship.

She tucks herself safely into this routine, and he does the same. Aside from the few Sunday shoppers who've braved the weather and need Andrew's assistance, it's a slow day, which is good. Love doesn't care for being interrupted.

Snatching random books, she relocates them to random shelves, lifting her brow at Andrew and wordlessly threatening disorder while he pretends to ignore her.

Love uses her arrow to poke at another book until it's wobbling precariously close to the edge. From the opposite side of the shelf, Andrew nudges the book back with his finger.

When they realize they're able to connect this way, Andrew declares, "Okay. All bets are off." They play tug-of-war. Her strength should give her the advantage, but he isn't a normal mortal, and feeling the worrisome force of his grip reminds her of whom she's dealing with, how he's affecting her.

Andrew sobers when he almost gets caught laughing at thin air by the shopkeeper. She bustles in, her hands on her hips. "Now, now. No having fun without me. Them's the rules," she says, expecting to see a customer.

"Private joke with an imaginary friend," Andrew says, disregarding the warning shake of Love's head. "I'm working, though. I swear."

"You've been holding out on me if imaginary friends are all the rage these days. Well, don't just stand there. Be a good host and introduce us."

Andrew's eyes flit toward Love, questioning. Gah! Love jerks to the side, hiding herself behind the nearest bookshelf. Which is a foolish move considering the woman is merely playing along with Andrew and can't see Love.

Besides, the chance at interaction is undeniably thrilling, and Love's already been to this woman's house. It's only fair to present herself. How much harm can that do?

Love pokes her head around the shelf, tiptoeing into partial view, her hands clasped behind her back. "Don't tell her my name," she begs Andrew.

He grins and makes a show of introductions, swinging his arm between them. "Miss Georgie, this is . . . Lily," he finishes, using the name Love had sarcastically offered last night.

"Here I've been trying to guess who this mystery girl is, and now I know why I kept getting it wrong. She's ethereal. You do have taste, Andrew." Miss Georgie's welcoming expression seeks out Love. Thankfully, her gaze doesn't quite latch on to her. "It's nice to meet you, Lily."

She feels a surge of trust toward this mortal pair. They're crazy. It's lovely to see.

She curtsies. "Likewise."

"God, this is weird," Andrew chuckles.

Miss Georgie turns to him. "Kiddo, I work in a world of stories. My warped mind's got no problem having an imagination. I'm weird. Let's be weird together." She winks, then returns to the register.

The rush of meeting her recedes too soon. Love ponders whether their exchange truly happened at all.

Andrew whispers, "Stay put." He disappears around the corner, then comes back with a pen and the notebook he'd been writing in when she first met him—he must have stored it in his backpack. He stands close to her, opens to a blank page, writes, and hands it over.

It's time for us to get real.

She wavers. Enterprising mortal that he is, he's stolen the initiative.

Don't pout. You said I was allowed to be curious.

"If you must," she yields. "By the way, you're not going mad."

You're a poor mind reader. I wasn't thinking about that.

"Good."

Why can I see you?

She glances at the ceiling. This is complicated terrain.

Aww, you don't know either, do you?

Of course she knows!

You're as clueless as me. You're stumped. You're incompetent. You're—

"You're unique," she says. "Only truly selfless humans can see me."

Surprise crosses his face. He takes a moment to absorb this.

His attractive hand starts moving again. *I guess that's a compliment.*

"Saying your nails are nice is a compliment," she remarks. "What I'm telling you is a fact. Your nails are nice, of course."

Thanks.

"You're welcome."

How long have you lived in the forest?

"For a long time, and no time at all."

Why are you there? What do you do all day?

"Raid nests and bully owls."

Is there one of you or millions?

"Yes."

How fun is it to mess with me?

"I'll tell you when I'm done."

We could be friends, you know.

Love falls silent. Friends. Even if his suggestion came with a set of instructions—one, *define*, two, *consider*, and three, *accept*—she still wouldn't know what she's supposed to do with the rest of it, this friendship. No one has ever wanted to be her friend before. Not even Wonder.

Please, tell me. What are you hiding?

Andrew could take his pick. She's hiding the stars, the snowfall, the soil, the human heart, and the laws of immortal destiny. Oh, and a romance novel in her right pocket.

Why are you alone?

This was going so well. She narrows her eyes at him.

"Kiddo—" They jump apart as Miss Georgie comes back. "Snack time. I'm craving a six-dollar slice of pumpkin-gingerbread goodness."

"I thought you were going to start baking pies yourself," Andrew teases.

"Uh-uh. You don't want to see that. I'd have an easier time cutting a potato with my finger than wielding a rolling pin. Providing you hold down the fort, show your Lily a good time, I'll pick you up a slice. Deal?"

"I don't make promises."

"That's my boy," she boasts.

The front door opens and closes with her departure. At Love's hesitation, Andrew insists, "It's okay. You could tell her your record player has started predicting your future, and she'd humor you. She's kind of, like, the local eccentric, but no quackery or anything. She's a superstitious dreamer. To her, anything goes. She's not going to go all town crier on us and tell people that I'm talking to myself, or that ghosts are infesting the streets or something. That would be a riot coming from her.

"She keeps to herself, like I do. She's a widow—used to be married to a playwright years ago. I think losing him made her retreat into stories. Instead of living with a bunch of cats, she lives with books."

"And playbills in the attic," Love adds.

"In a steam trunk," Andrew finishes.

Then Miss Georgie's a devoted believer in fantasy, which is why she sensed Love to begin with. It's fascinating only because it's innocent, because Andrew's power of sight is beyond the capability of people like this woman.

"She dresses like she belongs to history," Love muses.

"She wears charm pretty good, too. Fits her like a glove. Has ever since I was little. She was friends with my mom."

"Was?" Love asks.

He falters. "Yeah. Anyway, one summer when I was four? I caught a firefly in a jar and kept it as a pet. Whenever Miss Georgie would stop at our house for a visit, she'd ask to see it and say, 'Have you taken it out for a flight today?'"

They chuckle. Andrew glances over his shoulder and listens for customers. "We both knew the firefly would get away if I did that, but she acted like it was a typical pet, never made me feel awkward about anything I did or said."

"You're lucky to have her," Love admits. "It's nice to have someone."

Andrew sets the notebook down. "When we met there was no one in the forest with you. You looked officially alone."

Relentless boy with his tiresome stare. He won't let the

subject drop.

What's worse, his gentle comment causes a rock to lodge in her throat. She pretends not to care about her answer. "There is only me. I'm used to it."

"I don't believe you."

"Because you don't wish to."

"Wrong. I'm the selfless one, remember? My misery doesn't love company."

Her ears perk up. Finally, something about him. "You're miserable?"

"That's probably overstating things, but you've met my stepfather. You've met my 'friends,'" he jokes mildly. "The sun's not exactly shining in my world . . . It's winter, but you know what I mean. What people see is a kid who isn't surrounded by the most stable elders. There's nothing wrong with Miss Georgie, except that she calls me her 'kiddo' like I'm still twelve, which is kinda embarrassing." He looks bashful. "It makes her happy, though, so I don't care. I wouldn't let anyone say a bad thing about her. She's misunderstood. My stepdad is, too, and . . . Well, everyone at school judges me by my roots. I'm not overwhelmed by admirers."

"How do you entertain yourself?"

"Writing. I like stories."

She thinks of the note he wrote for her and what he said last night about Miss Georgie's attic, how it's good place for inspiration. "You fancy make-believe."

"I like that make-believe reveals the truth from a different angle."

"You're a philosopher," she muses.

"Another word for it is geek."

"Or philosopher."

"You're just flattering me because you haven't seen my comic book collection."

They laugh again. The tips of their shoes would bump if hers didn't come from almighty stock and have the stubborn habit of passing through his.

"And you like taking lone walks in the woods," Love prompts, still puzzled about that.

The texture of Andrew's face changes, emotions bending his features in the opposite direction of what they had been a moment ago. He steps back and mutters, "Yeah."

He returns to his work and doesn't speak. So she wasn't mistaking his prickly reaction when she brought up this mystery last night. Unfortunately, trying to figure out his secret thoughts at this point would be like trying to find the center of the ocean. It's too much, too soon for him.

She gives him his space and sneaks over to the romance section. Her fingers slip into her pocket and retrieve the paperback. Intending to put it back, she lifts her hand—

"Love?"

—and naturally gets caught. Grunting, she wheels on Andrew. He's standing in the doorway, his attention darting between her guilty face and the title in her hand. "So this is where you got the book. Man, I should have known. You've been a busy stalker."

"I was going to give it back," she chides. "This is me, Love, giving it back."

"Did you like it?"

The story was enticing. "Adequately done."

"Picky, picky."

Love swipes the flat of her hand through his shoulder, attempting to mock slap him, then regrets it as Andrew gasps. His reaction should make her chortle, but all it does is remind her how isolated she is from everything.

He rubs his shoulder. "You can take another one if you promise to return it."

The offer distracts her, and she grabs the first title she sees. On the cover is a classic painting of Eros leaning over the sleeping mortal, Psyche. Unnerved, she shoves it back onto the shelf.

"Not a fan of guys with wings?" Andrew guesses.

Eros in Greek mythology. Cupid in Roman myths. They're the same: not real.

Cupid is a disaster. She's read many of the pathetic tales—she couldn't take reading all of them—and nearly died of laughter, which is better than dying of insult. The dominant image is of him either wearing a diaper, which is degrading, or wearing armor, which is creepy on a toddler.

Eros, she can accept. In variations of his myth, and in paintings, he's depicted young but not infantile. He's strong and impressive to look upon. Sometimes he's mischievous—that much is accurate. And there are a few other details the myths got right—some emotions, a bit about the stars, her bow—but not enough. Certainly not the one about her gender, or about her having wings.

She turns toward Andrew, a heap of replies crowding her tongue, but she realizes that he's closed the gap between them. He chews on his lower lip, then releases it, letting it unfurl back into place. Its wetness shines beneath the overhead light.

He holds out a trembling hand and traces the shape of her arm, descending to her elbow. "You're like mist," he says. "You really don't feel this?"

Love shakes her head. "No."

But that's not entirely true, because this illusion of a touch has turned her into a current, this human has reached down to her bones.

Then his fingers curl right through her hip, and he lowers his voice. "How 'bout that?"

"No," she manages again.

"Just checking," he says sadly. "You're missing out."

It takes her a while to get past this disturbing remark. He sees the tragedy before him, confirming she's not deluded, that human touch holds sweet possibilities. Or it could be the siren's call of humans, and she's falling for it, because she's the poorest excuse for a goddess that has ever existed.

She screams that he knows nothing, that he's the lesser being and better not forget it. She flings books across the room and tells him to shut up, accuses him of gloating and rubbing it in her face.

At least, she fantasizes about doing this. In reality, she stays quiet as his wrist twitches against the air of her body, until the shop's front door opens with a *ping* and breaks the spell.

Love recoils from Andrew. She doesn't want another book or anything else from him, and the proof of it must clutter her face, because he frowns, stung by her rejection.

She wants to tell him not to worry. He won't be rejected by the next girl.

10

Still in a turbulent mood from her day with Andrew, Love steals into Holly's room the next afternoon and takes her confusion out on the girl's bed. While waiting for her to return from the bathroom, Love hops onto the mattress and bounces, her head pitching toward the ceiling, her boots crushing the perfectly-made polka dot blanket to smithereens. The ridiculous mini pillow flops over the edge. The springs creak.

Love feels a little better. A little.

She had no choice but to come here, to study Holly's life and how it might fit to Andrew's. Love had hoped to pursue Holly yesterday, right after parting from Andrew when his shift ended, but Love was too mentally unsettled by those hours spent by his side. She escaped to her tree instead, needing the peace and quiet so that her wits could recover properly, all the while muttering and chastising herself for being a lightarrow.

She could have trailed Holly at school today, but Love prefers order. As much as she enjoys cavorting through Ever High School, she wants to begin with the lovers' personal lives outside of busy classrooms first—that's how it always goes with her young targets, and she isn't about to change her routine.

Holly had mentioned her street name, Mayfair Court, to Andrew in the park, so it was easy to track the girl's friendly berry scent from there. To start, she's a tidy one. The bedroom is spotless, and the pencils—only pencils, facing down—in the jar on her desk all match. Her slippers rest at a set angle beneath a dress form modeling layers of necklaces. Pictures of her and Griffin line the rim of her full-length mirror without overlapping. In every photo, she's looking at the camera while he's looking at her.

As Love thumps up and down, she compares this place to Andrew's room. This morning, he'd idled outside his front door as if waiting for Love, craning his head and staring into the distance until finally slumping down the steps and heading to school. Hoping to snoop around for extra clues about his personality, she broke into his house once he was gone, climbing to his window and wrenching it up, glad that it was open and she didn't have to bust the lock to get in.

His bedroom was organized chaos. His minty, selfless scent lingered everywhere—the scent must come naturally from him, from his body, since she's still able to detect it. Three sloppily painted question marks graced the wall behind his twin bed. A tarnished silver bookmark engraved, *Love, Mom*, rested on the nightstand. Towers of notebooks and comic books and fables crowded the floor. Aged posters of science-fiction novels were taped to the ceiling, slanted and curling at the edges.

Love's bouncing subsides to a contemplative bob. Andrew's posters versus the scalloped wall decal—monogrammed with Holly's initials above Holly's headboard.

What else? Based on the images flashing on her laptop, the girl likes school sports and dances. Andrew doesn't strike Love as that type.

Holly adores her phone. She's spent a ridiculous amount of time fondling that apparatus, stroking the screen with the waning half-moon tip of her manicured finger. The phone plays a lot of peppy dance songs.

Andrew also isn't the pop-music type, nor is he a gadget boy. He owns a phone, but it's a peeling flip model, which he's used only once—to check the time—since Love met him.

Their families are polar opposites. Yesterday, she saw him chomp on burnt toast while enduring his stepfather's abusive grunts. By contrast, Holly's parents apparently both work from home, and the moment she arrived from school, the family had gathered in the kitchen to snack on homemade cookies and plan their monthly board game night.

The girl's closet is filled with delicate colors. Andrew likes black wool coats.

Love likes black wool coats, too.

Before heading to the bathroom, the girl finally put down her phone in favor of one of the romances she bought in Andrew's shop. So there it is. The lovers' link is reading. This isn't much to work with.

It does give Love an idea, though. During their frolic the other night, Andrew assured her that he's always at the bookstore, if not at school. He could be working another shift at this very moment. If Love could find a sneaky way to provoke Holly to venture over there . . .

Love abandons the bed and snatches the romance novel from the nightstand. A bookmark sticks out of page 152. She scans the story, then rips out pages 160 to 165. It takes place during a lovemaking scene, just after the heroine slowly, sensually undresses the hero, but before the hero returns the favor. She dumps the book back onto the table, pleased by the thud it makes.

This is the part that usually excites Love, the moment when she sets events into motion, guiding the lovers' paths like train tracks about to cross. The moment when her invisibility doesn't count and she has an effect on this world.

Yet the satisfaction doesn't come this time. Indeed, spite gnaws at her insides.

What is that girl still doing in the bathroom? Painting a circus on her face? Scribes have illuminated manuscripts faster!

Holly returns with thicker eyelashes and glistening lips. She pauses and surveys the beating Love gave the blankets. Frowning, the girl straightens out every wrinkle.

Love remembers the mismatched sheets on Andrew's unkempt bed. This isn't going to be easy. Her arrows are potent enough to bypass these details and infuse eternal love between them, but it wouldn't be an impeccable pairing. They need to establish a connection first.

The girl snuggles against her pillows and opens her book. Love settles herself onto the opposite end of the bed and lies on her back, her head hanging off the edge as she scrutinizes the ceiling, awaiting the inevitable.

A dreamy sigh drifts into her ears. Love rises on her elbows and follows the sound. Holly's engrossed in the story, twirling a lock of blond hair around her finger, blushing and practically swooning at the page's content. She must have gotten to the beginning of the steamy scene.

Love has read a similar book and was also swept away. She understands this girl. Right now, she could be like this girl. She wants to ask if the longing feels the same, if there's more or less to it. She wants to share questions and compare answers, to have someone to talk to, another girl to confide in.

Do you think real embraces are just as intense? Does it need to be with a certain boy?

This ardent side of Holly, stirred by passionate prose,

is telling.

Andrew is a writer. This might be useful later.

Love hates that it might be useful. She hates to imagine him writing something to this girl, the way he wrote to Love—or to picture him writing something more meaningful. Once they're together, will Holly have the same beguiled reaction to Andrew as she does to the book? Or will their private interludes be different? Better?

The girl's phone rings. Not rings, actually—it's a titanic sound that hollers for attention. Holly jerks in surprise and grabs the phone, dropping the book in her lap.

"Hello?" she asks.

"Babe!"

It's a strapping voice on the cusp of baritone, not quite old enough but trying rather hard to be. As the girl turns on the speaker, Love identifies Griffin's voice.

"I'm on my way, damsel," he says. "Keep your ears peeled for the stallion in five."

Holly straightens, scoots to the edge of the mattress, and swings her legs over the side. She checks the time on her phone. "You're early."

"I couldn't wait. I missed you. Can't I do that?"

"Yeah," she mutters.

"You sound annoyed."

"It's just, you didn't ask if you could come over already. You do whatever you want without thinking."

"Babe, come on. Are you still mad about Andrew?"

"Still?" she repeats. "It wasn't that long ago. Yes, I'm mad. You totally overreacted."

"Can't I defend my girlfriend? He keeps getting in your way."

The girl sighs as if she's heard this before. "I told you, he wasn't. Those were accidents. And how do you explain what happened at school today? You let him take the fall for the whole thing in the park. A teacher overhears you big-mouthing about it in the hall, and Andrew says it was all his fault, and you just keep your mouth shut."

Love's jaw unhinges. So Andrew willingly shouldered the blame for this beast.

"My record was already in the crapper," Griffin groans through the speaker. "Coach would've kicked me off the team if I got nailed again. Dude, they slapped Andrew's wrist! And he hit back, you know, made the first move and then pulled some tornado ninja crap on us."

Love smirks. Tornado ninja crap.

"Forget it," Holly says. "I don't want to go over this again. Anyway, I thought you were still at the varsity blood drive."

"Done and done. I only had to stick around for an hour."

"Oh."

At her obvious lack of enthusiasm, Griffin falls silent. On second thought, he might have delayed Love's plan. Does this mean the girl's not going to return the novel to Andrew's job? That was the whole point of ripping out the pages, but she hasn't discovered they're missing yet.

"I'm bringing those stupid marshmallows you like," Griffin entices. "Those mini vanilla ones, from that place you always talk about. Not the grocery store ones—I know you hate those."

"I don't hate anything," Holly replies.

"You hate me right now," he says, sullen. "I just care about you. I want to hang out with you. You're not gonna give me a second chance, babe?"

She softens. "I didn't say that. You have to stop being such a ..."

"A what?"

She picks up the book and stares at it. "A wolf."

"I'll make it up to you," he promises, then hangs up.

Love would scorn the girl's general taste in boys, but the idea of specially made mini marshmallows gives her pause. She has difficulty envisioning the boyfriend's big hands carrying a bag of tiny sweets. She can, however, picture him throwing them at people's heads in class.

Holly flops back on the bed, and Love does the same, returning to her original position. After a moment, a feminine gasp tickles Love's ear, making her sit up again. Holly has reached the torn section of the book, her expression scrunched like a sponge as she rifles back and forth through the text as if the missing pages will magically reappear.

"Just great," the girl complains. "And they lived happily-whatever-after."

Love's delight is short-lived as the "stallion" honks from the driveway, the call galloping through the room. She listens to the crunching sounds of resentment build inside the girl. Holly dumps the book on the bed, then grabs her puffy jacket and a bag dangling off the knob of her closet door.

Love grinds her teeth. The girl is supposed to go to bookstore now, to get her money back for the novel and accidentally run into Andrew. She's not supposed to go anywhere else today!

Snatching her bow and quiver off the floor, Love darts after the girl, who detours into the kitchen, saying something to her parents about Griffin and a date.

"He's early," the mother says.

"He'll learn," the father says.

Love follows Holly out of the house. Griffin drives a rumbling, restless sports car. He fills the interior to capacity, reeking of false machismo and buffoonery. Yet he beams at his girlfriend, his damsel, as if her beauty is the sole reason gravity exists, because something that amazing looking shouldn't be allowed to float away.

Circling the vehicle, Love glares at the miniature helmet—from that sport called hockey, she guesses—hanging off the rearview mirror and the *I'll huff and puff and run your ass down* bumper sticker. She wracks her brain. The girl shouldn't have tolerated her boyfriend's premature arrival. She should be heading to the bookstore, with her tinted lips and thickened lashes.

And this relentless alpha brute of a boyfriend is here instead of working overtime at a blood drive, where he could be contributing pints of wolf DNA to patients. It's clear he's possessive and likes to commandeer Holly's time. He's going to thwart Love's mission on a regular basis. She needs to stop them from driving away, stop the boy from "making it up" to the girl.

Griffin revs the engine—oh, brother—worried no one in this country will hear him. Sighing, Love rips an arrow out of her pack and shoots the front passenger tire. The iron tip slashes through the rubber. The gash emits a wheezing cry, and the tire deflates into a flabby black puddle.

"What the hell . . ." Griffin tears out of the driver's side, and Holly follows.

"It's okay," she tries to reassure him, but his grunts stampede her words.

He rants about the plan he had. The gazebo in town, her favorite coffee, the vanilla marshmallows, the blanket he brought. Too bad that plan didn't include a spare tire.

Holly ventures into the house and then returns with her parents, along with a litter of children who swarm the yard. One of the kids scales the car and proclaims, "I'm a knight, here to slay the enemy!"

Love approves. She points to Griffin. *There he is. Get him.*

"It just blew on me," Griffin explains.

"Have to call it in," the girl's father says, rubbing the back of his neck. "I don't have a tire that size."

Love sits on the hood, crosses her arms, and celebrates. The parents return to the house with the children (who've stolen the marshmallows from the car), but the lovers remain outside, shivering and talking. Love monitors the situation, making sure they don't find alternative transportation or a romantic form of distraction.

A tow truck arrives fifteen minutes later. It's driven by Andrew's father.

He gets out, chewing on something invisible while he surveys the damage. He glances at the couple standing there and squints his leathery face at Holly. "I know you."

Love tenses. The girl tenses.

"Didn't you walk my boy home the other night?" he asks.

"Your boy?" she peeps.

"My stepkid. White hair. Limp. Pathetic. Was that you with him?"

Apparently Griffin had no idea about this. His grisly expression says so.

The stepfather's gaze ticks between the lovers. "Little prick came home that night with a shiner." He strides up to Griffin and goes nose-to-nose with him. "I know you, too. You're McKee's boy. Lemme guess, you're the boyfriend, and that was your handiwork on my kid."

They size each other up. The senses flare. The venomous taste in Love's mouth, which is coming from the older man, has to be directed at Griffin. At last, Andrew's odious relative is going to defend him.

Before the boy can flex his muscles and deny everything, the stepfather wipes his hands on his uniform and swaggers backward, droning, "You shoulda gone for his bad leg."

Fiend! Savage!

Love despises her invisibility. She wants to be human just so she can get her claws on him, cripple him, and see how he likes it. She wants to hotwire the man's truck and ram it into him.

As the stepfather unwinds a chain from the tow truck, Holly gapes, and Griffin scrambles to process what he heard. Retaliation from him is certainly likely once Love brings Andrew and the girl together. The stepfather all but gave Griffin an invitation. These male mortals are violent problems that require muzzles to cage their wrath.

Love spits at the ground to get the unfortunate taste of an idea out of her mouth. There's one person who can help her take care of this problem, but she really, really, really . . .

. . . really, really, really . . .

. . . really doesn't want to ask for his assistance.

"What now?" he demands from behind.

Too late. The stars couldn't be more annoying. Even in the daytime, they're awake in that cursed sky, ready to help a goddess summon a god—whether that goddess intended to or not. Love rolls her eyes and wheels around to face her visitor.

Tunic. Fingerless gloves. Earring. Grimace.

Anger.

11

"I can't do that," Anger growls.

"Yes, you can," Love argues.

"No, I can't."

"Do it or I'll tell everyone in the Peaks that you're scared of snowstorms—"

Anger's whacks a container of engine oil. It flies across the auto repair shop, and one of the mechanics ducks at the last minute to avoid getting pelted in the head. The container smacks against a wall and hits the floor. A group of men twist and stare, searching for the culprit.

"Whoa," one of them says.

"Have I been drinking?" another one asks.

Andrew's stepfather pokes his hard-boiled head out from beneath Griffin's car. He scans the shop, then mutters, "Hate this ghost town."

That brings to mind the arrow Love shot into his house.

The repair shop's garage is filled with the sounds of tools drilling and rock music shrieking. The space smells of mortal aftershave, fatigue, and Anger. He'd been holding back. A true swat, and that container would have exploded. Or more to the left, and the rusted motorcycle beside them would have taken the blow and launched into the air.

He *is* scared of snowstorms. Given that, it's amazing he spends time in her sector at all. Only their class knows about his fear.

She quirks an eyebrow at him. He was so incensed by her summons—not that she called him willingly, and not that he had to answer if he didn't want to—that he refused to speak with her at Holly's house.

In the time it took for the stepfather to chain Griffin's car, Anger cooled down, grousing about having a job of his own to do. It was on the tip of her tongue to suggest that maybe he was in the neighborhood anyway, since he's been spying on Love, but she would prefer to ignore that fact.

They'd followed the stepfather's truck as it dragged the sports car away, with its surly owner tagging along. Griffin parked himself in the waiting room and is presently alternating between tearing through an auto magazine and texting his girlfriend. Love hopes Holly hasn't gone to the bookstore in the meantime.

Love wants her to, of course.

Of course. But not without Love to accompany her.

Her least favorite god broods next to her, looking tall and inconvenienced. Does that fierce expression ever exhaust his facial muscles? Would smoothing them out make his skin crackle?

"They're perfect targets for you," she argues. "A mere notch of your power will—"

Anger holds up his palm, effectively cutting her off. "Enough. You know I can't do what you ask, not outside of my territory and not impulsively. It's our law."

"The Fate Court will forgive you in this case."

"They don't care who's bullying your mortal. Matter of fact, they won't mind if the bullies cut Andrew open with a pocket knife and save us all this trouble."

"That is a cruel and unjust wish! It's beneath the Court and the stars, and you know it. The Court will care if these villains screw up my task."

Anger's palm falls to his side. "Screw up? Even your vocabulary is beginning to sound ... abnormal."

Human. That's what he was going to say.

Humans are not abnormal. They like books and writing, they aren't afraid of deities, and they have an amusing way of expressing themselves, especially when he—they—ugh!

"If I'm abnormal, you're a sissy," Love says.

"I see pettiness isn't beneath you," Anger drawls. "*A mere notch.* You think I'm going to do your bidding *merely* because you say these men are temperamental. Everyone in this world gets mad. What I do is about more than that."

"I know," she concedes, lowering her voice. Just because archers have the freedom to choose their targets—Andrew being the exception—it doesn't mean they're allowed to take advantage of that liberty by shooting whomever they wish. This is a mindful job. They've trained decades for it.

However, she's not asking for the moon. No one owns that.

She hadn't called out to him on purpose, but she'd figured that since he was here now, she might as well appeal to the peaceful side of his power. Like Envy and Sorrow, he can incite the emotion if it's necessary for human motivation or growth, to help mortals learn a lesson. But like Envy and Sorrow, he most often reduces the emotion to calm people down.

"I need help," Love says. "Trust me."

His laughter practically causes him to levitate. "Trust you."

She digs into the pockets of her soulless soul for an ounce of pride, something that signals she's offended. There's no room for ego, though. Not presently.

"I can't do this with them in the way. They're dangerous to my …" She sucks up greasy engine-oil air. "My target. They hurt him, and I don't believe they're going to stop. It will get worse. I don't know how to prevent it." That last part is hard for her to admit.

Fine. There might be wiggle room for pride.

Her mind drifts to Andrew. *What's he reading? Eating? Touching?*

What is cold to him? What is heat?

She thinks of asking him about this and that. She thinks of him and him and more him.

Who is he thinking about?

At the drum of Anger's fingers on his belt, Love's mind stumbles back to the present. He contemplates the wintry landscape, the stud in his ear flaring at her. "I thought you were a master at cunning."

"I marvel how you'd know that."

"Fine. Wonder blabbed that I've watched you now and then. You need it."

"If you say so," she snaps. "I need you to spy on me, I need you to watch my back, and I need you to keep those oafs from attacking my target, who's technically *our* target—the Court's target. So yes. You've won. Are you satisfied?"

Her throat feels uncomfortable. Living in the forest is a quiet affair, but since Andrew first pried a word out of her, she's been unable to seal herself back up. Everything inside her has been loud and hysterical since. Words have constantly been on the edge of falling out of her, into the world where she can't take them back.

"Watch out," Anger says. "Your voice is approaching high

tide. Any more of this gibberish, and someone might mistake you for Lunacy."

He's not helping that tide. She's dealing with two human inbreeds from the murky world of wicked, and Anger fancies this is a good time to reward her with mockery. Besides, there is no deity called Lunacy. It's not an emotion.

His finger-drumming stops. "If you want to protect your mortal boy, you'll shoot him before you're on the brink of collapse and the Court is forced to kill him."

Andrew is not *her* mortal boy.

Anger must see in her expression something awful because he deflates. He steps forward. She steps back. He checks himself, a covert and unaggressive emotion dulling his features. It's so unusual, so unsettling, that Love pauses, waiting for whatever is afflicting him to subside.

Another drilling noise spirals through the garage from one of those horrible tools, the sound coming from the belly of the shop. One of the mechanics hums to himself while another takes a cigarette break. Within the men, she inhales stress and depression.

The stepfather is the only one who smells empty. His whole life is narrowed to his task: harnessing a new tire onto Griffin's car. It's like the stepfather has squeezed anything resembling spirit out of his body. Love would almost call that a talent if it didn't mean complimenting him, and if she weren't determined to ruin him for eternity.

Eternity happens. An arrow slices through the air and plows into the man's heart. He rolls over groaning in pain.

Love turns toward Anger. He lowers his bow. "Never say I don't listen."

Because he's Anger, his strike is harder for mortals to recover from than her own arrows. It looks like the stepfather's having a heart attack. The other mechanics drop what they're doing and charge toward him, and he tries to sit up and bat them away, while one of the men rushes to the phone.

Anger cuts through the garage with Love on his tail and takes care of Griffin in the waiting room, shooting him in the chest. Love won't lie to herself. She enjoys watching him topple out of the chair and turn into the disabled creature he accused Andrew of being. Meanwhile, the mechanics are in the garage, too preoccupied with the stepfather to know what else is going on.

They'll both survive. And they'll behave themselves from now on.

Normally an archer decides how long the magic of their weapons lasts. It could be anywhere from an hour, to a year, to forever. The flash of Anger's arrows, their blazing light, indicates that he released life shots.

This is another reason why Love is different from other archers. The human race mates for life, so her arrows—the ones that incite love, and the ones that extinguish it—have a lifetime effect no matter what. That's how she crafted her weapons.

Her lust-provoking arrows are the only ones that she can give a time limit to. It would be nonsensical for them to have an eternal impact on humans—that would be another form of madness, hardly practical in the long run.

A wailing ambulance swerves into the parking lot. Its presence is unnecessary, but that's for the humans to find out later. Before they even reach the emergency room, the stepfather will be perfectly fine, as will Griffin, who still hasn't been discovered.

She and Anger retreat a few paces from the shop.

"Thank you," she says.

Anger shrugs. "We both chose iron. Maybe that means we

understand each other better than we think. Or we complement each other."

A joke would diffuse that look of his and what it makes her feel, but Love can't think of one. Her eyes drift over his shoulder.

Andrew.

He's standing at the back of the ambulance while the paramedics load his brittle stepfather inside. It looks like Andrew had been walking alongside the man's stretcher when he spotted Love. The mechanics must have called him, and he must have been at work because Miss Georgie is here as well, speaking rapidly with one of the paramedics.

His eyes drag from Love to Anger in surprise. Love's foot lifts to retreat a step, but then she feels something strange against her elbow, a quick but tentative pressure. A touch.

Anger's touch. He's reached out to alert her, or perhaps to steady himself since he's never been seen by a mortal before and is cowed by Andrew's selfless gaze. Then his fingers disappear. Damn him, he literally disappears, which makes them both appear guilty of something.

Andrew looks frazzled, confused. He stares at the place where Anger touched her. When they stood together amidst the bookshelves, and Andrew asked, she said there was no one like her in this world. No other boys who could touch her.

His expression shrinks the space between them. *You're a liar.*

That's what his face says. He climbs into the ambulance without sparing Love another glance. While Miss Georgie follows in her car, the emergency vehicle skids onto the road and speeds down the lane, the siren blaring, the red lights flashing at Love before the frigid landscape swallows them.

She doesn't understand why he's upset, nor does she comprehend the sudden restlessness in her fingers and toes. She may have lied, but it wasn't that bad. She didn't say she would tell him everything.

Or does he think Anger is her mate?

Well, let him. It's his problem, not hers, and that's that. She doesn't have time to play into this drama. The panic is unpleasant, and it's doing unfavorable things to her sanity.

She returns to her tree and tries to nap, but she tosses and turns—as best as anyone can toss and turn on a branch. The memory of Andrew's wounded expression at the auto garage, how it contorted the watercolor on his cheek, makes a mess of her. She has no book to read. The weather is boring. The snowflake ornament looks sad hanging by itself, but that's the way some things belong.

12

Tuesday. Andrew's still mad.

There's nothing Love can do about that, and there's nothing she *should* do about it. He hobbles to school early, without pausing to daydream at the woods, and spends his morning in the library while she spies on him, her face poking out from a gap in a bookshelf. He writes and thinks, his pen poised on paper, silent questions in the creases on his face.

Holly floats through a solar system of classes and friends. Griffin is no longer a violent boy, which, Love realizes, isn't as helpful as she thought it would be, even if it does protect Andrew. Rather than growing apart like they were doing after the boy attacked Andrew, Griffin redeems himself and mends his courtship with Holly. Before first period, he surprises her with marshmallows and lets her make all the physical moves, his tone not possessive like before. It melts Holly, and she willingly cuddles into the valley of his arms.

Love's attempts to matchmake are catastrophic. She waits until the administration lady, whose stack of bracelets rattles like a set of tambourines, goes the bathroom. She peeks in the student files to get Andrew and Holly's schedules and find out if they have any classes near one another—when they'll be close enough to urge together. Between their second and third periods,

Love stations herself in the crowded hallway and shoots Holly's purse from her hand. Whipping out a series of arrows, Love strikes the bag repeatedly, propelling it across the floor, right toward Andrew, who's opening his locker.

Love's aim and speed maneuvers the bag around students' feet as Holly chases after it. "Excuse me," she keeps saying.

She almost reaches Andrew when some Fatesforsaken pimply boy snatches the purse off the floor and hands it to her with a bucktoothed grin.

After lunch, Love steals Holly's wallet, intending to plant it someplace where Andrew will find it, compelling him return it to Holly later. He arrives at his Gothic literature class studiously early, dumps his bag on the ground by his seat, and migrates back into the hallway, to the water fountain for a drink. Love trots past him and tosses the wallet on the floor, close to his backpack, but not too close. However, the teacher enters the room, proceeds to stalk up and down the rows and drop leaflets of paper on each desk, and spots the wallet before Andrew returns.

During their fifth class, Love makes a final attempt. Using supplies from an art class, she creates two flyers announcing a fake book club that's meeting in the library after the final bell, then stashes them in Holly and Andrew's lockers.

Andrew, who shows up on time, learns from the puzzled librarian that no such club exists. She even makes a call to Student Affairs to double-check, then chirps the same information to Holly, who arrives five minutes after Andrew is already gone.

Love knocks her head against the nearest locker in frustration, making a crater-sized dent in the metal, which demolishes the owner's astronomy project inside.

By that evening, she's grouchy from having to avoid Andrew's sight and failing on a monumental level to force an encounter between the lovers. She prowls the length of Holly's room, plotting what to try next. Holly plants herself at the window seat and paints her toenails a seasonal tint of purple, which makes Love stop and stare down at her own boots. All the color she ever boasts is the white of her dress and the black of her hair.

Her finger stabs one of the girl's romance paperbacks, making it fall off the desk and land on the floor. The girl glances up from her pinky toe and notices the book.

The reminder is a stretch, but it works. Once her toenails are dry, she packs the book and leaves the house. Love gives a sharp nod. Without exception, disrupting mortal routines has been an asset to her job: mixing up reservations, making lovers stand in a long queue, flattening a bus tire—Love has a history with flat tires—to delay a couple waiting at the bus stop.

And now, destroying books. At the store, Love watches through the window, rubbing her hands together in anticipation. Thankfully, not only is Andrew working an after-school shift, he's also manning the register. Holly flushes as she waves hello, then impulsively scans the New Arrivals shelf, choosing a title for herself before heading over to him. She hands him the ripped paperback first.

Andrew flips through the pages. He says something apologetic about the torn section, then offers her an even exchange, and she smiles. Andrew ducks his head, the sides of his lips creasing. In shyness? In pleasure?

He accepts her newest purchase next and starts to ring it up. From her vantage point, Love sees the cover as clearly as he does. It's the book Love picked up once, displaying an image of Eros and Psyche.

Andrew's expression falters. She wonders if he's remembering a few days ago, when Love was here with him, when she met

Miss Georgie, and when his hand passed through Love.

"It's better than it looks," she hears Holly mutter. "It's mythology. I mean, obviously. But I mean, the cover doesn't do it justice. It's annoying when that happens."

"Yeah," Andrew replies, grabbing a brown paper bag for the book.

"I wonder if people could see him."

His head lifts. "What?"

Holly fiddles with her purse strap, her self-consciousness fluttering in Love's ears. "Oh, um, I was just saying, I wonder if people could see Eros. He was a god, so you'd think he was invisible. But Psyche was a mortal, and she saw him. Or maybe she was the only one who could, even though he didn't want her to. I don't know. That's just, you know, what this cover makes me think of."

Miss Georgie struts into the room. "What I want to know," she interrupts, "is whether people felt those arrows." She leans across Andrew to grab a notepad off the counter. "Invisible or not, good intentions or not, taking one of those suckers in the chest had to hurt. Don't forget to give the dame her change, kiddo."

She leaves the room again. Andrew blinks at her retreating form, then at Holly, then at the book, some new idea dawning on him. Love has accepted that she can't sense his emotions like she can with everyone else, but she's also unsure of what his odd expression means.

The register chimes. The lip pops open for change. Holly accepts the paper bag and hesitates, but then issues a quick goodbye, not that Andrew notices. He's too preoccupied by his own thoughts.

Love rubs her temples like humans do when they've got a headache.

Wednesday. Whenever Miss Georgie or Andrew is away from the register, Love studies the receipts and random lists scattered there with Miss Georgie's scribble on them. After memorizing the handwriting, Love picks a fantasy romance from the shelf, adds it to a pile of "special orders," and forges a home delivery request with Holly's address on it. In a small town like Ever, with an unforgiving winter, deliveries are one of their seasonal offers.

Andrew uses Miss Georgie's car to drive over to Holly's house. At the front door, the girl wraps her sweater around her chest to blot out the cold. "Um, I didn't order this," she says.

"Oh." Andrew clears his throat. "It was ... There was a note ... You sure?"

Her mouth quirks. "Pretty sure, since I was kinda just at the store yesterday. Remember?"

"Maybe your mom or dad placed the order."

She snorts. "Definitely not them."

"Our mistake, I guess. You can, I dunno, keep it."

Her smirk gets more pronounced. She thinks it's a ruse to see her. So much the better.

It's the exact impression Love was hoping this whole scenario would make. She waits a safe distance away and clings to her bow.

Invite him inside! Invite him inside!

They shuffle their feet at the threshold. Holly's expression grows agitated. "Look, you shouldn't be here—"

The door flexes open wider. Griffin materializes behind his girlfriend, and she tenses, bracing herself for a confrontation. But her concern is futile. Indeed, Andrew and Holly's flabbergasted reactions are priceless as they witness the villain play nice.

"Hey, Andrew." Griffin gestures to the paperback on Holly's behalf. "That was cool of you, bringing Holly a book while it's, like, snowing and stuff. Wasn't it cool?" he asks her, as if this situation isn't random at all, as if it's completely normal.

"It was," she agrees, her gaze riveted on Griffin.

"Holly loves to read," he says to Andrew with a chummy grin. "Listen man, about the fight, I was being a dick. You didn't have to take the blame. Sorry for not setting things straight."

Andrew is stupefied. "Did you really just use the expression, *setting things straight*?"

Griffin laughs. "Dude, you should come in and hang out with us."

Holly beams at her boyfriend. Andrew declines, hands over the paperback, and makes a dazed getaway. Love flings her bow into the snow and stomps her feet.

⌒

She is on the verge of a goddess fit. She needs to give herself a break before she does something extreme like match Griffin with the nearest slobbering hound. Rather than traverse the forest path, Love jumps from one branch to the next, putting miles between herself and civilization. She takes her time, moving through the woods slower than usual, tasting snowflakes on her tongue as they drop from the sky.

She takes refuge on her favorite branch, flopping onto the coarse surface with a grunt and glowering at the sky forever. Andrew and Holly aren't making progress, though it's obvious he fancies her pretty face. Love has forfeited her right to borrow books from the shop, so she has nothing to read during a much-deserved rest, and she has lost her snowflake ornament to the recent snowfall. Everything's an utter mess.

What's worse, Andrew hasn't wiped that bemused look from his face since he talked to Holly at the bookstore, seeming lost, then found, then lost again. It's driving Love wild. What's gotten into his head?

She festers, rests, debates. She can't afford to waste more time, but she's lacking ideas and experiencing a critical case of matchmaker's block. It prevents her from shadowing the lovers at school on Thursday, forestalling her until that afternoon, when she finally surrenders and returns to town. Still deterred about what to do, she reaches the main square and stops dead in her tracks.

At least now she knows what's been consuming Andrew's thoughts. Sheets of paper flap from windows and traffic signs, bike racks and doors. Some are crisp from the cold, others are damp from the snow. The people of Ever murmur to one another, reading each page even though the leaflets all ask the same thing.

It's hypnotic. It's his handwriting demanding to know:

Are you Eros?

~

Love rips open the door to the bookshop and deliberately slams it closed behind her. Andrew whips around, a stack of books spilling from his arms, startling an elderly couple on their way into the Classic Literature and Poetry room. Aside from them, the store's lacking customers at the moment.

"What do you think you're doing?!" Love shouts at him.

Miss Georgie darts into the main room, her hand on her chest. "Jehoshaphat!"

Andrew glances at the couple, then at Miss Georgie, and visibly relaxes, reassured that none of them can see what he sees. He addresses the shopkeeper while staring resentfully at Love. "Moody customer."

Miss Georgie groans. "What's wrong with people these days? Sometimes I think this town needs more stories—or more love."

"I'll find out for you."

The elderly pair shuffles down the hall. Miss Georgie trots back to the register. Andrew collects the books he dropped and arranges them in a pile on the floor, then jerks his head, indicating for Love to follow him. They head into the Nonfiction room at the back of the store.

"Answer me," she growls.

"No, you answer me," he says under his breath. "Are you Eros?"

"I demand to know how you came to that conclusion."

"The mice in my pockets told me. Did you know a group of mice is called a 'mischief of mice'? You learn something new every day."

"This is anarchy! You wrote the question everywhere!"

"Sure did. I guess I could have visited your tree and asked you straight up, but hey, then you could have just lied to my face, since you're so good at that. I figured I'd take you off guard. If I was wrong, you wouldn't even know who the question was for. If I was right, I'd get a reaction. A big one."

She lifts her bow and aims an arrow at him. He steps forward, ignoring the weapon. "The night I got into that fight with Griffin, you called yourself a myth. At my house, you said your arrows were peaceful weapons. Hell, the fact that you carry arrows at all. You fired one through our window. My stepdad had to be rushed to the ER from work because he was having chest pains fifteen feet from you. The last time we were here together, that book with Eros and Psyche on the cover freaked you out. You're strong. You're gorgeous. You're immune to the weather, and as dumb as this sounds, you freaking wear white. Your name is Love. I know Eros isn't a girl, but what else am I supposed to think when I see you the way I see you? And who was that guy I saw you with?"

"He—"

"Whatever," Andrew snaps. "I don't care about him. What did you do to Griffin? Instead of his usual prickish self, he's been acting like my best friend—and how interesting because my stepdad's being nice to me, too. He never lifts a finger for me, but this morning I found him wearing a goddamn apron and poaching me eggs. It may not sound like a lot to you, but it's jacked-up to me. And he bought me a new coat. What did you do?"

"Nothing," she fibs.

"Uh-huh." He chews on the side of his lower lip. "Right."

His mouth transfixes her. She tallies the possible ways she might explore it through taste and texture and movement. Her desire must be spreading across her face, clear enough for Andrew to see because his chest hitches, and his breath stops for an instant.

"Tell me what you did to them," he hisses. "*What* are you?"

The question chafes more than it should.

"I'm not a demon," she says, humiliated by the way her voice splinters.

His eyes waver, then soften. "And even if you were, I'd probably still like you."

This makes her think of his stepfather, the person Andrew should be able to trust the most, encouraging Griffin to hurt him. The watercolor on Andrew's cheek is now brownish-gold. Soon it will be gone.

Love could deny her myth. She could twist the truth.

No. She can't do either. His face and voice—his Andrewness—won't let her. Oh, Fates. What would it be like to finally talk to someone? To be known?

The yearning flaps its dusty wings. Love's resolve curls up, defeated.

"I'm not Eros." She lowers her weapon. "I'm Love."

He almost smiles. "We've established that."

She reaches out her hand, pretending he can take it. "Come with me."

"My shift isn't over yet."

"I say it is."

13

In the woods, her glass cottage emerges. It glints at them in the coppery, late afternoon light, nestled beside a frozen pond. Love had assumed that if Andrew had the power to see her, he would be able to see the cottage as well.

She sticks her arm out behind her, indicating for him to stop while her eyes skim the landscape for signs of Anger the spy. To her relief, she finds none.

This is the most ideal place to talk. She'd wanted to speak with Andrew on her own turf by the tree, but the sun had begun to set, dragging the temperature down with it. The frigid outdoor climate would hardly make a comfortable setting for a serious, and potentially lengthy, chat, even with him bundled up in his new coat. Though it looks good on him, made of light-gray wool, with the collar turned up around his neck.

Inside, she lights a fire while he removes the coat, setting it on a chair and browsing the round hearth in the center and the plump white bed. The Guides who trained her have sophisticated taste. They envisioned this place, then used the stars to create it.

Love would have liked to decorate it herself, with fun, youthful things like snowflake ornaments to hang from the ceiling. It's not that she's forbidden to add personal touches, but it's frowned upon. It's a tradition for the Guides to outfit their archers' dwellings, to wish the archers well in each new territory they're sent to, like a blessing. It would look ungrateful, disrespectful, for her to dress up the cottage to her own tastes.

She's never had a guest before, in any of the places she's lived. He fills the cottage with a fresh breeze, a sweetness in the air that makes the room smaller but bigger at the same time. She busies herself, mounting her bow on the wall and then shrugging off her coat, his note tucked in the pocket.

He watches as she tosses the wool garment on the bed. "You don't have a problem with the cold, but I still would have given you my coat."

"Yes, you're dumb about things like that," she says.

"One hundred percent dumb," he agrees, rubbing his hands together.

His fingers peek beneath the long sleeves of his shirt, which end just above the knuckles. She shocks herself by thinking of running a finger in the valleys between them.

His nails are blue. The fire in the hearth must not be warm enough yet. What else do hostesses offer mortal boys?

"Tea. I have tea," she says awkwardly. "It's good tea."

He hesitates. She despairs while he hesitates, then perks up at the immense feeling of seeing him close the glass door behind him. "Tea of the Gods? This I gotta try."

It's a favorite of her people. In the Peaks, meals are an eccentric blend of magic and labor. Her water pitcher replenishes itself whenever it's empty, yet a kettle dangles from a hook over the flames, the bubbles signaling when the liquid is ready to be steeped in herbs and flowers.

She brews him a steaming cup, aware that she shouldn't be taking care of him. That's supposed to be Holly's job. Holly would probably make him something different, one of those coffee concoctions whose names contain a conga line of frothy words.

Love removes the kettle and fills the cup, muttering to herself, "How can she be his type?"

"Whose type?"

She jumps to find Andrew behind her, all nosey and close. She thrusts the tea at him. "I made it too strong, but it shouldn't poison you."

He smirks at the wry joke and forgets his question. They settle on a rug in front of the fire, with Love draping a blanket over her waist and legs, mindful that her dress is too short for her to be sitting without it.

The blaze improves his complexion, flushing his skin, and the sight of his nails losing that blue tone makes her happy, makes her sad, makes her angry.

He studies the translucent walls. "If you can't feel the cold, why do you need a fire to warm the place up?"

It's not technically for warmth. The blaze is merely nice to look at, flickering against the white world and casting a mellow glow through the cottage. Love is about to explain that when Andrew waves off the subject.

"You know what? Put me out of my misery and get to the macro stuff first, but make sure it's the annotated version. I can handle it," he says.

She feels a grin sneak across her face, but she smoothes it over like a wrinkled blanket. "Ask me."

"Tell me," he answers.

She should have expected that from him. "I'm a goddess."

"The Eros type or the Aphrodite type?"

"What makes you think that? Those are love deities, but you haven't seen me target couples. You think I was after Griffin and your stepfather."

He raises his shoulders. "Yeah, but maybe you were trying to give them a shot of compassion or make them softhearted."

"In mythology, Eros has wings. Sometimes he's a little boy, sometimes he's older, but he's definitely not a girl. Aphrodite doesn't carry arrows. She's too busy being a vain whore."

"And you're not?"

"A whore?"

"Vain. Jesus. You think I'm that much of a jerk?"

"Of course I'm vain. I'm Love."

"It wouldn't matter if you were a frisky goddess, by the way. Wouldn't it be part of your job?"

Rrrrrr.

Andrew holds up his hands. "My bad."

She purses her lips. "The mythologies told in your world are wrong."

"We got the arrows right."

"I'm not the only one who carries a bow. Some of your beliefs are correct, but not all. My friskiness really wouldn't matter to you?"

Pink stains his cheeks. "So what's your mythology?"

"We're the Fates."

"Be more specific."

Love's brows knock together. She doesn't know what he wants to hear.

He waits, then chuckles. "You're not used to conversation, are you?"

"Says the teen hermit."

"I don't have friends, but I'd be better at it than you."

"No one is better than a deity at anything."

"Get over yourself."

She slaps the rug. "This is why I said for *you* to ask *me* questions. I cannot read your mind."

"We'll go slow. Here's an easy start," Andrew says, wiggling closer. "Where do you come from?"

"Another dimension. It's called the Peaks." She describes the landscape, akin to living on a lush moon, with purple blooming cliffs, starlit waterfalls, grottos inside mineral caves, and giant flying insects that resemble silver dragonflies. "And yes, there are more people like me, and there's a hierarchy . . ."

The Fates are the rulers of emotions, gods and goddesses who prevail over the mortal world. When they're young, they're split into classes—the same way humans are in school—and trained to be archers governing whichever emotion they were created for.

"Emotions," Andrew echoes. "Why not gods of deserts and goddesses of oceans?"

Love gives a noncommittal shrug. "I don't know. Do you know why your people are meant to exist?"

"Gimme your theory."

"I suppose because emotions dominate people in heart and soul. They're the roots of all actions and reactions. That shapes their fate."

He squints in confusion. "If a typhoon comes along, your emotions don't have much say in whether or not you die."

"Forget nature. It belongs to itself. Aside from the stars, we have no connection to it. That's why we can't burn or freeze to death, but that's also why we can't tell nature what to do."

"There can't be that many emotions around to make it a big job."

"Surprise, disgust, sympathy, gratitude, shame, hate, joy, bitterness, hope—"

"Okay, okay," he chuckles. "I get it. I believe you. Something tells me you're not gonna stop anytime soon."

Satisfied, she nods. "I was taught from childhood. How to control my strength and speed, how to interpret emotions and feelings, human motivations, the flaws and intricacies of mortality, the science of relationships, the weight and precision of an arrow and how to avoid catastrophe—"

"I'm picturing a bunch of militant cherubs. Make it stop."

"You make it stop. It's your vision."

"I mean, all my teachers were warning me about back then was not to eat the glue."

Love can't predict what's going to come out of his mouth. She likes it.

She explains how there are many classes, all representing different emotions, and all grouped by age like humans. Wonder, Sorrow, Envy, and Anger are in Love's class. Growing up in the Peaks, they were taught for fifty years how to master their powers and then were shipped off to the human realm where they serve whichever places need them most. Love's existence is mobile, traveling to new landscapes—it could be for days, it could be for years—only pausing when her class returns to the Peaks for an intermission every decade.

Each class learns from instructors called Guides. Guides are deities who used to do what the archers do, but have advanced in life. Once Love is their age, she will become a Guide. She'll give herself a new name, and create and teach the next goddess of love. And so on.

Andrew taps the rim of his cup. "So it's a generational thing. How does that work? If there's only one deity for every emotion at at time, that doesn't cover a lot of ground. You can't be everywhere in the world at once. From what you said, your class, and your Guides, weren't even around when you were busy training.

That's not much of an almighty impression."

"There is no such thing as almighty," Love says. "Nature itself may be the only force that comes close. Mortals and immortals both have their limitations and weaknesses, some are explicable, others are enigmas. My people do what they can, deciding which places most need their help at any given time. We have to choose with wisdom. We're quite good at it."

"Does this town need love more than a third-world country?"

"I've served those countries, and I will again, but even the unlikeliest of places are filled with heartbreak. Pick your battles, you exhausting creature. Not everything can be rationalized away, not us, not nature, not you, and definitely not your many religions."

"I didn't mean to annoy you."

"You haven't," she says.

"I'm not asking all these things because I want to know the reasons for everything. I'm asking because I want to know about *you*."

She relents. "It would be helpful, but I don't have to exist everywhere at once in order to make a difference. You'd be surprised how one spark of perfect love between a pairing can have a natural ripple effect on others." Andrew appears torn by her words, so she asks, "Do you remember what we said in the attic, about the stars?"

"I remember every word we said that night."

"There's grandness in mystery."

"I know," he agrees, yet something else still furrows his brow.

Love tells him that when it's an archer's turn to become a Guide, the instructor yields, the same way elderly humans do. They pursue interests like art, music, leadership. And everyone is ruled by the Fate Court, five deities who reign for a term of five centuries.

"Sort of sounds like our system here. To be honest, I was expecting something more elaborate," Andrew admits ruefully.

"Feel free to keep reading mythology," Love answers.

"So you have no family."

She flinches. "No. Our relationships aren't what your people assume them to be."

"Shit. I could kick myself. I didn't—that was thoughtless, I'm sorry."

She huffs to make it seem like no big deal. "We're made of something better than family. We're born from the stars. Your people were correct in associating us with them. Partly correct."

"Wait. How old are you?"

"Two hundred and one."

"Say what?!" At her laugh, he babbles, "No, it's just, you know, you don't act like it. I'm eighteen," he admits, then sits up straighter and adds, as if it will make up for the age difference, "I—I'm a senior."

"Don't panic. I was born in 1813, but I'm young for a deity. Like a teenager in your world. Our bodies mature until a certain point, to the equivalent of a human's late twenties."

"So you'll always look pretty. That's convenient."

"Of course," she says airily.

"You're young to score this kind of work, aren't you?"

"You had no trouble believing Eros was a strapping lad or that Cupid was an infant. If I'm not mistaken, your people make soldiers out of the youth."

Andrew looks chagrined as he checks her out. "You breathe. So I'm guessing you have lungs."

"Ugh. Yes. And we even have ears to hear, eyes to see, a mouth to taste, and everything."

"Hey, don't get sassy with me. Your sense of touch is limited, and you move pretty fast. It's not a dumb question."

"My sense of touch is fine. It's just nonexistent with humans."

"That doesn't mean I know where the differences begin and end. Do you eat?"

She points to a bowl on a table, loaded with apples and persimmons. There's also a plate with bread and cheese. She doesn't need much nourishment, and despite human assumptions, he'll find no ambrosia at her table.

He lifts the mug of tea to his mouth and sips. "What's in this?"

The way his forehead crinkles brings out the naughty in her. "Spring," she says, keeping a straight face.

"Spring."

"Yes. Peonies, dewdrops, a dash of the sunlight, the afterglow of sex—"

He lurches forward and spits out the tea.

With the blanket still covering her, Love rolls over laughing. "Cranberries," she giggles. "Only cranberries."

His eyes widen. After a moment of hesitation, he breaks down and joins her in laughter, his smile cutting her into a million pieces. Their knees almost touch but won't touch. Defiant, she scoots closer.

Her tongue darts out between the slit in her mouth and runs across her bottom lip. Andrew's grin fades. His stare caresses many places within her, and she wishes she could return the favor, but nothing of her can reach anything of him, except her voice. She wants it to slide down the arch of his neck.

His gaze shifts to her bed. "Do you sleep?"

"Yes."

"Do you get sick?"

"No."

"Can you get wounded?"

"Yes."

"Do you have tear ducts?"

"Huh?"

"Do you cry?"

"I don't—"

"Do you cry like you laugh?"

"Slow down—"

"Am I asking too much?"

"Why—"

"Do you think I care?"

"I think—"

"Why are you leaning forward?"

"Because—"

"You'd like to strangle me."

"I want—"

"I'm pissing you off."

"A human can't—"

"And you're clenching your teeth."

"Because—"

"You need me to stop?"

"No—"

"This is called an interrogation."

"I know—"

"Do you have a boyfriend?"

That last question strikes her like a cork between the eyes. He's looking at her now, really looking at her, with an odd, torch-lit expression. Not at the bed or the cottage or the rest of the world. Just her.

"He's not my boyfriend," she says. "He's Anger."

The orange glint from the flames whips across his face. "You lied."

"I did."

"You're not alone in this forest."

"I didn't lie about that, you dummy. I lied about there not being others like me. He was passing through, but he dwells in another part of the world. I *am* alone here."

"He's hot."

Love's mouth drops. Whether or not "hot" has something to do with temperature, mortals use this word to fawn over each other. "Are you—"

"I'm not gay. I just know he's hot. I know what hot looks like."

"Fine. He's handsome. Anything else you want me to say?"

"That's about it."

Andrew stares pointedly at her. From the looks of it, thunderstorms and human traffic jams are cluttering his mind. Doors are opening and closing.

He's jealous. The realization makes her feel silly and squeamish. She can't decide whether to glower or giggle some more. She feels like . . . a girl.

She wants to punch him. In the face. Hard. Cover that watercolor with one of her own. Then she wants to kiss it, softly, until she has no more soft left in her.

"Anger and I are not lovers," she says. "There wouldn't be a great deal of time for it anyway. Intermissions in the Peaks are short."

"Sounds pretty lonely," Andrew remarks.

She thrusts a lock of hair over her shoulder and notices how his eyes follow the movement. "Loneliness is a romantic notion conceived by humans. Immortals don't get lonely."

"Who takes care of you?"

She blinks. "I don't understand."

Even when he repeats himself, she's confounded. "I'm a goddess," she says simply.

He frowns. After a moment's thought, he asks, "And what do you like to do in your spare time? Besides climb trees and flash people."

"It's a forest. It's winter. Options are limited."

"Not true." He motions at the glass wall overlooking the pond. "Get some ice skates."

"That's a paltry human pastime."

"Meaning you don't know how."

Her head snaps in his direction.

"I could teach you," he says.

Something about his expression dares her to respond in a certain way. With regret, she runs her hand through his knee, reminding them of their own limits with each other. "It wouldn't work."

He gazes at his leg for so long she wonders if he heard her. But then he says, so quietly, "I want to touch you."

14

The effect on her is total. Her body is sprinting, although she's absolutely still. He pronounced those five words like they were conceived inside a sonnet. This is precarious on all fronts.

"We can't," she says.

"I want to touch you anyway. I want you to be real. I want to know what you feel like." His throat pumps as his eyes meet hers. "Have you ever . . . you know."

Oh, Fates. Yes. She knows, and now she knows how words feel. Down below, she's pulsating, opening. She shifts on the rug. What should she say? What answer does he want to hear?

She bites her lip, avoids looking at him, and shakes her head in reply. "And have you?" she ventures.

There's a shy slant to Andrew's voice when he answers. One word telling her that, in some ways, they're the same.

"Do you think about it? What it's like?" he asks.

"I do," she whispers.

"Me, too. A lot."

Does he mean he thinks about it in general? Or with Holly in mind? Love considers changing the subject, but her physical self has other ideas, other needs.

"What do you do about it?" he asks.

"The same thing you do," she guesses.

"Does it work?"

"Usually."

"It's not enough, though. I mean, it could be more. With someone."

Love can't bear to speak. Neither of them moves, but she feels them both imagining.

Her body. His body.

Shadows. Sheets. Sighs.

"Has Love ever loved?" he murmurs.

Love sucks in a breath. "No," she answers, though the word carries a bitter taste.

Sex, decadence, rolling hips and searching tongues—that exists where she's from. Lust, deities indulge in because it's fun. Camaraderie and fondness, too. But love is lost on her people. It's a human necessity, not an immortal one. That's why it took the Fates millennia to create her.

"So you can't identify with us mortals," Andrew says.

"A king cannot identify with a peasant. That doesn't mean he's unfit to rule over his subjects."

"I'm a peasant?"

"No, you're magnificent."

He maintains eye contact. "I want my fingers on you."

She can't resist. "Where?"

"Wherever you ask me to put them."

"Assume you had a choice."

"Your mouth first. It's plush. The first thing I'd want to do is shut you up with my fingers, run them across your lips, then down you neck, and further down, along every curve. After that, I'd make you shout, really shout while we find out how many different touches exist. I bet we'd learn a lot."

Her fingers comb through the rug. Moisture is beginning to

flow through her at an alarming rate while fire licks the air. This is the sexiest conversation she's ever had.

"How have I been assigned to this town for three months and overlooked you?" she muses.

Andrew runs his own finger along the rug. "We have invisibility in common. I told you before, this town doesn't think I grew up with the most stable elders. Try as I might to get people to notice me in a good way, they don't. Trust me, I'd like to impress you, but I am who I am."

"You're plenty impressive," she says. "Keep touching me with your words."

"Seriously, I don't know where this is coming from."

"I do," Love says. It's coming from a simple place. Unfortunately, humans tend to make it more complicated than it is. He's a boy who likes what he sees, and she's otherworldly, and they're alone. She understands the way he's behaving. It's how her matches act whenever they're about to lunge at one another.

It scares her because she knows better, because this is wrong. She has to take back that last request before he indulges her.

"We have to stop," she says

"I don't want to," he says.

"Please do it for me."

He considers, then finishes his tea. "Safe zone it is."

She's disappointed. She's relieved.

He talks about stories he's read, she describes stories she wishes someone would write. She praises humans for inventing airplanes, birth control, and music. He hums some of his favorite songs, and they debate the lyrics of one in particular. They mash up mortal and immortal slang. He complains about science classes but raves about his teachers. He recalls his first crush with gusto, and she resents him for it, and he teases her back to normal. She boasts about the first time she achieved a direct hit during archery practice, and he listens, and she smiles. They make fun of the mortal ritual called Homecoming, inventing alternative dances that take place underwater or are only accessible via mirages, but too soon they go quiet.

"What made the Fates choose Ever for you?" he asks.

She folds her legs to the side. "There are lots of needy people here."

"Lonely people?"

"Sometimes."

"Heartbroken people?"

"Sometimes."

He squeezes his mug. "Who else needs you?"

Love snickers. "Nearly everyone," she confides. "The human embrace is a gifted one, but a mortal's defect is in knowing how to choose a life mate." She pats her chest. "That's why I'm here. It's about perfection . . . ," she trails off.

Andrew's whole demeanor has changed. "You're saying you control what they feel."

Uh-oh. She senses him changing his mind about this conversation.

His laugh comes out sour, disbelieving. "You know, I've been sitting here, so overwhelmed by you, that I forgot why I came here to begin with. You're just so . . . That's what you did to Griffin and my stepdad, isn't it? You brainwashed them."

"I didn't. Anger did that. He controls the nature of wrath."

"Anger, your immortal buddy. The hot archer who's not your boyfriend but was just 'passing through' the right place at the right time."

Love points at him. "Take that back! He's not my buddy."

"So why'd he interrupt his busy schedule to shoot my

stepdad?"

Because I asked him to.

Andrew glowers at her. "When we got here and you made tea, you were talking to yourself. You said, 'How can she be his type?' *His* type. Who were you talking about? Me?" His eyes darken. "Am I one of your targets?"

"No," Love lies. "I was imagining who your type would be. That's all. It's in my nature."

"How can you do this to people? They aren't puppets to mess around with."

"It's always been like this," she argues, baffled.

"That doesn't justify it."

"It's the way of things."

"It's stealing people's free will!"

Offended, Love rises to her knees. "You're a mortal. You're not meant to understand."

His tea mug goes flying and smashes against the wall. "I know the fucking difference between right and wrong!" he yells, staggering to his feet. "You're no different than my stepdad or Griffin. You're just as cruel."

"We're not! We're benevolent. We nudge you down the right paths, save you from regrets and nonsense and choices that would end in spoils. Even more of your people would trip over their own foolishness and break their necks if it weren't for us. We tirelessly reduce that number by a considerable degree!"

"Bullshit. Mistakes happen and, yeah, some people don't learn, but that doesn't mean we're all stupid. That doesn't mean you're entitled to make us your bitches, so you can feel all supreme. You have no family. You care for no one. You've never been in love, and you're the one pushing people together? You guys don't know anything. I don't want to be magically wanted. *I* want

140

to be enough, but you wouldn't understand that. You're so perfect that you're seismically fucked up."

She feels yet another debilitating sensation: unworthiness.

"Andrew," she calls as he grabs his coat and heads to the door, but when he turns to face her, a brief and horrible silence pinches the room. "You don't know the way back to town."

There's no path, it's dark outside now, and his leg—

"Don't underestimate me. I can take care of myself," he says. "I don't need you. No one does."

"Whatever happened to your leg is because of him. I wanted to stop the bruises."

"Why would you do that?" he asks, then parrots her words. "The deal with my stepdad is, it's *always been like this*. It's *the way of things*. And *by* the way? Screw you. He didn't do anything to my leg. My mother did."

He throws open the door and disappears into the forest.

15

The fire snaps at her from the hearth. Andrew's words turn her into ash. Love stares at the shattered fragments of the tea mug.

He didn't do anything to my leg. My mother did.

She feels small as a crumb. She had assumed. Anger changed the stepfather forever because she assumed, robbing the man of the possibility to change on his own, to care about Andrew on his own. She took that from them.

Love doesn't move until midnight. Then she gets up, retrieving her coat from the bed and shrugging into it. She collects her bow and quiver—she doesn't need them, but she wants them close to her—and sets off into town. The weather is tame tonight except for fog coasting down the sidewalks. Houses reflect an indigo sheen that seems like a warning.

She passes a middle-aged couple that she matched two months ago. She hears the static whirr of their unflappable personalities as they march to their car, their boots raking through the snow. They stop beside the vehicle, the woman knotting her scarf while the man grieves over a scratch on the hubcap. They suit each other. They don't challenge each other. They're the same people they were before their first kiss. Their bond is flawless.

Love has saved them from tears, wild quarrels, pain, and regret. The same intense things Andrew has made her feel tonight, she has spared them. Isn't that nice? Isn't it?

Yet if she had the choice, she would repeat this evening, despite how much it hurt to see him mad at her, to see him leave afterward.

At his house, she pauses and gazes up at his window. He came close to figuring out her plans. Once he and Holly are together, how will his life change? How will Griffin feel?

In a different world, Love could leave them alone, leave everyone in this world alone. But where would that leave her?

"Are we doing the right thing?" she asks.

"Well now, that depends on if you want the mortal or immortal answer."

She turns. Wonder is beside her, her mouth caught somewhere between a smile and a frown.

"I want *your* answer. Do you believe we're doing the right thing?" Love asks.

"Love, you shouldn't punish yourself. You're trying to save us and the boy."

"Quit diverting. I'm talking about instinct, not duty or loyalty."

"Oh, really?" Reproachful, Wonder holds up her scarred hands. "And is this what loyalty looks like?"

Love clams up. It's not.

"I've disobeyed and paid for it," Wonder says. "You don't want to know what that's like. It's about time you regretted what you made Anger do. Of all the foolhardy things to request of him. Yes, you wanted to protect the boy from fiends, but you must be smarter about it, or you'll draw attention to yourself. Anger could get suspicious. He might slip and say something to the Court."

"He told you about Andrew's stepfather and Griffin." When Wonder makes no reply, Love says, "I had an excuse. I can't match Andrew with brutes on his tail. And I didn't *make* Anger do anything."

"Oh, Love. He's incapable of refusing you—," Wonder stops, swallows the rest of her words.

On that score, Love would beg to differ. There's no way in Fates Anger would do whatever she wants. He doesn't like her, doesn't trust her not to stray, doesn't have a problem spying on her.

"I told you there was another option if that boy matters to you," Wonder clucks. "Do you remember what I said about becoming mortal? If Andrew falls for you—"

"He won't."

"—and you fall for him—"

"I won't."

"—this will end differently. You don't have to kneel or serenade the sky or make a ceremony out of it. Your hearts will do the work."

"You're lying," Love says.

"If you pay attention, you'll know the moment it happens. The changes within you—"

She aims an arrow at Wonder. "If you don't be quiet, I will break your heart."

Moonlight and shadows splash across Wonder's face. "Too late for that."

Love's bow lands at her side. "Oh?"

"You're not the only one who ever cared for a mortal."

Oh. Back in the Peaks, on that day Wonder was tortured, everyone knew she tried to desert the Fates. The *why* of it was something she kept to herself, swallowing the reason she abandoned her post and fled deep into the mortal world.

The memory of Wonder's punishment assaults Love with glittering clarity. How Love defied the Court to protect Wonder and tried to keep their classmates from mangling the goddess's hands.

"There was someone," Wonder confides, the starbursts of her eyes dimming. "A boy. When we were still in training, my Guide took me to observe the humans. That's when I saw him on a ranch in 1860. He liked to sing and ride horses. He was dusty all the time." Her lips tremble with laughter, then sadness. "I don't know what came over me. I was filled with desire, yet there was also this little feeling, something soft and protective."

Dumbstruck, Love drops her bow and hastens to pick it up. She can't believe what she's hearing. That little feeling, that something soft and protective Wonder felt back then, it couldn't have been love, could it? No deity feels that.

"I used to sneak away to be near him," Wonder reminisces. "He had no idea I existed, but I didn't care. I didn't want to be assigned somewhere far from him, so I searched the Archives for a way to change that. I was so desperate that I hastened to the Hollow Chamber and found that scroll about undoing immortality. I thought, although he can't see me, he can still read messages from me. For months, I wrote letters and stashed them in his saddle bag."

Love gapes. That's forbidden. Even she wouldn't go so far.

Actually, yes. She might.

"In the Peaks, I used to listen to you speculate about human affection," Wonder confesses. "I wanted to ask you more, but I didn't dare. I thought perhaps what I was feeling could be close to love. The letters were my attempt to find out, to make the boy love me and bring us together.

"All it did was frighten and torment him. He believed he was going crazy, and I worried about him. I tried to run away from the Peaks, to hide somewhere and watch over him, make certain he recovered, but he was committed to an asylum. Then the Court found me. I managed to keep my Archive snooping to myself, but I'd done plenty already to deserve my punishment."

Wonder doesn't lose her grin, but her eyes mist. "When my hands were cut up, I pictured that boy dying without knowing me, losing his mind. I didn't have the chance to free myself like you do."

Well played. Love wants to laugh, though none of this is funny. She pities Wonder for assuming she needs to repay Love for the past, and for assuming Love could become a secondhand remedy for Wonder's regrets.

"What you're saying isn't going to work on me," Love cautions. "This isn't just about what I asked Anger to do. I want to know if what we're all doing is right. Please."

"I wish I knew," Wonder replies, rubbing her arms, shielding herself. "People rely on destiny as a comfort, a means to keep their hopes alive. It's ironic, is it not? I make people wide-eyed and starry-eyed, but by forcing them to admire things they didn't care about before."

"Stealing people's free will," Love quotes Andrew.

"That is a glowing way to put it."

She never had a problem with this, never thought about emotions being fabricated or about stealing mortals' choices from them, never considered it to be wrong, because her powers are her natural, stars-given right. According to one mortal boy, Love knows very little and will never know enough.

Is she too perfect? Is she *seismically fucked up*? Shame on her?

People may court sloppily, but they do it profoundly. It leaves their souls bruised, yet they're willing to experience it again and again, in new ways—searching, suffering, savoring. There must be something to that gritty, ordinary pursuit that makes it worth it. Perhaps it has to do with all that sweet touching.

Love draws an arrow in the ground with the toe of her boot, knocking the slush around. When she's done, she knows that Wonder is gone.

If I don't do what I'm supposed to, Andrew will die.

Because he's killing us. I'll be dead first. I'm dying right now. I keep forgetting. Silly me, I keep forgetting.

Sneaking to the back of his house, she finds the kitchen window is closed but not locked. She shoves up the sill and hops inside. The home smells of beer and longing. Upstairs, the stepfather sleeps fitfully, muttering a woman's name from the cave of his room, the heels of his bare feet punishing the sheets. Love tastes his grief and rushes out the door.

She skulks into Andrew's room. It's mystical at night, blue and silver as winter. Clothes and comic books scatter the floor. There's a book about mythology and blank paper on the desk, and there's the ever-present question marks painted on the wall, and the *Love, Mom* bookmark.

Mint wafts from the laundry basket. Love drinks in the scent. His bed. Him. In the center.

He's sprawled across the mattress, chest bare, a wall of skin rising and falling. She idles beside him, her heart picking up speed.

When he rolls to the side and smacks his lips, her throat tightens. Her hand steals up to caress him, but it passes through his body the way it would if she were dipping her fingers in water. She slides an arrow from her pack and carefully inches the tip between the tie at the waistband of his pants.

In one swift move, the arrowhead cuts through the knot. Andrew moans in his sleep, the sound floating through the air. Silently, she begs his pardon, then continues, maneuvering his pants down a fraction. She peeks at the V of his hips. He stirs against the blanket, moving nearer to the edge, as though in offering. This is the most she allows herself. Anything more would require waking him up.

She watches him for hours. She wants to be the sheets that cover his toes. She wants to be the ceiling separating him from the sky: above him, the first thing he sees before and after dreams. She wants to be the open window letting in the light for him.

If magic were easy, they could shrink into the pages of his books and live there. They should find a way to do that, to become so small, tinier than ants. They could hop from letter to letter. They could find scenes that describe coves and then discover one another's bodies there, lying in the sand together and drawing out each other's sighs. If she were to grow wings, he'd cut them so she couldn't fly away by accident.

Love takes out the note he wrote for her.

Who is this girl?

Who is she? A girl who's not a girl, who has a thousand trees but not one ornament. An archer who can strike him down, but who can never caress his cheek. A greedy goddess who creeps upon him like this without his permission, because it's in her nature to be selfish. A trickster. A traitor.

She removes her coat—his coat—drapes it over a reading chair, and sets the note on top of it. She tiptoes out the door, making sure not to look at him again.

It takes longer than it should to get back to the glass cottage.

She can't sleep, so she has a silent conversation with the glass walls. By sunrise, she knows.

She has fallen in love.

16

Light arcs across the translucent ceiling. It drags her into the past, to a memory of her very first bed, the moment when her infant eyes flashed open with life.

Other recollections follow. She thinks back on every crevice of the tale, from what she was told to what she remembers. The myth of Eros isn't the truth.

Her story is the truth.

It's not romantic.

17

There's a star that refuses to shine. It hides in the sky above the Peaks, where the Fates live. In the celestial realm of waterfall cliffs and moonbeams, the stars serve a purpose: to create deities. But this single star is stubborn and ignores its people.

For millennia, the Fates have controlled mortal destinies and reigned over humanity's fragile emotions—all except one, the most mysterious and coveted emotion of them all.

Love.

The Fate Court has toiled to create her, but unacquainted with the stirrings of love, they have never succeeded. In despair, they almost give up until the Guide of Wonder approaches them with an idea. "Love cannot be made on its own," she says with a winged brow. "It's a constellation. It must be made with a cast of emotions, and I believe I know which ones. In fact, the next generation of them have just been born."

So it is the perfect time. Four Guides—the mentors of Anger, Envy, Sorrow, and Wonder—are tasked to create Love. Anger and envy to fuel passion. Wonder as an intricate blend of happiness, admiration, and awe. Sorrow for heartache and longing.

At nightfall, the Guides flock to a glass dome that has existed since before humans thought to invent observatories. On the center dais, painted recreations of constellations grace the floor. Above the *artwork, an elegant silver funnel that the gods call a stargazer—not quite what mortals call a telescope, but close—is poised upright. It aims toward the sky, supported by posts that coil like vines at the ends.*

The Guides join hands around the mouth of the stargazer, harness their magic, and beseech the sky. But deities banding together is too much for the stars to handle, and unexpectedly, the canopy above goes dark. Only one star is left flickering. Once dull and useless, it now winks down at them. Indeed, a stubborn little thing.

With a flash, it burns out and reappears in the Guide of Wonder's palm. The other three deities surround her, peeking down at the rare and glimmering seed. Soon enough, the banquet of stars return, and when asked, they confirm what the Fates hoped. And the glimmering seed becomes a goddess.

Everyone kisses on the night Love is finally born. From the young deities to the old ones, eyelids fall shut and tongues explore the deep wells of open mouths. It's a good time to celebrate, to touch and be touched.

Meanwhile, in her room, the arched spine of a bow hangs on the wall above Love's crib. The braided wooden bars cage her in as she reaches up and flaps her arms like wings toward the members of the Fate Court, who've come to view her. They grin with pride and amusement at the needy gesture. None of them thinks to pick her up and stroke her back, nor caress the pudgy skin around her face—it's just not done among their people. And why would the tiny goddess yearn for such a thing?

After they retire, Loves blinks at the void above her. She whimpers in confusion, waiting for someone, anyone, to walk in, to kiss her or pat her head. She waits and waits.

And she waits.

⁓

They live in open cottages on stilts over a vast, dark blue pool of water. On the way from their homes to their lessons, Love whines while the other archers ignore her. She doesn't want to train. She wants to play and roll down the purple blooming hill, or better yet, push Envy down the slope just to see how fast the god can tumble.

In a misty enclave, their group sits in a semicircle, their short legs dangling off their chairs. They listen to the four Guides declare their class the most exceptional in the Peaks.

Love purses her lips. Envy, Sorrow, and Anger have never acted exceptional. They only act mean, calling her a misfit whenever they feel like it. Wonder is nice, offering secret smiles behind her hair, but no more.

Other deities, from younger and older classes alike, aren't unkind. Yet they don't seek Love out, either. She's the only emotion they can't relate to, which makes her a precious oddity.

During the lecture, she glances sideways at Anger, who jerks his head away, his profile shifting from puzzled to irritated. He'd been staring at her.

After their lessons, Love attempts to make friends with the class. At the top of the hill, she asks, "Want to race down?"

Wonder brightens at the invitation, but Sorrow grunts and leaves without answering, pulling Wonder along with her. Anger's mouth twists, emitting a sort of mean-spirited pleasure that doesn't quite reach his eyes, then struts off on gangly limbs.

Envy turns to Love with a flourish. "What do I get if I race you?"

"My respect," she volleys back. "If you're lucky."

"Is that all? I want you to swoon for me. I want a kiss."

He lunges. The bud of his puckered mouth descends with the finesse of a hailstorm and pelts her lips. It seems being nice will get her nowhere.

She trips him. It turns out, he can tumble quite swiftly down the slope.

⁓

She has come of age. Her class is still socially allergic to her, but the landscape of the Peaks, where she climbs and swims, hides and daydreams in private corners, is her refuge.

Her Guides are a comfort. In the beginning, she learned about the definition of love, an unending string of delicate rules and complexities that unraveled before her and snagged into various knots in her mind. The instructors were patient.

Now she's ready to advance. According to the Guides, the nature of love involves lots of touching. Sometimes the touch is fierce and lustful, like how the Fates touch. Other times the touch is delicate, which is a mortal inclination.

She learns about flirtation and attraction. The art of human self-consciousness and the antidote of flattery. Gestures and innuendos. Deities arrive to demonstrate how desire affects the body, and it looks delicious, and a great part of her wants to feel it—the skin on skin, the wild noises, the rhythm.

Yet it also seems hollow and meaningless. She wants it in a different way.

The Guides escort her to the mortal realm to observe. Love witnesses touches the likes of which she's never seen. Knuckles brushing hair from a lover's forehead. Palms cupping cheeks. Touches that give, not just take.

The power to make humans touch that way will be hers, she re-

alizes. These people belong to Love. She can make them happy. She can take part in it.

From then on, she's spellbound.

⌣

It's a lovely morning, the air fragrant with dew. She stares into the distance and imitates a certain type of touch, curling her finger into the cove of her upturned hand, leisurely and reverent.

A whistle makes her jump. Envy shakes his head at her as though to say, absurd. Anger taps his bow against his thigh and stares at Love like every second she exists makes him madder. Sorrow and Wonder huddle off to the side, but they also saw what she was doing.

Wonder's expression is emphatic. Who knows why.

Humiliated, Love juts out her chin.

Time for archery training on the hill. Wonder spends most of it talking rather than shooting. Envy is too busy comparing himself to the others to focus. Sorrow's motivation sinks with each target she misses. And Anger thinks cursing at the arrows will make them do what he wants.

Usually, Love has the best aim in her class—truthfully, of all archers in the Peaks. However, she's not concentrating today.

In an exquisitely condescending tone, Envy deems her too soft to be a goddess. He volunteers to touch her "lovingly" and pokes her backside with his arrow plume.

Love drops her weapon and launches toward Envy. Anger holds her back while her fingers claw at the air, struggling to reach the ego spreading across Envy's face. "Let me at him," she growls.

The god balances his bow across his shoulders and loops his dark arms over the ends, using the position to puff out his chest. "Love, I'd be honored to let you at me."

"You're one of us," Anger reminds her, his heavy breath rushing into her ear. "You'd do well to remember that."

It's true. She would. What god or goddess cares about being cared about? She never sees anyone else reaching out for affection. It's simply that, the way her people regard mating, something is missing. Or perhaps she's as strange as they say she is.

Even worse, being the goddess of love comes with sexual responsibilities. She must know the emotion inside and out, experience it in every way. That means she must one day consummate with a god or goddess of her choosing.

Love vows not to. Not unless it happens in the way she wants.

The Guides created her out of foresight and sheer luck. Whether there's another stubborn star in the sky remains to be seen. The point is, she can't be replaced easily. She's their gem, often excused for the wicked things she does: threatening to scratch Joy with an arrow, losing her temper and throwing a fit or a punch, fixating on human touch.

Nevertheless, her instructors won't be pleased to hear her plans, nor will the Court. Law dictates that they can't force her into a bed, though they will certainly discipline her until she gives in. She's willing to take that chance.

Anger lets her go. "Stop acting like a human," he snaps.

"Make me," she dares.

⌒

In the mortal world, the Guides introduce them to human landscapes: cities and villages and deserts and jungles.

One of these places is a town caked with snow, where a blizzard rages. Surrounded by flurries, Anger's pupils dilate. He clenches his bow while the four archers pretend not to notice his distress.

Love finds him later in the Peaks. He's hunched over and sulking inside a shimmering mineral cave, where a grotto ripples and cyan-colored plants grow within the shadows. This would be a glorious opportunity to mock him. Too bad she's in no mood to get into a skirmish.

Anger bows his head. "What do you want?"

"Why were you scared?"

"Get out of here."

"Storms can't kill us."

He clears his throat. "It looked angry. That's one kind of angry I can't control."

There are many things they might not be able to control when they're sent away. It's impossible to predict. She both fears and longs for that.

Love sits beside him. "It was brave of you to stay. I would have run."

"No. You wouldn't have."

That's possibly a compliment.

"I had to stay put. Retreating like a lightarrow would have embarrassed us all." He rubs the back of his neck. "What happens to one of us happens to all of us."

Love's hands steals out to . . . to what? Squeeze his shoulder? Offer the kind of touch he won't appreciate?

He pins her with unblinking eyes, guessing her thoughts. She yanks her arm back.

"You need to stop that," he warns.

⌣

He's right. Love needs to stop. Now she learns why.

The Court makes everyone watch what Envy does to Wonder. The barbed sound of torture fills Love's ears. She opens her mouth.

Wonder screams. Her wails mine their way through the chaos and seize Love's heart. The sight of the goddess's head thrown back as Envy lashes her makes Love's eyes water.

Wonder was disloyal. She tried to run away from the Peaks, to abandon her people. It was a traitorous act, something to do with a mortal.

Punishment of this nature is an uncommon event. All deities in training have been instructed to stand close and witness Wonder's introduction to pain. Love has been ordered to sharpen the blade and hand it to Envy. Instead of shackles, Sorrow restrains Wonder's left arm and gawks at Wonder's bloody knuckles. Anger secures Wonder's right arm and stares blankly ahead.

His earlier words slice through Love's mind. What happens to one of us happens to all of us.

Classmates are responsible for one another's punishment. In private, Love had caught the haggard look in Envy's eyes, though he concealed it once they were in public. No deity is bred to cower.

Before his hand comes down on Wonder again, her arms spasm. "Please," *she begs, her face as shriveled as a dying flower.* "Sto—"

"Stop!" *Love hurls herself toward the goddess, shielding her from another blow.* "Stop!"

The members of the Court regard her with tapered eyes and ominous expressions.

Anger gets to her before any of their shamed Guides can. He seizes her by the shoulders and hauls her kicking and screaming from the scene. The last thing she sees is Wonder's wrist twitching in her direction, attempting to reach out for her.

The Court orders Love stripped and locked in a pitch-black room with no tastes or sounds or smells. The days blur together. Amid the haze, and without warning, Anger's hand slips beneath the door crack, illuminated in a sudden gray sheen.

Love is offended. It's not the moon, or words, or rest, or his pity that she wants. What she wants is a damn blanket to cover herself with.

"I'm naked," she warns him.

Anger pauses, his wrist suffusing with color. "Why do I bother?" he vents.

His hand disappears. She cackles at how easy it is to harass him.

The cackles turn into sobs. Love realizes what she was too delirious and impulsive to register a moment ago, the one of kind of touch she longs for. Anger just offered it to her.

She thrusts her fingers under the door, searching, scratching the ground, making contact with nothing, wishing he would come back.

⌒

Silence at archery practice.

Envy lacks his usual swagger.

Sorrow studies the undersides of her arms more than her target.

Anger looses one arrow after the other, not sparing Love another glance.

Wonder rubs her bow with a cloth to warm up the weapon, her fingers too bruised to do it right.

⌒

Time to go. The others have already left. It's Love's turn now.

The Court agreed that if leftovers of her radical nature exist, solitude and matchmaking will stifle it. A few decades of that, and she will be desperate for a deity plucking.

She wants to leave and doesn't want to leave. She will miss her Guides and her safe niches in the Peaks. She shouldn't miss her class, since they've gone back to mocking her whims—well, except Wonder—but belonging to people is better than being alone.

"Remember," Wonder's Guide instructs. "Humans are sacred so long as they can't see deities. It's unheard of, but don't let your guard down. Eyes open, always."

Anger's Guide adds, "Your weapon is a part of you. Your power, your breath. As you have magic, it has magic."

Sorrow's Guide gifts Love with a white dress. Envy's Guide thinks it should be shorter.

~

She likes it in the mortal world. She finds naughty, uppity ways to occupy her free time.

However, it's not enough. Every night, she hugs herself to sleep, like the embrace is her little secret. It's not just an affectionate touch she wants. She wants to be matched.

Love wants love. From the way it looks, it must be wonderful.

18

It's awful. This business of being in love.

Like Wonder said, there's desire and a little feeling that's soft and protective. And for Love, it goes beyond that. It makes her feel anger, envy, wonder, sorrow.

At dawn, she paces, hates her boring white dress, muses about comic books, fairy tales, and myths. She invents scenarios in her mind that involve touching, the rustling of his coat, the mess of his hair. She grabs a pen and paper, and writes his name, the tails of the letters entwining with hers.

Love + Andrew

Andrew + Love

A + L

She tries to talk herself out of loving him, but this love is a wild animal racing from here to there inside her. It's impossible to catch, impossible to kill.

She is a buffoon. It can only be love.

Hoping to explain herself to him, she sets off into town. If she can't have his kisses, it would be nice to have his friendship for this brief time. It's a dim, drowsy winter morning, all inky blue from the early hour. She reaches his house but finds that no one's there.

The bookstore, then. That's where he'll accept her apology.

The laborious effort of walking around Ever sets her on edge. Snow pulls her boots down and makes each step count in a way it hasn't before. She actually feels the distance between her home and his work.

As she travels through the main square, she crosses paths with a male couple that she matched. The two men hold hands as they step into a coffee house, which emits the aromas of roasted beans and chocolate. They were enamored from the beginning, she barely had to strive to bring them closer together, and they look happy.

Are they? The affection was there before she came along, but afterward how much of their love was their choice, their doing? Has she served any pair well?

A supple orange light illuminates Miss Georgie's bookstore from the inside, the sight relaxing Love. The sign says the place is closed. It's rather early for Andrew to be here, but he could be preparing the shop for the day. Love opens the door cautiously, then tiptoes inside to the tune of a clarinet swirling through the space. Jazz again.

A candle blooms beside the register where Miss Georgie sits, her hair swept into a loose chignon at her nape and an open tie-blouse popping out of her vintage tweed skirt. She's scribbling something into a ledger. It's a cozy atmosphere, shelves of children's books surrounding her, stories with woodland critters painted on the covers.

Love keeps her footsteps light as she migrates to the other rooms, finding them vacant, then returning to the main room, also still vacant. She chances one more peek in the children's section. Miss Georgie hasn't moved from her spot, her head bowed in concentration.

"He's not here," she announces without looking up.

Love freezes next to the fairytales, shock hitting her square in the chest. The woman has to be talking to herself.

Miss Georgie's head rises, her eyes scanning the room. Love sags with relief. The shopkeeper senses her enough to call out, though she can't see Love. Fanciful humans have done this before, desperate to believe a strange breeze is the ghost of someone they lost.

"He's in school," she says, reminding Love that it's Friday. "But you're here, I bet."

Love clamps her mouth shut, willing the shopkeeper to give up, which she does, returning to her ledger as if nothing occurred. Love shuffles toward the doorway, wanting to get out of there quick.

"Of course, the kiddo forgot his essay yesterday." Miss Georgie grabs a stack of stapled paper, holds it above the candle, and lets it go.

Love leaps toward the essay and catches it inches above the flame, then realizes her mistake. In her grasp, the papers appear to float in midair before the woman's eyes.

"Aha." Miss Georgie wipes her hands. "Oldest trick in the book."

Indeed, dammit. Love is impressed and grouchy over such a basic error. She refuses to move, arm stretched out, the essay hovering until Miss Georgie plucks it from her fingers.

"Lily, isn't it?" the shopkeeper says, setting the essay on the counter and peering in Love's direction. The taste and scent of the woman's emotions suggest piqued interest—as well as a motherly type of feeling that's hard to decipher. "Well, I won't beat around the bush, Lily. You're trespassing, so I like you already. I approve of a spirited girl with the balls to go after what she wants. But ..." There's no mistaking the protective glint in

Miss Georgie's eyes. "I also like a girl with honorable intentions. Let's talk about the kiddo."

Love steps back, quite scared.

"I've known him since he was a tadpole. I've seen the way he looks at pretty girls, but when he introduced you to me? Lily, that was a whole new level of swoonery. The kid melted. I should be troubled since you're a ghost and this isn't going to end well, but that's not my style. I live too much in my head for that. Plus, these days, people have deeper relationships online than in the flesh, and I'll tell you what, there's plenty of fictional characters who've ruined my life.

"I'm keen on making sure my kiddo's happy. That's the problem here, Lily. From one day to the next, he's gone from smitten to somber. It's not a good look for him. He dwells on the positive side of things. I'd like to keep it that way."

Her voice thickens, wanting to make certain Love hears her. "Do you know what it's like to lose someone you care about, Lily? I'm not talking about a puppy love breakup. I'm talking about really losing someone who's irreplaceable, out of nowhere."

No. Love doesn't know what it's like.

Miss Georgie knows. Andrew said she was a widow. It shows in her downturned lips and the lonely shimmer of her wedding ring, which Love hadn't noticed until now.

In reply, Love pinches the candle between her fingers, dousing the flame, guessing that's how it feels. Like a light disappearing from inside her.

"Yep it's almost like that, but not quite," Miss Georgie acknowledges, a thread of grief in her words. She grabs a matchbook and relights the candle, the fire bursting to life with a hiss. "I take it no one's ever been that important to you."

Love shakes her head, not sure whether to feel lucky or tragic.

The woman tosses down the matchbook. "No one deserves to know how it feels, trust me. I don't want Andrew to suffer because you left without a word, or did something worse. He's already carrying enough loss on his shoulders.

"My kiddo can be a snarky pain in the ass, I know that. But he's a *noble*, snarky pain in the ass. I know he'll treat a girl right, open doors for her, carrying her bag if it's too heavy, write sappy letters to her. He deserves somebody who'll care about him just the same, so whatever your business is with him, make sure it's the decent kind. I have a pitchfork in my closet, right beside my fabulous hat collection, and I'm not afraid to use it."

Love resists the urge to hang her head. A human woman is lecturing her, grilling her about a boy, as if Love were a normal girl. The feeling is unprecedented, intimidating, and more exciting than she would have guessed. It sucks the apprehension out of her.

She understands why Andrew cares for Miss Georgie. Love envisions spending time with this woman, dusting or sweeping while Miss Georgie jots down figures. In a fantasy world, this woman—or some other caring soul—would teach Love mortal things like how to cook, and tell her about those life-ruining, fictional characters over supper. And she would scold Love, as parents do, for coming home late on a school night. It would be pleasant to have that, to be protected the way this woman protects Andrew. A simple life.

Love recalls the notes Wonder wrote to that boy in 1860 and the way things ended. The visual of Wonder's mutilated hands should alarm Love. Ramifications like that should prevent her from picking a blank leaflet of paper off the counter, from stealing Miss Georgie's faithful pencil from behind the woman's ear.

It doesn't. This won't change the outcome of Love's job. She merely wants the chance to win this woman's approval. How to do it? What to say?

I'd like your blessing to be his friend . . . No.

I ask your permission to be his friend . . . No.

Fates. Andrew would say Love sucks at this.

Honesty about her feelings would be melodramatic and unwise. If it were harmless to reveal, Andrew would be the first to learn what's in her heart. She needs an alternative, words to express what he means to her and what she must do. A promise that he, and Miss Georgie, both would appreciate.

The slow jazz melody struts from the speakers. In the candlelight, Love summons her nerve and writes. Miss Georgie watches in amusement as Love finishes and then slides the leaflet across the counter. Love tiptoes back, hands folded respectfully behind her as she waits for judgment.

I will take care of him.

The woman chuckles, her mirth chiming between them. Love delights in this secretive moment, knowing a repeat performance is unlikely.

"You're excused. Oh, and forget the essay," Miss Georgie says, grabbing the stack and dumping it onto another pile. "Ain't nothing but my inventory."

Love's mouth drops open. Another trick! The mortal is cunning.

"And Lily?" Miss Georgie winks. "Say hi to the kiddo for me."

⁓

He stands outside the school library and scans a bulletin board on the wall. The boy is looking good in a fitted blue sweater that emphasizes his shoulders. With more time at her disposal, she might grow obsessed with those clingable shoulders, now that she has seen them bare. A lot of him was exposed while he slept and she toyed with his clothes. Sneaky her, she doesn't regret that.

Nearby, another of her former matches nuzzle each other against a locker: a guy as slim as a broomstick and a mousey girl with braces strung across her teeth. In another life, that is how it could be for Love and Andrew. She could be a real girl trotting up to him, doing something silly to get his attention. She pretends, fixing her hair as she heads his way, dodging students as though she truly needs to.

At the last minute, impulsiveness gets the better of Love. She opts for a theatrical approach and leaps right through the profile of Andrew's body.

It's not funny. He whips around, his back crashing into the wall. "Christ," he hisses.

People laugh and whisper as they pass. Perhaps she overdid it. In spite of her invisibility, Love feels the quick thrust of the crowd's attention. Worse, Andrew's attention as he stares at her in disbelief.

"Hello," she says, rueful.

"Hey," he says. He licks his lips, taking in the sight of her standing in the middle of his school. He's about to say something generous to match the sudden thaw in his eyes, but he stops himself, rethinks it, and turns to the board. He's decided to ignore her. She has a problem with that. They're in public, but not so much as a murmur from him? It's not like Andrew. If she could, she would grab his shoulder and yank him back to her.

No. I must be humble. He's vexed with me.

Checking that no one's watching them anymore, Love snatches a fountain pen—a boy who actually uses a fountain pen!—from the side pocket of his backpack. She uncaps it and pokes the tip against his hand, making his fingers twitch.

"Now you must acknowledge me," she jokes. "I've made a mark on you."

Andrew rounds on Love. "You've made lots of marks on me. You just don't see them." Before she can appreciate the sentiment, he crosses his arms. "What do you want from me, goddess?"

Love takes the question far more personally than she ought to. She crosses her arms as well. "Last night, you were a guest in my home. You broke my cup."

It's not the answer he wanted. She can tell from the way his face breaks apart, expectations reduced to rubble. "Well, you broke my trust. Guess those gods you raise hell with haven't taught you to apologize."

I apologize teeters at the tip of her tongue. "You could have listened to my side of things."

"Go ahead," he says in a dry tone. "Talk."

He's staring at her like he's so righteous, and she's a demon come to maul innocent people. She would need a Greek chorus to help fully express what that does to her.

Maybe she doesn't love him after all. Or maybe this rapture can be . . . turned off?

On the bulletin board, a page framed with decorative swirls announces details for the calligraphy club's next meeting. The spelling is fine, but the grammar is poor.

A quick inspection of the hall assures her that no one is looking. She uses his pen to correct the mistakes. Finished, she caps the pen with a smack of her palm. "My world has a destiny as much as yours does," she contends. "This is what I was born and bred to do."

"You're saying you can't change or view things differently.

That's a crap answer."

"Without my bow and my power, I have nothing. What purpose do I serve?"

"That's no excuse for using people," he bites out.

"Fates, keep your voice down. I'm right *here*."

"Are you really?" he counters, flinging out his arms. "Will you ever be *here*?"

The hallway goes silent. Kids have stopped to gawk, unsure whether to hoot, record the spectacle on their phones, or put a hockey rink's worth of space between Andrew and themselves.

He flushes. Love swallows.

At two centuries young, her body has the power to ascend cliffs, outrun motorcycles, dance in the midst of earthquakes. Her senses have access to innermost feelings. She's brandished her weapon, leapt into the air, and struck a person down before her feet hit the ground. She has loosed two arrows at once in order to hit her targets simultaneously, taken shots in absolute darkness and in a club with a pulsing strobe light. Her eyesight, her aim, is flawless.

She is supposed to be flawless. This crowd has nothing on her.

Yet she's mortified. She has embarrassed Andrew and herself, and it hurts because this isn't her world, so he has to take the brunt of it. She wants to rescue him from their prying glances.

Holly does it instead. "Andrew, there you are," she chirps, cantering toward him with her halo of golden hair and waving as if they planned on meeting in this spot. It works. Her approach breaks up the scene, and students go on their merry way while playing with their phones.

Andrew glances toward Love, mad but unwilling to leave her alone. The longer they stare, the more his demeanor wilts, beseeching her. He wants to understand. He wants to understand why she went after his stepfather, why she goes after people she doesn't know, unconcerned about them after her work is done.

Andrew walked out on her last night. She gave him reasons not to trust her. And here he is, wanting to understand.

It's futile defending herself. He is incapable of accepting the truth, and under his scrutiny she's unsure whether she can accept it herself.

This morning, she intended to make amends. She promised Miss Georgie she would do right by him. Both attempts have flopped. At least this ripe opportunity with Holly will fix the latter, help him bond with her in Griffin's absence.

What Love wants for herself hardly matters, nor does the pang it causes.

She jams the fountain pen into Andrew's bag. "No," she answers, feigning indifference. "I will never be *here*. Get used to it."

His wonderful shoulders sink, and with them, any hope of keeping his friendship fades. Without looking back, he strides away to meet beautiful Holly halfway. This is good. Love repeats a mantra in her head. *This is good. This is good.*

"Hey, you," Holly says with forced cheeriness.

"Hey back," Andrew says, shrugging his bag higher, doubtless to conceal them from Love, the residue of their quarrel apparent in his voice. "What's up?"

"Nothing," Holly responds automatically. "Um, I wanted to say thanks. I liked that book you brought over the other day, from the store."

"Oh," he says. "Right. I'm glad."

Love purses her lips in agitation. Andrew isn't as chatty with others as he is with Love. This time, it could be that he's aware she's watching them.

"Did you hear there was supposed to be a book club starting? I stopped by"—Holly motions to the library door—"but no one knew about it."

"Me, too," Andrew says. "Things get screwed up by Admin all the time."

"Yeah. Weird." She loiters, playing with the zipper of her jacket until he regards her quizzically. "Okay well, I'm having a party tonight," she says.

Love scoffs. Andrew isn't a party person. But this is good.

When he doesn't respond, the girl adds, "It's cool if you have plans, though."

He shakes his head and sighs. "Look, you don't have to do this."

The comment pricks at Love. He thinks Holly's inviting him out of pity.

Holly realizes it, too, and backpedals, which is rather endearing to witness. "No. No, I . . . I honestly don't get why people were staring at you. I mean, I talk to myself all the time," she says lamely. "I'm inviting you because you're a friend. It'd be cool if we were . . . friends."

Andrew is momentarily startled, then to Love's relief and misery, his words take on a humorous lilt. "You know, if you wanted free books, all you had to do was ask. You don't have to bribe me."

Holly grins and shoves him. "Whatever."

Laughing, they stroll down the hall together. As they go, Love cranes her head, honing in on Andrew's thumb swiping at the pen mark she made on his hand, rubbing the ink to make it disappear.

That night, Love weaves through the dancing bodies at Holly's house, making sure to avoid Andrew but keeping close enough to do her job. Her heart twists watching him wander from room to room, staring at family pictures in the hallway, acting like he doesn't care that kids are casting him looks.

Music thumps from the speakers. Heads whip back and mouths gulp amber liquid from shot glasses. Orange dots of light flash in different areas as people light cigarettes.

As Andrew weaves through smoke toward the back porch, he passes a beer-touting trio of boys. One of the guys has a giant, leaping nose and a chin pimple to end all pimples. He calls over the pumping speakers, "What's Andrew doing here?"

"I heard Griffin kicked his ass. Poor boy can't take a hint about Holly."

"I heard it was the other way around. The limp gave him magic powers."

They snort with laughter. Love whacks the bottoms of their cups, one by one, popping them into the air and splattering the boys' clothes. Everyone nearby goes nuts and heckles them, raising their drinks in the air in a sloppy toast.

Andrew disappears outside, thankfully forgotten. She lets him go and trails the sound of Griffin and Holly upstairs. Her bedroom door is ajar, but they wouldn't notice if Love opened it anyway. They're busy.

On the bed, Holly giggles while her hulking boyfriend multitasks, nibbling her neck and stroking locks of her hair. He used to try too hard and too much, but he's different now. He's gentle, confident, patient—fake. Maybe he could have learned on his own how to be a lover. With time, and without an arrow, he might have learned to calm himself and curbed his aggression, making room for Holly's own flaws to peek through, for both of them to learn from one another. An imperfect but authentic courtship, with its smudges and smiles, belonging to them and no one else.

Love thinks of Andrew alone outside, going home to his father, sleeping beside the bookmark engraved from his mother who isn't there, going to work with Miss Georgie, who is also alone. Andrew wants someone to want him, only him, as he really is.

Love wishes he could have that. At least when it's over, he won't know the difference.

Swallowing her remorse, she chooses a lust arrow and shoots Griffin, giving his passion a temporary jolt, enough to make him greedy and overeager, not forceful but pushy—just enough to get Holly mad at him. His entire frame shudders from the impact, and then he swoops in, urging her backward onto the mattress, covering her body with his weight.

Holly squeaks before he licks his way into her mouth. She clings to his arms and wrenches him back. "Slow down."

"I want you so much, babe," he pants, tugging at the secrets beneath her shirt.

"Wait," she says, more insistent. "Wait a minute."

In the doorway, Love squeezes her eyes shut. This boy was vile to Andrew, but he adores his girlfriend. He wouldn't pressure her like this.

Andrew wouldn't want Love to manipulate them. He'd detest her for it.

Love doesn't want to manipulate them, either. Griffin won't get violent, because the shot hadn't been that strong, because she would never give anyone a shot that strong. And even if some wicked twist of nature intervened, if things unexpectedly got out of hand, out of her control, she'd stop it by whatever means necessary, even if she had to knock him over the head with a lamp.

It's no consolation, though. She's made these humans into

puppets. She's disgusting. She's fucked up, like Andrew said.

I'm sorry, she thinks over and over. *I'm sorry.*

Griffin buries his head in Holly's shoulder. His mouth worships her, dominating her with a selfish kiss, and her hair gets tangled up in the roughness of his hands.

Holly writhes. "You're too heavy."

"You feel so good."

"Not here," she protests. "This is crazy."

"No one's gonna walk in."

"Freaking hell, Griffin!"

Leave her alone!

Love's libido boost means that he'll be like this for a good ten minutes. If she wants to stop him before then, without causing him physical harm, there's only one way. With a growl, she whips out an arrow, one that will permanently erase his love for Holly, and aims.

Too late. Holly shoves him away so hard that he hits the floor with a monstrous thud.

"What the—," he hollers, lurching to his feet. "What's wrong with you, Holly?!"

"With me?" she yells. "What wrong with you? You've never been like that!"

"Like what? We were kissing."

"You were totally *not* in the mood for *kissing*."

Love's head darts between them. *It's my fault. He didn't mean it.*

Griffin's face falls. "I thought you wanted to."

"Not like this," Holly says, exasperated. "There's a party downstairs."

He yanks at the roots of his hair. "I don't get you, you know that? When are you going to knock it off and want me back?"

"I do, you jerk!"

"Yeah? Well, it's not something you're proud of."

He storms off and slams the door on his way out. Through the window, Holly and Love watch his car blast out of the driveway. The girl slumps onto the bed, tears leaking down her face.

Love feels like a fool. With the right arrow, she could have obliterated Griffin and Holly's feelings for each other long ago, made things easier instead of maneuvering around those feelings. That's usually the solution when handling love triangles. This whole time, Love forgot to consider that.

Guilt flares inside her. Yet that would have been just as cruel, wouldn't it?

Once Holly gets her crying under control, the muffled music seeping into the room lures her back to her guests. Either she's unaware of the mascara smeared beneath her eyes or she doesn't care. People give her looks. They must have heard the shouting upstairs and witnessed Griffin leave. A pair of girls coo over Holly while, from various corners, other girls roll their eyes at the drama and mutter to one another.

Holly claims a headache and retreats to the back of the house. Love isn't fond of having to follow her like a shadow. Besides, if this girl wanted to be alone, she should have stayed upstairs.

No one warns her that Andrew's outside. They probably forgot him.

Love and Holly pause at the screen door and watch him on the porch swing. He's hunched over, writing in his notebook, ignoring the frosty air. His white hair blends in with the snowy landscape. Somehow, his presence manages to soften the harsh edges of winter.

A sad but comforted grin lifts Holly's mouth, which Love can relate to. It's precisely how she feels whenever she sees this boy. She wants to go to him, but it's not her place. After Holly shuffles through the door, Love cranes her head to get a decent view through the screen.

"Hey," Holly says.

Andrew glances at her in surprise, as if suddenly remembering where he is. "Hey."

"No, it's okay," she says when he moves to get up and leave. "Griffin's not here anyway. I mean, not that that's why you'd ... you know." She settles beside him, the swing croaking beneath her. Love's hand chokes the doorknob when Andrew's leg brushes Holly's.

The humans pretend to study the sky. Actually, Holly pretends. Andrew regards the stars poking holes into the darkness with guarded scrutiny, like he doesn't trust them to stay up there.

"You came," she says.

"Yeah," he answers, still fixated on the sky. "I was curious."

She laughs. "That's a new one."

Andrew doesn't speak for a moment, then sets his pen and notebook beside him. He rubs his hands together, tucks them between his knees. "Rough night?"

"The worst."

"The worst sucks," he agrees.

More silence.

Holly blows her bangs out of her face. "I know what Griffin did to you was wrong, and he won't admit it, but he's a good guy once you get to know him. He really is," she insists.

Andrew shrugs. "You would know."

And more silence. Lost silence.

Without warning, a dam splits open. "Last year, I had appendicitis," Holly blurts out. "Griffin stayed in the hospital all night, bought my parents coffee and stuff to eat, played with my brothers so Mom and Dad could get a break. He went to my house and packed my favorite books and got me, like, a dozen of these little vanilla marshmallows." A weak chuckle escapes her. "He has no clue I hate marshmallows. I once acted like I liked them, just as a joke. Like, oh they're life-changing, haha. But Griffin took it seriously and buys them for me all the time now. It makes him happy to think I'm happy.

"But sometimes it's, like, too much. I know where it's coming from. His parents pressure him about school and hockey. I tell him he's amazing all the time, that he's important to me, but it doesn't stick. He never thinks he's good enough. 'Nice guys' make him angry, like he won't be able to compete, so he gets jealous and possessive. Honestly, I was beginning to think he was getting over that. The last couple of days, he's been incredible, but tonight it started again. He seriously messed up. Oh, God." She rolls her eyes. "I'm ranting. It's not like you asked."

"'S'okay," Andrew says. His attention is back on the stars, but Love knows he's listening.

"We don't really know each other, and I'm saying all this personal stuff."

"I don't mind," he answers.

"You're just easy to be around. My friends don't get it. I guess that's why I read books instead of calling them. I want to know how other people fix the bad stuff. When things happen, how do they make it better? It's stupid, right? So stupid."

"It's not," Andrew says. "Stories help that way."

Holly gives him an appraising glance. "Thanks for tolerating me," she says, reaching out to pat his notebook in gratitude but knocking it off the swing. "Ugh, I'm a spaz." She beats Andrew to it, plucking the notebook off the floor before he can and pausing at an open page.

"*A girl made of iron, of white dresses and lonely smiles,*" she recites. "*A wingless, remorseless, clueless body. This wild girl is not my girl.*"

Love blinks. He's been writing about her!

Holly shakes her head. "Wow. Who is this? Do I know her?"

Andrew snatches the notebook. "It's no one."

"Oh, I didn't mean to . . . ," she rushes to say, then changes direction. "The writing's beautiful. She sounds like she's everyone to you."

He sneers as if to say, *Love would definitely like to think so.*

"You're mad at her," Holly guesses.

"You think?" he gripes.

"I know the feeling. Griffin was crazy tonight. God, why does being with someone have to be complicated?"

They ponder the ground as if the question has fallen from her mouth and landed there. Love does the same. Why is the complication worth it?

As she looks up again, the sight of Andrew's profile gives her the answer. It's complicated, it's worth it, because . . .

"Because it matters," Andrew says.

Indeed, Love thinks. Because it matters.

It takes him forever, but eventually he covers Holly's hand with his own. She grins meekly at him. "You're sweet."

He smiles back. It's a pensive grin, but it's there. It's for her.

Holly's eyes skip over his face for a long time. "I don't know why I'm bringing this up, but I remember in eighth grade, you used to give away your lunch, every single day, all year, to that poor girl who didn't have lunch money."

Love's chest clenches. That sounds like something Andrew would do.

"What was her name?" Holly prompts.

"Iris," Andrew answers without missing a beat. "Her name was Iris. How do you know about that? You and I weren't friends."

"I noticed you," she demurs. "That was when I realized you were cute and nice. Anyway, it's not complicated with you."

"I haven't said much," he points out. "Wait until I start talking."

They laugh. Love yearns to draw him back to her where he belongs. Instead she stands there like an idiot, letting herself be forgotten.

Andrew sobers. "It's not complicated with you, either."

Holly glances at his hand over hers, then up at him. The rhinestones of her eyes hold his attention.

Love tastes the syrupy flavor of Holly's intent. "You delivered that book to my house even though I didn't order it. You're always so quiet that I thought maybe it was your way of reaching out? Because if it was, maybe we should . . . find out what uncomplicated is like. See if it's better."

"How?" he whispers.

Her eyes drop to his mouth. "I have an idea."

Andrew catches her meaning and boldly laces her fingers with his. "So do I."

There are some moments that don't require Love's intervention, moments when human nature works on its own. Laughter, clinking glasses, and pumping music bound from inside, but outside a fissure cracks open in this icy world. The porch swing sighs as these two mortals move closer to each other, while a helpless goddess spies on them.

The pair waits, then chuckles when nothing happens.

"What are we waiting for?" Holly says, angling her lips upward.

Love wants to shut her eyes, to look away, but she can't.

Holly and Andrew can touch. They do touch.

They kiss.

19

The worst part is that Love feels their kiss. She feels the determination as their mouths mesh together. The embrace is cautious but curious, visibly turning Andrew to putty. He kisses her back, leaning in and searching for more.

More. He wants to have more.

When his mouth opens to fully take Holly in, he holds her face and kisses her deeply, with no intention of stopping. Ever.

Madness crawls through Love. She sinks her teeth into her lower lip, bottling up her feelings so that Andrew won't hear her. It takes her several attempts, bow lifting and dropping, and lifting and dropping, before she surrenders. It's the perfect time, but she can't do it. Not yet.

Let them enjoy each other for real first.

Love thrusts up her chin. She walks away slowly and in a daze until she passes through the swaying, roaming bodies. Rancid, giddy emotions swarm her from different areas of the party like winter flurries.

She rips open the front door—"Dude, did you see that?"— and marches across the lawn. She halts beside a group and pretends to join them, chuckling along, her mirth heightening to a lunatic crescendo because she has no idea what's so funny. She's arrived too late to hear the joke.

It's no use. They can't see her. She doesn't belong.

Frustrated, Love smacks a guy's drink out of his hand, then selects an arrow and shoots a mild dose of lust into his heart. The boy stumbles backward. His eyes glaze over with hunger, looking for someone, anyone at the party, to be with. He won't attack people, but he'll certainly make a clumsy dolt of himself, and for the next few minutes, until the ardor wears off, people will think he's drunk.

Andrew is with Holly. The mortal swine's not thinking of Love at all, even though just last night he professed his desire to touch her. Maybe Holly will ruin everything by drooling on him or tasting like a rotten vegetable. Miracles do happen.

Love raises her bow, about to target another soul who has gotten in her way.

"Let me know when you're done rioting," a voice grunts.

She stops. Anger festers beside her with his arms crossed.

"Don't you have protests to break up and crimes of passion to thwart?" she asks.

"Yes," he says simply. "If I could snore through your self-destruction, I would. You must think you'll be praised for delaying the inevitable and looking incompetent at best, untrustworthy at worst." He gestures toward the party, appalled. "Corrupt as well. Shooting mortals without tact? Where did our Guides go wrong with you?"

"Leave the Guides out of this," she warns.

"Don't you understand? All this romantic prattle is wilting your sense," Anger raps. "I've known you to be naughty but not vicious."

"This is almost over. Andrew and the girl's tongues are currently entwined."

Anger applauds. "Bravo. And so what? That wasn't your doing. I know because I was there. I was at the back porch—"

"Spying again," Love says, unsurprised.

"I saw it for myself. They were ready, you had your chance to shoot them, but your bowstring went slack. I defied the laws of reason and helped you by taming those other two mortals, yet you're still too daft and besotted to get the rest right. There's a word for it. Let me educate you: It's called hopeless."

"Anger—"

"Curb your appetite for the boy and finish this!"

"Let go of me," Love seethes.

He glowers down to where he's suddenly clasping her shoulders. Repentant, he yanks his hands away. She rubs the place where he seized her.

Strong. His touch is so strong. Supposing he were able to love, Anger would do it strongly. If he gave her comfort, he would do it strongly as well. He would hold on, if she asked him to.

Another girl is tasting Andrew's mouth. Meanwhile, Anger could be holding Love. However infuriating the god is, she changes her mind and wishes for the latter scenario. She could use a pair of arms around her, a hint of strong.

Anger must sense her thoughts because his demeanor shifts. It ignites his entire being and kindles a long-deprived need to the surface. His eyes dark, he advances, and Love permits him to, transfixed by his intensity and the commotion it causes low in her belly.

Stars, this is inconceivable. This is Anger. *Anger*.

He's about to grasp her once more, on the verge of further complicating her life, when he stops. The trance breaks as he examines her, suddenly horrified. "For Fates' sake, look at you. You're pale. You've got shadows beneath your eyes. Your body will turn gaunt within days at this rate. This isn't a game, Love!" he thunders. "This is your life!"

Her stomach churns. "You wouldn't understand," she says, crestfallen.

His eyes narrow to slits. "I'm not going to help you be frail. Grow up, goddess."

Love walks away. To his credit, Anger knows better than to pursue her.

In the main square, she detours and breaks into a clothing shop. Running her hands over a shelf of pajamas, she discovers a bundle of soft azure cotton: sleep pants and a pretty shirt, and underwear called boy shorts. Something to cover herself. Something human.

She changes into them, balls up her white dress, and stuffs it into her quiver. She decides to keep being stupid and heads straight to Andrew's house, flopping onto the porch and waiting.

And waiting.

"What are you doing here?"

Andrew approaches with an accusatory frown, his grip tightening on his notebook. She stands, fidgets with the pajamas, feeling silly when he fails to notice them.

He's disheveled and ruddy. His gray coat was closed at the party, but now it's split open, and he smells like berries. Like her.

Love wants to put her white dress back on. "Where were you?"

"You overhead me and Holly at school. Figure it out for yourself."

"Must have been a fun party."

"It was. I had a real good time with her, actually."

"Indeed. I saw that."

Andrew balks. "You were there?"

There's no way to explain why. That wasn't supposed to come out anyway.

He rakes a hand through his hair. "You had no right to eavesdrop. That conversation was between us."

Us. They're an *us* now.

"You weren't doing much talking," Love criticizes.

"Right," he laughs bitterly. "I forgot how much you people care about our privacy."

"So I've lost you, then."

In an instant, sadness washes over his face. He has trouble meeting her gaze, his features pulling in two different directions. "Love ..."

Her name has never sounded so alive. She doesn't have the will to conceal what this means to her. Or maybe part of her wants him to see her hurt.

She asks, "Was it nice?"

"This isn't fair."

"Was it nice to touch a girl? Be touched back?"

"Stop it," he says. "You can't do this. You can't follow me to work, and to school, and to parties, and expect me to be okay with that. You can't be my friend, then lie to me, then push me away, then hold it against me for spending time with someone else, then come here and act like I belong to you. You're only interested in me because I can see you. I'm a toy, and you're lonely!"

"No. It's because I feel sorry for you!" she shoots back.

Hurt contorts Andrew's features. "You're lying," he insists, but his voice cracks at the end, doubt creeping in.

"You're not supposed to see me. I didn't trust you at first and had to investigate, and then yes, we had our friendly moments. And when you learned what my people do to mortals, you became upset, so I felt obligated to mollify your nerves before they ran amok. As for the party, you're a fragile thing—you proved that in the park when I saved your hide. I figured Griffin's vengeance might be a roadblock at Holly's house, and I would have to play the guardian yet again. I'm grateful that I was wrong. You're quite the burden."

That last part is true. He is a burden, and she loves him for it.

"I don't care a fig about your company. It was a minor diversion," she finishes, detesting herself for this speech and what it does to Andrew's face.

To his credit, he bounces back quickly, his expression smoothing and concealing the pain she'd just seen there. His eyes sharpen in the dark. "Huh."

What does *huh* mean?

It means, "Then maybe I'll just call Holly tomorrow and hang out with her."

Love snatches the notebook from him, takes advantage of his shock, and opens it to find another passage about her. *Glass eyes and lying mouth. Hands that slip inside my chest and find my heart.*

Clipped onto the inside cover is the note he wrote to her. *Who is this girl?*

She yanks it from the clasp. Cursing, Andrew lunges, rescuing the notebook and bending it in the process. He's not quick enough, though. She only needs that one page, the one that refuses to go away. She tears it apart, ripping it to shreds.

The papers fall like snow and puddle around Andrew's shoes. He sinks to the ground and gathers the soggy pieces gently, quietly. The sight destroys Love.

He looks up at her, so very, very sad. She wants to fall to her knees beside him, to bow her head and beg his pardon. Why is she doing this? Why can't she just be good to him? Why does she always make these mistakes? Why must he matter so much?

He rises, his words cutting through the air. "You don't need to touch me in order to hurt me. You break my heart without lifting a finger, and that's why tonight happened."

Love holds out her hands, imploring. "Andrew, wait. I—"

"I wish I never met you. Get away from me."

It appears he doesn't need to touch her, either, in order to make her suffer. She doesn't know what to do with this terrible, stinging feeling, and she's tired all of a sudden, and still desperate to fix this night, and furious because the more she tries, the worse it will get.

In his eyes, everything about her is wrong. And she agrees with him. And she can't take it.

"Fine," she snaps.

"Fine," he snaps.

Neither of them moves. She loathes to be the one to leave, or the one left behind, and she wonders if he feels the same.

"On the count of three," he suggests.

She nods. On three, she whirls away and hears his hobbling footsteps across the porch. After a few paces, she glances back to see him disappearing inside the house. The light pops on in his window, then clicks off a moment later.

When she gets back to the glass cottage, she studies her reflection in the glass and puckers her lips. In her mind, she imitates Holly. She bats her watery, damsel-length eyelashes at Andrew: *Oh, woe is me, boy-I-never-paid-attention-to-before. I'm a fictitious heroine who's claimed by the wrong rogue, and I'm going to impress you, the social commoner in our high school kingdom, with my introspective side. We should find out what uncomplicated feels like. I have an idea. Oh Andrew, wanna try?*

How long did they kiss? How many times?

Love has never cried before. She checks to see if she has tear ducts, but her reflection is too blurry to tell.

20

After Andrew goes to work the next morning, she checks the first-floor windows of his house. They're all locked, so she scales the wall. It's difficult to dig her nails into the shingles and hoist herself up. By the time she reaches the second story, she's panting.

Love startles when she tries to lift his bedroom window. It's also locked.

She summons her rage and shoves the pane up into the ceiling, prying the hinges from their sockets. In his room, bits of paper litter his desk, pieces of the note from last night. She remembers him collecting them, clutching them to his chest while wishing she didn't exist.

Love sits cross-legged on his floor and spreads out the papers. This should take seconds, but she works slowly like a mortal, forgoing speed. As it is, she's not certain she'd be quicker. She is wilting because of him.

She uses tape and gives life back to his words. The page is finished but scarred everywhere. She rereads the whole thing, baffled how he ever saw her as someone ethereal.

Who is this girl?

Love borrows one of his pens and writes her answer.

She's not a girl. She made a mistake.

Please forgive her.

She sets the note on his pillow and leaves. In her cottage, she brews tea and stokes the fire. The flames' height is a good sign that Andrew will be comfortable when he returns and they find a truce. Soon, he'll read her words and miss her as much as she misses him.

He'll trek sideways across the snow, and in this secret place, he'll have more things to say and ask.

Love watches the sky expectantly as it shifts from light to dark. She listens for his footfalls. The fire needs more logs. The rug where he sat across from her looks worn. Dipping her finger in the tea, she discovers its texture has changed, meaning it must not be warm anymore. She empties it out.

Andrew's not coming back to her. Maybe he called Holly like he said he would. Maybe she invited him back to her lair after his shift. Maybe he's there now, kissing her and inhaling her dragon breath behind Griffin's back.

Love gives up waiting, gives up hoping. She climbs into bed and curls into a shell.

Now she knows what regret feels like.

21

A knocking rhythm intrudes into her dream. She opens her eyes and rolls over—and tumbles off the bed. Swatting hair out of her face, Love bounds to her feet.

Andrew stands a few feet from her, just inside the door, his cheeks bloodless from the cold and his new coat spanning his shoulders. Outside, the branches netted around each other quiver in the breeze. The sky is a gentle shade of afternoon blue. She slept all night and nearly the entire day.

Andrew's gray eyes rake over her pajamas, then settle on her. "I lied to you."

Hello? Good morning? Excuse me for breaking into your invisible glass cottage?

Nothing of the sort. "I didn't have a good time Friday night. I hate parties."

He waits for her to respond. He cares that she cares. She cares that he wants her to care, but he probably doesn't want to know that she knows he cares, because he'll think she only cares because he wants her to, and then he'll be mad, which doesn't make sense because as long as she's doing what he wants there shouldn't be a problem. Then she'll be mad because *he* should *know* she wouldn't fake caring for him, but anyway showing that she cares is as bad an idea as showing that she doesn't care, because either way he'll care even more, and that will make her care even more, and she's not sure what any of this means because she's lost track of her thoughts, which is making her mad, and once she gets mad, it's only a matter of time before he gets mad.

Sigh.

"Hate is a strong word," she says.

"You okay?" he asks, stepping forward. "You look like you have the flu. I thought goddesses couldn't—"

"It's temporary. Drama and sleep deprivation will fatigue anyone."

He nods. "Holly and I kissed. We got carried away."

Love seeks to control the conversation before he expands on that. She doesn't want to talk about their kiss, or think about their kiss, or picture their kiss, or guess how many kisses they've shared since, or consider what else they're planning to do together. "In case you're wondering, Eros doesn't give out sex advice. Not for free."

"If you had a tail, I would yank on it."

"If I had a tail, I would also have claws."

"Not just a goddess but a bully," he observes.

"Maybe you should write that down," she suggests. "With all the details you've collected, you could write a novel about me. I'd make an infuriating character."

"I kissed Holly."

"I heard you the first time! And I know. I was there, remember?"

"It just happened, and ... You don't want to hear this."

Not particularly. But in a way, yes, she does.

"She was upset about Griffin," he explains. "And I couldn't stop thinking about what you said in school. It stung, and I just wanted it to stop. I tried, but I couldn't do it."

"Have sex?" Love asks between her teeth.

"Knock it off. We didn't get that far. I wouldn't have."

Neither would Holly. She sucked Andrew into a kiss less than twenty minutes after Griffin left, but she's not the type of girl who would have done anything more.

"Why did you come here?" Love asks. "On the porch, you walked away from me."

"You let me walk away."

"I thought you abhorred me for what I did."

"What you did to my stepdad, to Griffin, to my notebook, or to me?"

She ducks her head and says in a tiny voice, "My actions ... And the things I've said ... I didn't mean it."

Andrew kicks the ground with his heel, choosing his words carefully. "If Holly hadn't made a move, I would have kissed her anyway."

Love sees blood red.

He speaks faster. "She needed someone to make her feel better, and I was there, and I needed the same thing. There was some chemistry between us, so we followed it. I hoped I could find something with her. But the whole time, I was remembering that day in the bookstore with you, when we goofed off. I remembered you dragging your finger, with its curious little bend, across the bookshelves, and how it drove me nuts.

"I was kissing Holly, and I was really into it, only because I wasn't thinking about her. All I could think about was you. How you didn't want me the way I wanted you, how full of lies you were, how that crushed me. I wanted to believe that I could care for somebody else. I did a bang-up job failing, you know. No matter how much I kissed her—and trust me, we kept going—I imagined your mouth, which pissed me off, because let's face it, you're snobby and entitled."

A tender look softens his face. "You're also funny and fierce and protective. You didn't judge Miss Georgie when you met her. You have a hard time saying you're sorry, but when you do apologize, you mean it. You want to belong to others, I can see it. We haven't had much opportunity to connect like friends do, but I'm one hundred percent attached to your laugh.

"I accept the mistakes my family made because they're my family. Since I'm an asshat, I thought I'd have a choice with you, that I'd be able to walk away if you disillusioned me or turned out to be a blood-sucking creature of the night—and okay, I would have bailed if you were evil . . . Or maybe not. Knowing myself, I'd want to save you. But you're not evil. The point is, I'm realizing you're the same as everyone else in my life, only a thousand times more potent, and that has nothing to do with where you come from. I can grit my teeth about what you do, but I can't control how I react to your laugh. I would rather be near you, see you touch everything but me, than be holding any other girl. I like being with you, Love. Playing, talking, fighting, not-touching. Tell me you keep showing up everywhere because you like me, too. Please."

Is this really happening? Love's head spins, but she'd better not swoon. That would be outdated, ungoddess-like, and humiliating.

Her voice carries through the space. "If you approve of me feeling the same, then yes. I do like you."

His lips twitch in the most charming way. "Soooo, can we talk about this?" He raises his arm, with the black coat draped over it. "And this?" He pulls out his note, patched with glossy tape strips.

"I did my best to fix it," she says. "I never wanted to ruin your words. I brought them back to you one night."

"While I slept," he fills in. "That's when I dreamed about you. I dreamed you came into my room while I was asleep. You were really there, weren't you?"

"I was."

"Your hand went through my chest. You used your arrow on me."

Remembering the waistband of his pants and the torn knot, she asks, "Did you like the dream?"

His ears turn a buoyant rosy color, begging to be nibbled on. "Every bit of it. Why didn't you wake me up?"

"You were furious at me."

"Fury can be an aphrodisiac."

She snickers. "Stop."

"I think if we could touch, the last thing you would do is tell me to stop."

His words curl around her knees like smoke. He may have kissed Holly, but he's here in this room with Love. She's got knots in her hair and most likely grid marks from her pillow across her cheeks, and she has nothing to offer him. Yet his fondness for her hasn't rusted. He's chosen to be here.

She sits and pats the mattress. He rushes to settle next to her and reaches for her hand, but then he makes a fist, remembering it's no use.

"I think we would kiss now," she theorizes.

"I know we would," he says.

"Let's imagine that."

In answer, he draws nearer. Their legs blend like paint colors, he braces his forehead against the outline of hers, and they grin, fantasizing about their lips meeting. She wishes she could taste this moment.

His gray irises adore her. She soaks up the feeling and sends it back to him.

He inches away, euphoric. "That was beautiful."

"We can pursue more beautiful."

So they do. Andrew removes his boots, and they climb into the bed together, facing one another. She runs her hand gently over the outline of his features, his neck as he swallows, the knob of his chin, and the large freckle on his jaw, careful not to let her touch slip through him, imagining what his skin feels like, pretending that she knows. When his eyelids drop closed, it's easy to believe the contact is real.

He pretends to touch her, too. His fingertip eases down the slope of her nose, then across the curve of her ear, and up to her temple. She's amazed by the tissue-thin moan that floats out of her when he brushes his palms over her cheeks, as if to cup them. He stays like that, sliding his thumbs over the shapes of her cheekbones.

They try to explore each other's faces, to see if it makes a difference. And it does, because they tremble and sigh in response.

There could be much more. It dawns on her that there are other ways to affect one another.

Andrew's mouth lifts into a smile. "Whatever you're thinking, it seems like fun."

"Remember what we talked about last time you were here?" she asks. "When we spoke about pleasing ourselves to our own thoughts?"

"You mean, touching ourselves."

"That. Indeed."

Andrew is quiet, but the swish of the blankets as he moves closer reverberates in her ears. He tilts his head, his breath on her chin. Oh, his breath.

She can feel his breath! How?

He makes a throaty sound. "I want to be with you."

This is wrong, but she quells the doubt lingering in her mind. Matchmaking can wait. She has two more days.

Two days. Then she'll betray Andrew. Fates, let her have this time with him.

"Show me," she says. "Show me how you touch yourself."

"Are you sure?"

"Don't make me repeat it. We can feel each other this way."

His shaky hands pull back from her. Her cheeks almost feel the loss, the shift of air, the absence of weight.

Andrew is not shy, not with her. The zipper comes down, and he tugs himself free, and he's glorious to see. His eyes glitter, trusting her, as his palm runs down his stomach.

"I can't believe . . ." An astonished laugh bubbles from between his lips, then stops altogether, catching like something in a net.

It's all so much. His eyes squeezing shut, his body twisting in bliss, his torso rising like a landmass that Love wants to live on forever. It creates an effervescence in her mouth, which builds with each disjointed noise Andrew makes.

When she reaches out to slide her hand through his rhythmic one, he calls out her name, and Love welcomes the sound between her thighs. She doesn't wait for him to finish. She wants to be *there* with him. Her hand slips beneath her pajama pants, and Andrew stills for a second as he realizes what she's doing, but then he continues. Their eyes lock.

"Feel me?" he says.

"Yes," she answers.

"Me, too. You feel incredible."

Winter colors flash in front of her, spinning faster and faster.

Blue sky. Purple wounds. Silver flurries. Her dress. His coat.

Her fingers move as erratically as his hips. His fist is her body. She emulates the pace of his arm, and he holds back for her, and they climb higher. At the top, they find a way to collide.

22

He returns to her on Monday after school. When he knocks on the glass door, she opens it and nervously thrusts a winter posy of needle branches, coiling twigs, and coralberries toward him.

The force of the motion startles Andrew. He stares at the tiny bouquet choked in her fist, his lips kicking up in a sweet grin when she fails to explain herself. "Are these for me?" he prompts.

Love nods. "For you."

That's all she manages to get out, annoyed by her bashfulness and the tremor of uncertainty in her voice. The season gave her few options for blooms, not to mention she was picky about each stem she selected in the woods.

He tortures her with his silence for all of three seconds before accepting the bouquet with an expression of genuine delight. "Thank you."

He likes it.

Love finds herself standing taller. This is what feels like to make him happy.

Andrew carries the posy with him as they take a stroll through the forest, talking about random, insignificant things, each topic swirling into the next. He says that he'd put his arm around her if he could, like boys do with their girlfriends. At the word *girlfriend*, Love seeks a distraction and lobs a snowball at him. He sets his little bouquet safely on the ground, then retaliates, ecstatic that his snowball makes contact with her shoulder. They play and then collapse on the ground, facing opposite directions, their heads next to each other.

They crane their necks and swap indulgent grins. She knows they're both thinking about her bed. The things they did there.

"Say something," she orders.

"We've been talking forever. Do we have to, or can we head back to your place?"

It doesn't take a psychic to know that he wants a repeat of yesterday. She rolls her eyes and pretends to kick him, her leg passing through his. "Typical lad."

He pretends to hip-bump her. "Immortal tease."

"You have something about me on your mind. I'm eager to hear it."

"What makes you think it's about you?"

"It's always about me," she responds smugly.

"Fuck, you are such a little—"

"For such a morally good, self-proclaimed geek, you have quite a pagan tongue."

He perks up. "You like it?"

"I wouldn't be me if I didn't."

"All right, I've been philosophizing on how you match people because they need to be perfect for each other. Call me crazy, but I don't think people are supposed to be perfect for each other, like with tastes and morals and coordinated lifestyles. That's convenience, not love."

Love wrenches her coat closed. "I'll thank you not to nullify my purpose in life."

"I'm not saying this to get you upset," he vows. "But it's not all about you. It's about your targets, as you call them. People, as I call them."

"To those *people*, fate is this"—she flicks her wrist—"this fantastical thing, written in the stars, that leads to chance meetings and romance. It makes humans feel special. It's alluring until one puts a dress on fate and arms it with a bow. According to you, if the world could see me, its people would hunt me down. Hypocrites."

"First of all, you're gung ho about perfection, not actual love. If two people are special to each other, they'll gut each other, they'll challenge each other. It's inevitable because what they say to each other matters more than what anyone else says. Second, that's exactly what makes it amazing. People struggle together, learn what it takes to heal, when to step up or back off, when to meet in the middle, make sacrifices. They inspire each other, become better people for it.

"I don't date, my parents didn't have a model relationship, but I listen to Miss Georgie's stories about her husband. I read books. I see people in love at school. And being with you, *feeling* with you, makes me dig deeper. A messy love is a real love. It can't be faked. It's something that ... grows. It's like best friends and lovers and family all tangled up. Yeah, we like the sound of fate, but we also want to know we had something to do with our life, that we earned our love. I know I do."

His hand dives into hers, letting their fingers swim together, and he pins Love with a hopeful expression. She can't handle it, can't handle anything he said.

Seizing on the subject of family, she asks, "Where's your mother?"

Andrew twists away and speaks to the sky. "Dead."

"I'm sorry."

"I'm sorrier than anyone on the planet. I was a seventh grader, and she was a clinically depressed mother. She sped off an icy road and rammed us into a tree in the woods. I think she did it on purpose."

Love rises on her elbows. "Why?"

"Short story, she wanted things she couldn't have, namely my real dad—he left her when I was in elementary school." He chuckles wryly, oblivious to Love's troubled silence. "When I was little, I thought my family was invincible, that they had all the answers to stuff like, *how do I conquer my fears?* I thought they could fix anything: broken toes, famine, animal extinction. I realized I was wrong after they split up. No one could snap Mom out of it, not even Miss Georgie, and they were best friends. My stepdad got elected as the Rebound Husband but couldn't cure her, so she flipped life itself the bird. He's bitter. Or I guess he's not bitter anymore since you brainwashed him."

"Do you resent them?"

"Nah. The guy raged all the time because he was heartbroken. Sure, he got physical, pushed me around, but he never flat-out hit me. He didn't have it in him. He let bullies take care of the dirty work. Hell, I bet he was glad about Griffin, like that would toughen me up so I'd rage, too, keep the man's anger company. It made him feel like a wimp for not getting over the past like I did.

"Talking about Mom like this isn't my favorite thing, but I'm not pissed like he was. I miss her. She suffered, but she cared about me. She wanted to take me with her."

With her? As in *with her*?

Love pictures herself dashing across the driveway, swiping that innocent boy out of the car and dragging him away before his mother turns on the ignition.

Andrew ruins the vision. "Sometimes I feel guilty for surviving the crash, like I left her alone."

"You didn't. You kept other people company."

"It sounds nuts, but I wore these plaid slippers to her funeral. It was the last gift she ever gave me. It didn't feel right wearing a suit that didn't mean anything to her, but at least I could do something about the boring fancy shoes. My stepdad was afraid I'd make a scene in front of everyone if he ordered me to change out of the slippers, so he waited until after everyone left our house to throw a fit. It was worth it. I wanted to say goodbye to her the right way, sharing something with her.

"I go to the woods each year, around the same time the crash happened. It feels better to face things and then remember the good stuff. That's what I was doing when you jumped me."

Love slices her finger through the snow, drawing around his arm. "I could have paired your mother with your stepfather. They would have been happy. If you had the choice, would you have stopped me?"

Andrew starts. She stops drawing, realizing she just used his tragedy to validate her existence. Though it's impossible to miss the veil of temptation in his expression.

"Good shot. You're right. Then she might still be alive," he contemplates. "But then I wouldn't have met you."

With a groan, Love lands back in the snow, accepting the stalemate. The advantages and disadvantages of what she does wars in her mind. She creates one kind of bliss for people while robbing them of other kinds of bliss.

"I like to think my mom brought us together." Mirth lights Andrew's face. "Do goddesses get shy?"

"Pfff."

"Looks that way to me. You're blushing."

"Ha. Never."

"Well, I wouldn't control people the way you do, but I'm a fraud. I'd have wanted my mom happy and alive if I had the choice. The human in me might have taken you up on those arrows, I don't know, in a moment of weakness. Let you strike her and my stepdad. It wouldn't have been right, but it would have taken away their pain. How could that have been bad?"

His eyes cast down. "My stepdad keeps making me breakfast while I keep waiting for him to detonate and go back to his old self. It's not really him, but I'm glad about that—I'm glad for him, not me. It's nice to see him doing okay. You're making it hard to regret that."

Love's chest tightens at his words.

He scrambles to his feet and retrieves the winter posy. "Enough angst. I got me some plans for us."

When they return to the cottage, he sets the bouquet in a cup of water beside her bed, grabs his backpack, and leads her to the frozen pond. She makes a sound of apprehension when he pulls two pairs of ice skates from his bag.

"I said I would teach you," Andrew says.

She shakes her head. "I can't."

He misunderstands. "Still not getting immortal sleep, huh? You look it. We don't have to. Maybe the walk was enough."

"That's offensive. I'm fighting fit," she declares, the denial crawling across her tongue. "I meant, this is silly."

"Love."

"It's for children."

"Love."

"Human children."

"You won't fall," he promises. "I won't let you. And if I do screw up, and you land on your ass, I'm the only person who'll see it."

Love stares at him. Those pale lids and lips, that trustworthy face. He won't laugh at her if she falls. Her coat might flap open, and he might have a chance to look up her skirt—which is fine since she's wearing the new boy shorts—but he won't laugh at her.

She can climb the tallest tree, hop from branch to branch. She can do this, too.

They lace up their skates. It's impressive that he guessed the right shoe size for her.

On the pond, their blades cut across the ice. She bites her tongue in concentration, ignoring her shaky elbows and wobbly limbs and labored breaths, determined not to ruin this simply because he's killing her. He skates backward, using a broad stick to bridge their hands and guide her around the rim. He's good at this, despite his limp.

When she's ready, he pulls the stick away. Love yelps, her arms flapping, then straightening, then gliding. They make it to the center of the ice, where they spin slowly, grasping the stick and giggling.

Snow begins to fall and powder the woods. Love cocks her head toward the sky, noting the signs.

"I think a storm is coming," she announces. "A mighty one. Sometime tomorrow."

"You look sexy in that coat."

She catches Andrew admiring her. "Why—thank you."

But he has more to say. "I wanted you to keep the coat because I thought you were freezing, but also because you looked unbelievably sexy in it. I like you for all the reasons I said yesterday, and for more reasons the longer I'm with you. Lying in the snow, I wanted to roll you toward me, warm you up with my body. Learning how to skate makes you smile, and that makes me smile. I forgive you because you matter. You can wreck me, and I'll still forgive you. I can't help it. I have it bad for you, Love."

He waits. So she does the only thing a goddess can do when a mortal boy is declaring himself to her: She tips her head back and lets the snowflakes land on her tongue. When he sees what she's doing, Andrew cants his head to the side with interest.

"Try it," she says.

They arch backward and stick out their tongues, letting the ice slip down their throats. Andrew stops and grins, causing an avalanche inside her. And she thinks, *I made that happen.*

She could do this over and over, make him stumped or speechless, guarded or relaxed, joyful or pained, see his face in its different forms. If she could do this, she could be content, and she would let him do the same to her. And so much more.

He holds out the stick. "Come here. I'll take any type of close."

She reaches out. Her fingers brush against his. Just like that.

A touch. He touched her!

Andrew's eyes widen, and life stops, and they both stop. A split second of indecision, and Love scuttles backward with a gasp, almost losing her balance. She spins around, intending to flee, but he drops the stick, and his arms catch her from behind. They swath around her middle and hold tight, surrounding her with a delicate, terrifying weight, robbing her of breath as his chest—his heartbeat—thumps against her back.

This is how it feels to be Holly. This is how it feels to be like everyone else, brittle and comforted and unsatisfied. A desperate need to release these feelings builds and overwhelms Love. She wants to scream. So she does.

When she's done, she relaxes into him with an exhale, her muscles slackening. How strange to fit her body to a mortal's, how unfair that it's never happened before.

He turns her around and buries his face in the side of her neck. "Are you okay?" he whispers.

She rests her forehead onto his shoulder. "No. Yes."

"You feel like a magic trick, like a magician pulled you out of his hat and gave you to me. I could hold you all day and night. What the hell?"

Indeed. How? How, how, how?

Oh, Fates. It's his influence on her, the way she couldn't outrun him or sense his emotions, the way she loses bits of her powers each time she's with him. Touching must be no exception.

"It happens the longer we're with humans," she mumbles.

"What?" Andrew's voice sounds haunted, angry. "You didn't tell me!"

That's because she didn't expect this. She would need more words to explain, but his embrace has taken them all away.

"Okay. We're going to overdose," he says. "We need to get inside."

That would require letting him go. "You said you could hold me all day and night."

"I'm not going anywhere."

Yes, he is. But not yet, not without a kiss.

She pulls on his coat, pulls him to her, their chests bumping, trembling. His lids lower a fraction. She senses his willingness and pushes past her fear, moving slowly. Andrew closes his eyes, sighing as she grazes his mouth with her thumb, discovering the soft contours of him.

He likes this, she notes.

When her nose touches his, she is lost. Until tomorrow, she owns him. He may not love her, but he wants her.

Her lips brush against his, over and over, gliding against him, teasing him with her breath while his hands plunge into her hair.

A tiny noise curls from his throat.

"I've thought about you this way so many times," he says. "I wanted you to be my first kiss. I wanted to learn how to taste you."

"You still can," she murmurs against his mouth. "Let's take care of each other."

"Oh, Love."

"Ask me to kiss you."

"Kiss m—"

She seizes his lips before he can finish, parting them with her own, swallowing his gasp. Her arms scale his shoulders and encircle the back of his neck as their mouths slant over each other. His sweet tongue passes through her, catching her with eager, innocent flicks of honey and winter, driving her a little bit insane.

As their ice skates make gentle slicing sounds over the pond, the kiss restores her blood to its former glory. She attacks him with it, deepening the kiss. Its texture is new to her, the thick nook of air between their mouths different from the air around them.

Unleashing a gruff, needy sound that is distinctly mortal, Andrew slips his hands into her coat and grips the sides of her dress. His hands dip lower, sneaking beneath the hem and over the boy shorts she stole. He smiles against her lips when he discovers them, then drags his fingers under the fabric, cupping her bare backside, rubbing in small circles and drawing a mewl from her. She falls into his lips, thinking that maybe kisses have a bottom. Maybe she can find it, and if she does, that's where she will hide.

23

Love walks backward, drawing Andrew into the cottage by his collar. He's flushed and thoroughly kissed, and the sight fills her entire head. She sees nothing but him as she rids herself of her own coat, then yanks his off his shoulders. He tries to assist her, fumbling with the sleeves in a hurry, but ends up stuck with his arms behind his back. His cute smile tugs at her.

"Help me?" he asks.

She loves hearing this, the way he needs her for the simplest thing. She thinks of the couples she's matched, how often the boys would ask this of girls before making love. So often those boys seemed uncertain of where to aim themselves, needing the girls' hands to guide them through uncharted space.

Help me?

She wants Andrew to ask her this in a dozen ways before the night is over.

Love, I need you to help me.

I need you.

Help me.

She tosses his coat to the floor and rips open the front of his shirt.

He inhales. She blinks. They chuckle.

Should they talk each other through this? Does he take the

lead, or does she? He's the mortal, but she's the myth.

She finds her voice, and it feels right when she says, "Touch me like you said you would."

He maneuvers her against the nearest table—"Hold onto me"—sweeps her off her feet, and drops her onto the surface. He's dazzled, but his movements waver, checking with her before continuing.

When she nods, his irises darken to an unfamiliar shade. Grabbing the backs of her knees, he gives one eager tug, sliding her to the table's edge until her thighs flank his waist. The fruit bowl beside her rattles. Apples and persimmons tumble and roll across the ground.

"First, your mouth," he says, running his pinkie over her lips. "Then your shoulders." Dragging his hands down her neck, he removes the straps of her dress, mapping her skin. That same honeyed taste from their kiss on the pond flows freely through her mouth.

His touches are a downpour. From her shoulders, he moves on to the places he didn't have the chance to list that night when she first brought him here. He drags his fingers to the front and palms her breasts, her nipples surfacing beneath his thumbs. Next, her stomach, then the dip of her back, then her legs.

Then her ankles. The contact causes her to burst, turning those ankles into the universe.

"Then"—he kisses her lips—"your heart."

Yes. There's her heart. He found it for her.

They thread their fingers together and go still, feeling her pulse race, losing themselves in it, falling into it, and then doing the same with Andrew's heartbeat. They take their time, paying attention, relishing.

At last, she notices the blue tint of his nails. "You're cold."

"Not possible," he jokes.

If she can't be human, she wants to be irreplaceable, a girl that he can't find anywhere else. She pushes him away and hops off the table, straightening the hem of her dress. The action is intentionally girly and coy. It drives Andrew to close the distance once more, but she stops him.

"Wait," she says, taking his hand and leading him into the bathing chamber.

He lets her ease off his pants, watches as she undresses him, stares at her like she'll disappear. His abs form a beautiful grid of skin and muscle. She memorizes the curve of his backside, the scar across his leg, the V of his hips and the way they revolve because of his limp.

The question he asked her flits through Love's mind: *Who takes care of you?*

The tub fills on its own. His mouth parts in relief when he sinks into the water and rests his head against the rim. She offers him a wicked smirk through the curtain of steam, and his eyes follow her as she climbs into the bubbles, soaking her dress in the process.

"I can see through your dress," he flirts with a dopey grin.

"I can see more of you."

"C'mere."

She slips behind him, bending her limbs on either side of his body, making the water ripple. He relaxes against her, and she kisses the wet hair fanning around his right ear and cradles his torso. Together, they watch his fingers thaw.

Afterward, she grabs a pair of towels and lets him peel off her dress. They dry each other, their hands drifting, wandering. It isn't until he pulls on his boxers that she understands his train of thought. He believes they have time to take things slowly. He doesn't know it's their only night, and maybe there's a part of him that isn't quite *there* yet, isn't quite ready to fully trust this.

She wants to keep going, but she won't push it. She's selfish, but she's also in love.

The sun sets. They start a fire, eat apple slices, and climb into bed. She makes a comment about how bouncy a bed is with two people in it, and he challenges her, and they play-wrestle in the blankets, both fighting for dominance. It turns out he's also ticklish, and oh, boy, it's fun making him laugh so hard that he's gasping for breath, his body shuddering with joy.

Under the blanket, she crawls over to him, eager for his arms, and he opens them to her. Her head nestles into his chest. It's incredible that a pair of bodies can link together like this. His hands travel over skin and sinew, a whisper of a touch along her frame, which he calls a coastline. She rolls her eyes but imagines his words finding their way onto a page someday.

"Do you like being a goddess?" he asks.

No one has ever asked her that. Deities aren't trained to consider it because there's no alternative. She does like being a goddess and wielding a bow.

Or she used to like it, but she's not good at anything else. She tells him so.

Andrew taps her nose. "There's more to you. Matchmaking inflates your ego, but when you let your guard down, I hear it in your voice, I see it on your face, how much you want people to feel love and find it with others. You could do so many other things with that kind of passion."

Her question sounds small to her own ears. "You believe that?"

"Of course, I do. Don't doubt yourself, Love. You're clever and sensitive. You don't need magic or power to do good. That good is

211

already inside you, I know it is. Humor me: If you had to do anything else, what would it be?"

Coming from him, the praise fills her with pride. She snuggles deeper into his arms. Maybe she would bring people together in other ways, or help ease their suffering from heartbreak, or create a place where couples could go to celebrate what they have. Maybe.

Love regards the dome of stars beyond the roof. Assuming she could truly do anything else? "I would do it as a human. Whatever it is."

He follows her gaze. "Show me which star is yours."

The star that birthed her doesn't shine, but she knows where it is. Love points east to a gap between four freckles of light. "There," she says.

"I don't see it." When she points again, he says, "It's dark."

"It's stubborn."

Andrew winds his fingers into her hair and tucks her close. She sketches his watercolor bruise as they drift off to sleep. And this is what it's like to feel safe.

Yet in the middle of the night, Love wakes up. She doesn't need as much rest as he does, so she listens to his even breaths, feels him rise and fall beneath her cheek. He's peaceful, while she's restless. She wiggles to the other end of the bed, coaching herself to be nice instead of naughty. Huffing, she twists away and beats her head against her pillow.

Quietly, tentatively, she turns back around and scoots closer to him. In her mind, it takes years to reach his body, days for her hands to inch down the blanket, hours for her hands to make contact with his abdomen.

The embers from the fire skip into the air. She drags her fingers across his muscles.

Then waits.

Keeps going.

Andrew sweats while dreaming, dots of moisture rising from the hollow between his collarbones. She traces the circumference of his belly button. It's adorable.

Her index finger moves along the elastic band of his boxers. Every blood vessel races to the center of her body as she tosses possibilities around in her head like marbles.

And then Andrew's waist rises off the mattress, giving her permission.

She pauses, sheepish, before tugging the boxers down his legs, kissing his bad knee on the way. When she hovers above him, his eyes scan her in the dark, awed and expectant.

She stares at him questioningly: *May I have you?*

He nods and arches his body, offering himself. "Do whatever you want to me."

Now she knows what it's like to shiver.

Her pajamas land on the floor. Andrew barely has time to admire her nakedness before she climbs on top of him, her thighs split and splayed across his lap, and she bends forward, taking his mouth and tongue with hers. It's a hectic, reckless, precious kiss.

He lets her explore him, from lips to neck, shoulders to stomach, arms and hipbones, and down, down, *down*. She likes the way he bucks against her, the desperate little sounds he makes, telling her what to do and for how long. He squirms, but she pins his wrists to the bed.

Just wait. Just feel. Just be patient.

She is careful not to bite.

With a groan, he grabs her and rolls her over, dropping between her thighs. He jerks his head to knock the bangs out of his face. "Can you get—I mean, I'm not prepared."

"You don't have to be," she assures him, explaining that deities can't conceive.

"Everything that's happening right now matters to me," he says. "I want you to like it."

"I want that for you as well."

"And, um . . ."

"I've never done this," they both remind each other.

Then afterward, as his mouth pants against hers, they have.

After shyness, and eagerness, and their bodies strained and seeking, and his mouth tasting her breasts, and her fingernails digging into his skin, and his hardness, and her wetness, and him asking her to *help*, and a teasing start that causes her to writhe and him to curse, and a thrust of his hips, and her insides clenching him to the brim, and sudden pain, and a pause, and their mouths brushing, and his thumb trailing beneath the sheets to find her in the darkness, and him pressing down on the spot where her nerve-endings spark, and her saying *yes*, and his gentle movement within her, and a clumsy rhythm that builds into steadiness, and a sharp ache, and his back hunching, and her knees rising, and her begging for him to *please*, and him begging her for *more*, and a chorus of stunned moans that get louder, and their bodies locking together.

After all that, they have done *this*.

24

And they do *this* again. As the sun rises, she makes love with a mortal boy, tangling herself up with him, their limbs raging. She worries that being with a goddess will be too much for Andrew. At one point, she feels his heartbeat sprinting, pumping against hers. She's about to suggest they slow down, but then he grins and, to use one of his favorite words, tries this sweet *fucking* thing with his hip, and she gets dizzy.

They discover the meaning of *deeper*, the significance of *faster*. Her back arches and she conquers the world as Andrew releases a strangled cry.

After, he lies on top of Love, still inside her. She winds her fingers through the damp hair at the base of his neck. Wrapped around his body, she suspects that she'd been wrong about her immortal affect on him—until he whispers into her neck, "Holy shhhhit."

"I know," she agrees.

Their pants turn into chuckles. They share an exhausted, breathy kiss and then press their palms together, the way they did at the bridge. This time, their skin makes contact.

Too soon, Andrew eases out of her. Instantly, she misses the fullness, the closeness of him.

Flopping onto his stomach, he rereads their special note.

She clambers onto his back, her body flush against his, resting her chin on his shoulder as he traces the tear seams. If they stare at it long enough, the note might fade and reveal a scandalous message beneath, words they can see only at the right hour, in the right light. The note will predict their future, including things like flowers and ticket stubs, backpacks and locker combinations, the smell of soap in his hair, him reading aloud to her, her hogging the blanket, fights about nothing, wet kisses about everything.

"Wanna see what I can do?" he asks.

"Yes," she answers.

Love wants to see it all.

Not just that. She wants his voice on the phone, with a mouth full of food, in the middle of laughing, caught up in a sigh, on the verge of weeping, raw from shouting, annoyed with her, moaning for her. She wants a life with him.

He folds the note into a paper bird, then dabs Love's nose with the beak. That's what he can do. She wants to give the bird a name, but she can't think of the right one.

Perfection has so many flaws. The Fates haven't learned that, but she has. An hour like this is much better with Andrew's chapped lips and Love's matted hair, the note she almost destroyed and this invisible home that doesn't truly exist.

25

"I'm the one you're supposed to match next, aren't I?" Andrew asks.

The blanket is a tent over their heads, illuminated by the orange light of the fire. Love jerks back, too startled to work up a good innocent act. She watches his profile glowering up at the sheet.

He says, "I can't believe it took me this damn long to figure it out. The day I got into that fight with Griffin over her, you asked me if I liked Holly. Then you had that god, Anger, shoot Griffin to calm him down. Then you turned up at Holly's party and watched us. She's the one you're matching me with, isn't she?"

Love's shock wears off. She waits until he faces her, then she nods.

He scrubs his face with his palm. "You weren't going to tell me."

"I had no choice. I was protecting you."

"Jesus, you need to quit doing that."

"Andrew, please—"

"If you promise that every minute we've spent together wasn't fake, and that you weren't playing me, getting me to trust you just so you could deceive me, and that last night wasn't some cheap immortal farewell fun to you, I'll believe it. But I need the truth."

She fights to keep her voice steady. "That's not how it was. You made pretending impossible. I didn't expect you to matter to me."

"There has to be a way out of this."

"There isn't."

"In stories, there's a catch. We could do research. We could go through the Fates' history and hunt for loopholes. Don't they have records? What have you tried? What are you not telling me? Don't give me that hopeless face, Love. I'm not going to bend over. I didn't think you would."

"But I would. I'd do anything for you," she says simply.

"Then don't do this," he begs. "I don't want Holly."

You will.

"You think she's pretty."

"Every guy in town thinks she's pretty. So what? Sure, if there was no one else, I'd be interested in Holly. Is that what you want to hear? Yes, I'm into her. I'm not going to lie about that. But I'm more into you. And even if that weren't true, I wouldn't want anything to happen like this."

"You bonded at her party. She read your notes about me." Love knows her jealousy is irrational and moot. She needed for Holly and Andrew to form an attachment. "The way you looked at each other—you smiled at her. You held her hand."

"She was in tears," he argues. "She's nice to me. I felt bad for her, we were both pissed at people we care about, and yeah, our feelings reached critical mass."

"And you kissed her."

"And I had sex with you! And I'm still here. It's obvious who I want."

You want me because I'm a goddess. You're enchanted.

"You'll be happy. I'll make sure of it," Love insists.

Andrew rolls over, facing away from her. "I'll make sure you're wrong."

They fall silent, listening for sounds that don't come.

⌒

Andrew has ditched his classes, having reasoned that it's only a half-day, but he has to work at noontime. He's takes care packing the winter posy into his bag.

Love walks him out of the forest, past the playground where she saved him from Griffin. The wind is building, picking up speed as a prelude to the impending blizzard she predicted yesterday. Her quiver is shockingly heavy on her shoulder, forcing her to hunch forward. Aches reveal bones and joints she didn't know she had, and the air is making her skin feel strange, uncomfortable, trembly. She sinks further into her coat. So this is what it's like to wither.

"Are you sure you're all right?" Andrew asks.

No. I'm dying. For a few more minutes.

It's the tenth day. The Court is expecting a bull's-eye.

"I'm tired. You wore me out," she pretends to flirt.

He doesn't smile. "Let me carry your stuff."

"It's fine."

With an indignant huff, he grabs her weapons and stumbles, unprepared for the weight. Adjusting himself, he fixes his gaze on their boots pushing through the snow. "Why did you bring your bow?"

Time to lie again. "I have another couple to take care of."

His feet stutter to a halt, then he keeps going, his limp rigid and clunkier than usual. Considering what she admitted this morning, and his personality in general, it's a miracle he accepts her answer without suspicion.

He trusts me.

Yet as they walk through Ever, he keeps a tight grip on her hand as if he knows. He *knows* this is the end for them. He knows from the maddened way their bodies moved last night.

From across the street, they stare at the bookshop, at the town ripe with the scent of chimney smoke. Lights glows from inside houses and businesses. A truck loaded with firewood rattles by.

This world. His world.

His wish to be loved for real, for who he is, crushes Love. More than anything, she wants to give him a choice about his fate, but there is none.

"What'll happen if you don't match me?" Andrew asks.

"You'll die," she says.

His face knots with confusion. "I meant, to you. What will happen to you?"

This boy is impossible. He's been told his life is at stake, yet he's not thinking of himself. She knows nothing of love. She has thrown away all she's learned and replaced it with him.

"You said immortals can be wounded. Can they kill each other, too?" he prompts.

"It won't be so bad."

He grabs her face. "But they'll hurt you."

"Something like that," she mumbles, telling him how she's the first of her kind, too valuable to execute, but not too valuable to torture. "I'll be punished. I'm not certain how. The Fate Court is creative," she answers. "I cannot refuse this order."

"Why? Why is it important?"

Andrew's willful expression leaves little to the imagination. He won't give up without a fight, much less walk away, which is what she needs him to do. Damn him.

She breaks down and wades through the story, omitting her time limit and Wonder's claim about how deities become mortals. What good would it do? He cares for Love, but not to that degree. He couldn't possibly after knowing what she is, after all that she's done. She would never deserve Andrew or be suitable for the likes of him.

He blanches to discover that he's responsible for the lives of an entire domain of gods and goddesses—and the fact that she can't carry her own weapon—merely because he has the gift-curse of pure selflessness.

Her selfless boy who gave up a year's worth of lunches to a poor girl named Iris and took the blame for a fight with Griffin. Her Andrew, who offered his only coat to a deity who didn't need it, who tried to frighten him. Her boy, who let his father rage and use him as an emotional dartboard so the man could expel his grief. Her love, who feels guilty that he didn't accompany his mother to the grave so she wouldn't be there alone.

Her Andrew, who worries more about Love's fate than his own.

Selflessness. She feels the meaning of it. It's a wholly giving feeling. It's love.

Selflessness, which destroys her people's selfishness. What the Fates do isn't evil, but it isn't noble, either. Humans are sacred to them only as inferiors, as people to govern instead of serve.

Nevertheless, her kind doesn't deserve to die for it. Andrew knows it.

He bows over, bracing his hands on his thighs, sucking loud gusts of air through his nose. She would give him the choice if she could, her own fate be damned.

Holly's a good girl and will make him smile. That gives Love comfort.

When this is over, she will find a new way to matchmake people. A fair way, if possible. She will relearn her power, do things differently. Maybe the Fates can learn with her. Somehow, she will discover a balance with mortals.

Love's hands tremble for Andrew. She longs to soothe him with her touch, but she's afraid of doing it wrong. The most she dares is tucking a lock of hair behind his ear. It seems to work.

Straightening, he squeezes his eyes shut and then opens them. "Okay," he whispers. "When will it happen?"

This she can lie about as well. "Not for a while."

His head lists to the side. "You're about to tell me not to come back. That I can't see you anymore."

"Andrew—"

"If I'm right, I don't want to hear it. Please, just . . . Don't say it."

"May I say something else?"

"Yeah. Lots of something else."

"Be a tad greedy sometimes. It's good for the complexion," she chokes out.

"You're good for my complexion," he jokes back before his face crumbles, and he yanks her into a hug. Tears sneak out, but she sucks them up, worried that if she lets them escape, they will turn her into water. She'll freeze like snow, melt, and disappear.

They share a tender kiss until she breaks away. *Don't go, don't go, don't go, don't go, don't go, don't go.*

"Go," she says.

He shakes his head in defiance and kisses her once more. Then he turns away, not looking back, his limp creating that signature trail through the snow, promising her that she'll always know how to find him.

That's when Love cries. She covers her face, allows herself a minute of it, then wipes at her cheeks. She waits like a hunter as snow begins to fall. On time, Holly drives down the main road and parks in front of the bookstore.

Snowfall, Love thinks sarcastically. *How romantic.*

In the glass cottage, Andrew had dozed off before getting ready for work, and Love took the opportunity to pluck the flip phone from his backpack. After scrambling to figure out how to work the stupid thing, she located Holly's number—as Love hoped, they must have swapped numbers at school, or maybe at the party—and sent her a text. Pretending to be Andrew, she typed a request to meet at the bookstore after school, saying that he and Holly needed to talk.

The girl slides out of the car, biting her nails. Love senses the girl's torn emotions, fear clashing with guilt and uncertainty. Also, affection.

She loves Griffin. She likes Andrew.

Following Holly inside the store but keeping a distance, Love feels better. The air's indoor texture counteracts what she felt on her skin in the woods, calming it somehow. How odd.

She moves deftly, peeking around the corner to find Miss Georgie recommending a book to a customer—a young man, college-age, in a beanie hat and mittens.

Andrew's at the register when Holly approaches. Surprise and embarrassment crisscross his face. They babble over each other awkwardly, tripping on their words.

Just then, his stepfather barges into the shop, striding past Love. He takes one look at Andrew and sags with relief. The man's face isn't as leathery anymore, and he's more perplexed than irate as he butts into the lovers' conversation.

Love strains to listen. It's difficult over the music, the customer, the whoosh in her ears.

" . . . been worried about you," the stepfather exhales.

" . . . call next time."

" . . . gotta get to work."

From the looks of it, Andrew has a hard time accepting the man's affection. He pats Andrew's back, which makes Andrew stiffen. Through the window, he watches as his stepfather drives off to the auto shop.

Holly waits to finish their discussion. It's a clear shot.

Love swipes the right kind of arrow from her pack. The iron is dense and heavy, dragging her arm down twice before she nocks it to her bow and draws, her breathing uneven. She steps into the open doorway. No one can see her except for the person that matters most, the boy who will forget she exists, who's about to fall in love.

It will happen quickly. He won't know any different.

Miss Georgie plays detective over the rim of a book. Outwardly, it appears that Andrew has made his choice and that "Lily" the specter is gone. It's going to be true. Holly will be the bright spot in his day, will get to know Miss Georgie when Holly meets Andrew here at the end of his shifts. Later, Miss Georgie may dare to ask about Lily, and Andrew will say, "Who?"

Love fails to muzzle her sob, the noise sweeping through the bookshop. Andrew's shoulder blades tense. The instant he pivots and his eyes lock onto hers, there's a charged moment of confusion, then terror. Then betrayal. She never said it would be today.

She looses the arrow. It tears across the shop. It disappears into his chest, the impact ramming him into the counter.

The customer and Miss Georgie flank Andrew, asking if he's okay. To them, it looks like his bad leg has given out. Meanwhile,

Holly grips his arm. Love aims and fires again, and the girl careens into a shelf. The place quakes as the snowfall outside whips into a blizzard.

Andrew and Holly stumble to their feet, and glance at each other, and don't look away.

That's all Love can bear. She flees, barreling through the door, causing it to slam open and shut. She sprints across the street, obstinate tears stinging her eyes and forming icicles on her lashes. The blizzard is a thick curtain. She can barely see. Her arrows have morphed into iron monsters clanking against her frame, and gravity fights to pull her down.

Through the forest, she propels herself past one landmark at a time. *That tree. Now the trail up ahead. Now a little farther to that bend. A little farther.*

The gale whisks pinecones and branches off the ground. Her boots sink into the white landscape. That discomforting outdoor sensation returns to attack her. The closer she gets to the glass cottage, the harsher it becomes, stinging her skin and making her teeth clatter. She feels the bizarre need to pull her coat closed to block out the storm.

She glances down and gasps. Her fingers are shaking. The nails have turned blue.

What is happening to me?

She shot her targets. She should be healing!

An evil wall of wind shoves her sideways. She stumbles to the ground, her weapons scattering. Blindly reaching out for them, she grabs hold of a slim, pointed object that bites her, and the pang intensifies because the snow is wet and something else. A sharpness rips into her blue-nailed hand. A thin line of blood carves through her palm.

Then she sees it. One of her arrows lies on the ground. She

reaches out and places her shaky fingers on the stem, touching it to confirm what she already suspects: It's an arrow that invokes love.

And the tip is red from where it sliced her.

Love screams.

26

Defenseless. Terrified.

Deities bleed. That's not what she fears.

She scrambles backwards, trying to escape her wound, gaping at her bloody hand while snow pelts her face. Being cut with this type of arrow, and being matchless, is a plague. She's about to go mad with unrequited love. It must be happening now because she's wheezing, crawling across the woods in her haste. The snow hurts.

The blue nails. The little bumps in her skin. These are human responses to temperature. She's cold!

Her mouth opens, but she can't make another sound. This time, someone else screams. It's a voice she loves, howling through the trees, roaring her name. It gets louder, wrestling its way through the storm. Not only is she on the verge of losing her mind and turning into a mutant, but Andrew's looking for her, even though he's supposed to be making goo-goo eyes at his intended. Why can't he be predictable?

Love retreats as far as she can from the voice. He can't catch her, can't see her like this. She attempts to climb a tree, but her arms wobble, and when she loses her grip, her knees grate against the bark. Torn skin. Beads of blood. Rawness.

Now she knows what pain feels like.

The cold bares its teeth and lashes out at her. She tucks herself behind the tree and presses a fist to her mouth because she's frozen, everywhere is frozen. How do mortals endure this?

"Love!"

Andrew shouldn't be out here. The storm will bury him.

"Love!"

Why, why, why? He knows she can take care of herself.

Then again, he should be love struck. His memory of her should be gone.

"Love . . ." Her name thins and gets swallowed by the landscape. He could be hurt. If she doesn't help him, he'll freeze to death. He's an idiot!

She shuts her eyes and pictures a place where the dizzying sun beats down on them, where they're nothing more than kids in a safe place, confessing to each other what scares them. Then she moves, scurrying on all fours, searching, shivering.

Finding. Andrew's body, slumped unconscious in the snow, materializes through the curtains of white. His face has lost all trace of color. Of life.

"No!" she yells, shaking him and smearing her blood on his clothes. "Andrew, no!"

Feeble mortal breaths. No response. She is going insane, and she's filthy and bleeding, and she wants to bury her face in the crook of his neck and stay there, waiting for the answering touch that won't come.

She grunts, straining to loop his arm over her shoulder and carry him. His form is an anchor tugging her down each time, and there's cold, and her wound, and madness looming.

They collapse. Dazed, crazed, her head lolls onto his chest in surrender. The snow is beginning to feel good, blunting her of sensation, alleviating the gash in her hand. The trees spin, the branches multiply. The world is so white. Her dress is so white. Andrew's face is so white. There's blue in the distance, but not a blue shape or object, not even a blue mist. Just the shade itself. She sees the sun, too. She's missed them both, but now they're here with her. If she can reach them, she'll be fine. Maybe she can drag Andrew to the sun, and then they can go to sleep.

Movement in the distance. A filmy silhouette approaches, kneels, and sharpens into focus.

Love raises her head. It can't be. The very comfortable snow is pushing her to the brink, making her see things. That's it, because Anger wouldn't dare be here right now.

Anger is afraid of snowstorms.

The god cocks his head at her, despair cutting into his face, his ear stud twinkling. He thrusts out the words with a great, big shudder. "Don't hate me for this."

Hate him for what? He's here now. He will haul Andrew and her to safety, and Andrew will live, and everyone will live, because she's completed her task.

Anger tilts his gaze toward the sky. Above, a dot of light pokes through the storm. A star. The sight leaches the exhaustion from her, sucks her out of her drugged state. He's sent a message. To whom?

To them. Five figures who march forward in unison.

Love has always viewed them as marble statues come to life. Their carved, polished features so prominent, two gods and three goddesses, once archers like her, now rulers. They renamed themselves after timeless things that escape her mind as she struggles to focus beyond their ancient eyes.

The Fate Court.

One dark goddess draped in a prism of gossamer, her gown whisking up around her ankles and off her shoulders, the material flapping like butterfly wings. Another goddess with purple hair like Sorrow and black slits for eyes. And another goddess of hypnotic, androgynous beauty, made of pale skin and swathed in white lace—frost itself.

A god with a hawkish nose and hair down to his waist, framed by two braids. And a cloaked god with slanted brows that trap him in an eternal frown.

These are the first faces she beheld from her crib. Growing up, she spent hours emulating their walk and the richness of their voices. They used to be her saviors.

Today, Love must be her own savior, for they are not here to humor her. They spread out and form a half-circle around her. In the midst of a tempest, their posture is flawless, enhanced by the flurries corkscrewing around them as though obsessed with the Court's presence. What does it matter that the blizzard started before the deities arrived? They've sparked a craze in winter, and the snow is going berserk not knowing what to do with itself. It's relishing her kind and killing her Andrew.

Guh. That's untrue. Nature wouldn't react like that for anything but itself.

Her mind is embellishing. The Court's splendor makes that easy.

Ice. Spasms. Agony.

Love gathers Andrew against her chest in a feeble attempt to keep his body warm. Intuition prompts her to block him behind her hair while she turns to Anger, desperate and scared.

The archer gives her a terrible, mournful look. He rises and shuffles backward—back, back, back with her class. Envy, Sorrow, and Wonder. They're gathered behind the Fate Court, watching with slack jaws.

Why are they here? Love has done what she was supposed to.

She bundles her wounded hand into a fist to staunch the blood, mortified that they might see what she did to herself. "W-what d-do you want-t-t?"

In a synchronized move, the Court answers. They raise five bows nocked with arrows.

Archer arrows carry the magic of emotions. They don't kill.

But the Court's weapons do.

"Move away from the boy, Love," the god with slanted brows commands.

But why? This isn't fair. The danger is over.

Her gaze swings between the deities. It lands on Wonder, who's silent and locked in a stupor. The rest of their class stays quiet, too, instead of speaking up or doing something, anything to stop this.

The pinpricks of treachery assault Love's throat. They never claimed to be her friends, but they were raised together, and yes, she hoped Wonder would become a friend someday.

It's Love's fight, then, with her blue hands and sliced palm, with her clacking teeth and small frame racked with cold.

The god repeats in a silky, impatient tone, "Back away, Love. You've grown too ill to have an effect on the boy. Your arrows have failed. He's still a threat. We'll take over from here."

"No."

"Release him. Now!"

Swallow. Tremble. Defy.

"F-f-fuck y-you," she seethes.

Five pairs of eyes spark with disappointment. It's as though she has betrayed them.

"Anger," the god barks, his cloak slapping the air. "Seize her."

Anger hesitates. "Perhaps we should wait and see—"

"Restrain your peer, archer! Protect her!"

Love growls as her classmate dithers, then advances on her. She flings herself across the snow and snatches her arrow with her good hand, her fingers gripping the stem. Lurching to her feet, she barrels into Anger and desperately, haphazardly swings the tip at the god's face. He knocks it from her grasp with more force than he intended because he gives a shout of dismay when the blow sends her crumbling against Andrew. Her wrist beats a nasty rhythm against her skin and has her seeing spots. She cries out over his apologies.

"Love, I-I didn't mean—"

"Dammit, imp. Forget her wounds and grab her!"

It's been too long. It's too cold. Is Andrew's heart gone now? Is he gone?

A soft voice flutters to her ears. "Love ...?"

Andrew. Love looks down at his ashen face. She knows that face like she knows the stars. His eyes yield to her, weak but aware.

Then they widen at the sight of the deities and the five deadly arrows poised in his direction. Those eyes of his blaze, misinterpret, and conclude. She opens her mouth to assure him they won't fire, not with her in the way. They wouldn't dare. She won't let them.

But for once, Andrew is faster. With a groan, he surges to his knees, grasps her by the waist, and hauls her out of the way. Love tumbles into Anger's arms. She vaults forward, arms and legs flailing against the god's grip.

"Stop!" she bellows. Desperate, she burrows her teeth into Anger's hand, but he doesn't flinch.

No. He grunts. He staggers back under the jolt of Wonder's elbow ramming into the side of his head, the Court too focused on Andrew to notice.

Anger loses his grip on Love. She tumbles to the ground and lands on top of a bow—her bow.

"Draw!" the god shouts, and the Court pulls on their bowstrings.

"Love," Wonder says under her breath, kicking something across the ground.

It's another one of Love's arrows.

The next moments swirl into a dream, taking forever and an instant. Wonder catching Envy and Sorrow's eyes, issuing an unspoken plea. The pair swapping stunned, uncertain glances and then making a choice.

Sorrow's expression saying, *I will if you will.*

Envy shrugging. *Why not?*

From behind, the archers tip their bows at a steep angle, pointing at a massive tree looming over the Court, its thick branches netted so tightly together in different places that small mounds of snow have collected in the webs. Envy and Sorrow fire in rapid succession, their arrows hitting enough of the branches to make the tree quake. Small avalanches plummet onto four of the Court members.

The impact momentarily bewilders and distracts the rulers, except for the cloaked god with the slanted brows, who stands a few feet ahead of them. He ignores the commotion and hones in on Andrew.

It's Love's turn. She's frail and numb, and the iron is unwieldy, and the gales rage, clogging the air with white. But while she may have lost most of her strength, she hasn't lost her aim. Another kind of blizzard surges through her blood, pumping her with energy. Twirling the arrow between her fingers, she nocks it to the bow.

Andrew slips and slides on all fours. The god shoots.

Love releases.

Flight. Two arrows catapult in Andrew's direction and meet in an explosion of light. His body pivots, limbs flopping, and crashes into the snow where he goes still. The blast shoves Love backward.

The flare dulls, then vanishes to nothing.

Nothing.

27

Then her lids open. And it's something.

The blurred edges of her cottage take shape, the furniture and the crackling hearth. Beyond the glass walls, the sky's ripe moonlit glow indicates that it's evening. Her body feels funny, divided into sections instead of whole, parts of her strained by movement, other parts liquefied. Rolling onto her side makes her wince. Her feet are especially strange, as if there's no blood flowing there, forcing her to wiggle them—ah, much better.

Love wipes away the crust nestled at the corners of her eyes and rises on her elbows. She gapes at the bandage encircling her hand and wrist, distressed when she bends her knuckles and feels resistance.

A weight stirs beside her. It smells like mint.

"Andrew," she says, whirling around.

He's passed out on the bed, as naked as she is. His body is trembling, and sweat is beading from his neck, but he's breathing. She brushes the hair off his forehead, then yanks her fingers back with a gasp. His skin feels demanding, reminding her of a steaming cup of tea.

He should be with Holly. Or he should be dead.

Voices drift from outside. Love grabs a blanket and wraps it around herself, then rushes out of the cottage. She stops short, arrested by the biting presence of the cold. The blizzard is over, but a few feet from her door, a wall of snow—nearly two feet high—has invaded the forest.

It makes little impression on her guests. Standing beneath an umbrella of stars, the four archers round on her, weary and grumpy.

Except for Envy. "Hubba hubba," he says, admiring her bare limbs. "Look who's awake."

"What happened?" she asks. "Where's the Court?"

"Shh, my nymph. Pace yourself."

"You need more rest. You've been asleep for only eight hours." Wonder, who almost let Andrew die, who waited until the last second to help, has the decency to drop her gaze from Love. "How do you feel?"

Love glowers. "How do I feel? How dare you! I did my job and—"

Sorrow scoffs. "Keep telling yourself that."

"Listen before you judge," Anger cautions Love, leaning against the cottage wall and drumming his fingers on his hip.

She's going to combust. "Don't tell me what to do!"

"Please, let me explain," Wonder's plaintive voice reaches out to Love. "When Anger sent the message to everyone that your arrows didn't work on the lovers—"

Didn't work on them?

"—the Court practically raised the sky. It was a frenzy. They believed you were fading swifter than expected and had grown too weak for your weapon to have an effect. But I knew. I knew why the arrows didn't work. I just *knew* it. You've changed."

Love almost drops the blanket. It becomes clear. "Am I . . . ?"

Wonder forgets herself. She beams, clapping her hands together. "Your hearts have bonded. You're mortal. Your strength and speed and powers. All gone."

Immediately, Love knows when it happened. It was yesterday on the pond, when Andrew taught her to ice skate, and she was happy, happier than she'd ever been in her life, and they tipped their heads back to swallow snowflakes, and then their fingers brushed. She'd misunderstood that moment, assuming they were suddenly able to touch because she was weakening further. But no, it was because they'd fallen for each other.

And then they kissed. It was her first kiss with Andrew. Her first kiss ever, when her lips parted like a chasm and she felt a new kind of texture: pure, rousing warmth on her tongue. Warmth!

Her frailty this morning, when it was difficult to carry her iron arrows, wasn't because she was dying. It was because she'd become human—healed, but human.

Because someone loves her. Andrew loves her.

Love's eyes sting. She blinks down at herself, prepared to find a whole other person. She rubs her arms, wiggles her ears. She turns sideways to the glass wall and presses the pads of her fingertips into her cheeks, testing the consistency of her skin, searching for the real Love somewhere in the alternate reality of her muted reflection. Lastly, she studies her bandage with fascination.

Wonder recaps, "Sorrow stitched you up."

"Don't look so surprised," Sorrow chides Love. "I've been around plenty of black and blue humans to know my way around *this*." She removes the needle that she always wears pinned to her collar and holds it up. "Never fear. The flames sterilized it—I think."

Love strives to put her thoughts in order. Words that Anger's Guide once spoke return to her.

Your weapon is a part of you. Your power, your breath. As you have magic, it has magic.

If Love no longer has magic, neither do her weapons. When she became mortal, her arrows lost their matchmaking power. Now that she thinks on it, she never actually saw the lights flash in Andrew and Holly, which is what normally happens when her arrows make contact.

However, since the arrows were never created with the intent to kill, weren't forged to draw blood when fired from her bow, they remained benevolent at their physical core, sparing Andrew and Holly from death when Love shot them. Indeed, the arrows' speed knocked Andrew and Holly off balance, but the impacts weren't deadly.

Of course, without a bow, arrows can inflict small wounds on their own. Also not life-threatening, but that explains the cut on Love's hand, minus the magic it should have had.

"I didn't realize," she says. "I was in the bookshop when I loosed the arrow. Andrew's stepfather, Holly—they didn't see me. I was invisible."

Sorrow groans. "You're welcome for the stitches, by the way."

"Actually, they could see you, bow and all," Wonder amends. "It's likely they weren't paying attention. Most mortals don't look closely at the world around them. They see what they expect to see."

Everything did happen fast. Love released her arrow and ran. Only Andrew saw her. Miss Georgie might have caught sight of Love if the woman hadn't been preoccupied.

Envy swaggers over to a hedge of snow and signs his name into the white while saying, "Apologies for the scare with your boy. The Fate Court thought he was still toxic to us. They had to take action."

"I-I couldn't let them know I poked around in the Archives, found the scroll, and encouraged you. I didn't know how they would react," Wonder confesses. "I'd hoped you would realize what was happening and say so. I hoped the Court wouldn't shoot, not with you blocking the boy. I wanted to help you, but I was paralyzed. I didn't expect things to turn out as they did. I couldn't move until the last moment. I made a blunder of it."

Love's resentment ebbs. She can't blame Wonder for fearing more torture. Besides, Wonder did help in the end, as did Envy and Sorrow.

Wonder explains that she rushed to tell Envy and Sorrow about the scroll before their appearance in the storm. The archers knew Love might be human, and Andrew might be harmless, so when Wonder wordlessly begged them to stop the Court, they caused those little avalanches with their arrows. Their rulers were too sidetracked with Andrew to register the bits of defiance occurring around them.

Anger was out of the loop. Wonder hadn't had the chance to inform him, like she had with Envy and Sorrow, because he'd already been in the woods, because he'd been monitoring Love as usual.

"I revealed everything to him minutes ago," Wonder says.

"Once the Court left," Anger finishes, then addresses Wonder with sarcasm. "Thank you for cuffing me in the head, by the way."

"You're welcome," she beams.

It should hurt that the Court isn't here to say good-bye to Love. It does and it doesn't. The recollection of them shooting Andrew churns her stomach, mistake or no mistake. Perhaps they guessed that she'd rather not see them, or they've tossed her from their minds, deeming her unworthy for wanting a human over them.

According to the archers, her arrows lost their powers, but they could still fly. Her aim had intercepted their ruler's death shot, whacking the god's arrow off course a hair's width from Andrew's chest. The collision and the explosion of light—which had come from the god's arrow, not hers—thrust everyone to the ground, knocking Love unconscious.

Once the deities regained their senses, Wonder pointed out the gash on Love's hand, and the bloody arrow, to the Court. The rulers were able to discern what type of arrow it was and balked, because the cut should have driven Love mad.

Feigning ignorance, Wonder encouraged them to consider all they knew from the Archives, asking if there were any means by which Love's weapon could lose its power like that. The rulers speculated and appealed to the stars, who responded to the call and affirmed Love's mortality.

Wonder hangs her head. "They think you discovered the scroll on your own."

Love smirks. Let them believe it. Let the archers safeguard the truth, lift it from Wonder's shoulders, and splatter it across Love's legacy. It's not farfetched in light of her mischievous ways and fetish for mortal affection.

"The elite class of the Peaks no longer. That's us now," Envy says with dash of petulance. "Once a valuable constellation of archers, now we're no better than a bunch of black holes."

A tendril of worry, and indignation, creeps into Love's voice. "Elaborate, please."

Sorrow clutches her chest and does a remarkable impersonation of Joy gossiping. "Haven't you heard?"

What Love hasn't heard is that everyone in the Peaks knows what happened. Amidst the uproar about the scroll, that an unsung mortal nearly vanquished them, and that Love prevented it—though not in the way they would have predicted—her people's beliefs remain unchanged: To feel love isn't in their nature. They consider Love the obvious exception—and a deserter. She wooed a mortal and abandoned her people for a lowly existence. That's why the Court isn't here, as she'd suspected.

Their class has become the laughingstock of the Peaks. The Guides are shamed. Envy and Sorrow are publicly pitied for being saddled with degenerate peers. Wonder's own past with a human has been resurrected. And their class has been reduced by not one, but two.

Anger has been banished from the Peaks.

"What?" Love hisses, her head whipping toward the god.

Anger looks like her distress offends him. "I hit a nerve, so to speak." He cracks a rare but droll grin that further startles her. "Turns out, I'm not rebel material."

He confessed to the Court that he hadn't reported everything he saw while monitoring Love for them. He'd taken matters into his own hands and withheld news of her budding attachment to Andrew, suspecting the Court might venture here to see it for themselves, discover her playing with fire and delaying the match.

Shielding Love has cost Anger. He will be living in solitude, wandering the human realm without purpose, neither of that world, nor of the Peaks.

Love fights to keep her knees from buckling. None of them deserve this.

"It's my fault," she says to the ground, unable to meet their gazes.

"You *are* human, already getting cottony on us," Envy drawls, that pompous grin of his restored. "There's no need to worry, nymph. However blemished you've made us look, we archers have plenty of time to get over it."

"Well, it was my pleasure," Wonder announces, folding her scarred hands in front of her. "But I will come back to haunt you if you let my efforts, and Anger's, go to waste."

Love promises she won't, then peeks at the god. "Where will you go?"

Anger bugs her with a patronizing sneer. "I'll live. Longer than you."

Loves stares at him. If the Court hadn't ordered him to report Love's progress with Andrew in the first place, Anger might not have been there to summon the rulers, and they wouldn't have tried to shoot Andrew.

But if Anger hadn't been there, she and Andrew would have died in the storm.

Wonder loses a trace of her luster as she reminds Love of something they discussed early on, back at Love's tree. "Your memories will fade over time. You can see and touch us now only because you were once a goddess, and you still have your memories of that life. You're still connected to us in that way, for a little while yet. Once you lose those memories and forget we exist, everything will change. It's the final stage."

What's left of Love's confidence melts into a puddle at her feet. She will forget her past.

Her home in the Peaks. Lush cliffs and caves, purple flowers and silver light.

Her Guides, who were proud of her, who inspired her, who made her feel like she belonged when her peers didn't.

The Fate Court, whom she admired for two centuries, and still does in her own way.

Her bow skills will wane along with her memory. She will forget matchmaking and all she learned in exchange for this realm, with its hospitals and accidents, earaches, food poisoning, body hair, and the annual bone-chilling arrival of winter. Unpredictable daily life. Countless pairs of mortal eyes fixed on her.

Love is petrified. Yet it cannot be close to what Anger must feel, losing everything, everyone, all because of her. She will miss the chance to beg the Court on his behalf. She will forget that she caused this. She will forget him. And Envy, and Sorrow, and Wonder.

She doesn't deserve to forget the bad. Nor does she deserve to remember the good.

"Your love ties you to each other, so Andrew's memory will fade as well," Wonder says. "The otherworldly parts of your time together will vanish, but you'll remember the friendship and love, and the Fates will live on."

They'll keep ruling over mortal hearts. She won't get the opportunity to fix that, either, to argue for a change. That isn't her destiny.

She wants to be with Andrew. For him, she would have willingly sacrificed her immortality anyway, her memories. Nevertheless, she would have liked to be granted the choice, to have made that decision for herself.

Now she understands what it's like to have that taken from her.

Fate versus free will. There should be a balance.

The Fates may alter their views one day. To that end, she needs to do what little she can before her past becomes a blank slate. She reminds herself that even one small act, one small word, can evolve into something greater, with hope and the help of others.

She looks to Wonder. "What we talked about that night

in front of Andrew's window. About us doing the right thing. Remember it. We need to relearn what fate really is, what free-will is, what's in a mortal's heart, what's in a deity's heart." She peers at the ground in realization. "We need to find a deeper bond with each other, in the Peaks. We need to stop turning up our chins when we feel like crying, calling affection undignified, denying our fears and flaws. Perhaps we need to deal more with ourselves, less with humans."

There's an awkward silence. Love lifts her gaze to archers, who are all watching her. She spoke as though she's still part of the *we*. They don't acknowledge what she said. They don't dispute it, either.

Wonder smiles. "I will remember, you may count on it. I'm an Archive diva."

"They'll have a hell of time replacing you," Envy says to Love, his wit resurfacing. "I will, too. I had plans for us, if you know what I mean." He nudges his chin toward the cottage. "Hope you're not attached. The cottage is going to disappear once you and Andrew leave it together, which could be a while with the snow piled like this. We doubt the rest of your little town is faring any better, so if there's no search party looking for Andrew soon, rest assured it's because they're either trapped indoors, or they can't make it through the forest, or both. We'd love to use our mighty muscles and plow the area for you lovers, but you know how it is. We've overstepped our boundaries once today."

Understood. Disrupting nature is forbidden. Aside from the stars, nature allies with no one, and the archers have already manipulated it by shooting the trees and propelling that heap of snow onto the Court's heads. Her peers aren't about to test their limits twice. Who knows how nature would retaliate. Best to quit while they're ahead.

The elevation is low, the snow is powdery rather than hard and wet, and the cottage is set in an open part of the forest. The snow will melt in two days, if the sun decides to shine.

"In what condition you both leave the cottage is another story," Sorrow says. "You got lucky in the storm, but the boy has a fever. Little things like stitches, we can do. Illness is out of our hands."

Love thinks of the way Andrew's skin felt when she woke up. Fear hatches in her chest. Humans are sacred, but sickness is a destiny the Fates do not control, won't dare try to interfere with.

Wonder pats Love's cheeks. "I wish we could do more."

They can cross long distances directly, but not short ones, like to Ever's hospital. It doesn't matter, though. Popping up at a faraway hospital is impossible as well, for the archers can't ferry Love or Andrew with them. Such ability to travel is an individual gift.

"Um . . . ," Love clears her throat. "Thank you for two hundred years. And for helping me."

Envy blows Love a kiss. She humors him and catches it.

After he's gone, Sorrow shakes her head as though Love is the strangest person she's ever met. "Don't rip those stitches," she warns, then disappears.

Wonder steps closer to Love. "What a dazzling journey, to start over. Yours is a tale for a blank scroll. I'll volunteer to write it."

"Make me clever," Love requests.

Wonder tucks her chin into her shoulder, a saucy gesture for her. "That and more. You stood up to the Fate Court for a mortal. Our people can deny it all they want, that they're incapable of love, that you were an exception, but your story has struck them, and it won't be forgotten."

"You have beautiful hands."

"Liar." She glances between Love and Anger, and whispers, "Be gentle." With that, she dissolves, her hands the last to vanish.

A thick coat of silence envelops the woods. Anger studies the frosted pond, a smooth silver coin reflecting the moon and stars. "I saw you kiss him out there."

Not what she expected. Not by a longbow.

Love was expecting a ruthless comment or snide exit speech. Instead, the words *saw* and *kiss* leap out at her.

He gestures to the pond. "The goddess of love feeling a mortal's touch before my very eyes. Your powers were slipping, and you didn't care. Reckless little thing, you are."

Her next question shocks them both. "Did you watch us make love?"

It's rare to behold a stunned Anger. He covers it up with an insult. "No, thank Fates. That would have repulsed me. I came back the next day, hoping you'd gotten your taste for him out of your system and were ready to save the Peaks. Instead, I get here in time for your arrow to falter and whatnot."

"Why do you hate me?"

His head jerks toward her. "I don't. I don't hate you, but we're the same arrow. We're iron."

"Love and anger are not the same. I will not believe that."

"That's your choice."

"And it's your choice not to give me a real answer." She's not in the mood for riddles, but suddenly she's nervous. If he's being evasive, it means there's a stronger reason why he has scowled at her all their lives. And that reason has to do with the way his eyes shift to the cottage, where Andrew is, and then back to her.

"Forget it," she says.

Of course, once she says it, he chooses not to. "I don't hate you," he enunciates, yanking the words like roots from a hidden place inside him. "I've never *hated* you. Get it?"

The woods grow silent, creating a tension that's more intrusive than whenever Love and Anger bickered in the past. Her back sags against the cottage wall. "Oh. I ... I see."

"Like I said, love and anger are equal in many ways."

It's more than that. Deities aren't bred to be overwhelmed by the emotions they serve, however that's not the case with their class. She's witnessed Sorrow's depression. Anger has what humans call a short fuse. Envy is occasionally prone to spite. Wonder cares enough to find things out. And Love is Love.

Wonder revealed feeling something tantamount to love for that boy she tried to contact. Anger has just done the same. Perhaps Envy and Sorrow are capable of it as well. Perhaps it's the unique way of their class. They are the veins of love itself. The inclination to love may have been swimming inside them undiscovered this whole time, and perhaps someday the rest of the Fates will follow suit.

For the first time, Anger's gaze isn't hostile. "I watched you long before the Court asked me to keep track of this chaos with the boy. I watched you whenever I could, a glimpse here and there, abandoning my post too often, for over a century. You were so different from us. That could have gotten out of hand.

"I used that excuse, as the leader of our class, when I first went to the Court about your boy. Too bad they stopped believing my case after a healthy interrogation, and I admitted I wasn't reporting everything I saw between you and him. Something told me not to." He gazes at her. "You looked too damn happy to expose."

"Anger."

He chuckles quietly. "Don't say my name, please."

She bites her tongue.

"You're not a straight shot, so to speak. You don't make being a fellow deity easy. You frustrated me, but I adored you anyway."

There was the day Wonder was tortured and Love tried to help her. Anger visited afterward, when Love was confined in the dark. He reached out his hand, offered a loving touch. And she mocked him.

All these years, his incessant lectures about behaving herself were the product of concern, of what he kept secret in his heart. She must have driven him crazy.

"I think this belongs to you." Anger holds up the snowflake ornament she'd lost, scratched but intact. When the archers came to warn her, he paid attention to her tree, her surroundings, more than Love realized. He always has.

She doesn't know what possesses her when she moves forward. She pauses inches from him and frames his face with her free hand, tipping it down to hers. Maybe she owes it to him for the ornament, or for his own hand materializing under the door that day when the Court locked her up, or for the way he braved a snowstorm in order to watch over her.

Love belongs to Andrew. It's Andrew who needs her right now. But this is farewell. It's his banishment, and her fault, and his only moment, and the only comfort she can give. And perhaps …

It's a spark, a sliver of what he could have made her feel someday, what he could have meant to her, with time.

"May I?" she whispers.

His eyes fall closed. "Yes."

It's a mere brush of her mouth on his cheek, but it's no less urgent, no less profound. Anger exhales, his breath rushing, trembling against her skin. He leans into her kiss, his arms encircling her waist, holding her in that strong way she predicted he could. And she lets him. And, as she hears his relieved sigh, it makes all the difference.

She breaks away. "I won't forget you."

"I wish that were true," Anger murmurs, stroking her face, seeming to drink in the sight of her. "Again, I'll live. Make sure you do, too."

She will try.

28

Andrew mumbles incoherently throughout the night. He's no longer blue or stiff, no longer a part of the snow. He's the opposite, thawed and listless, but it isn't helping. He teeters on a dangerous precipice. Each cough tips him closer to the edge and terrorizes Love.

She has witnessed countless mortals fall ill, yet she's an unprepared amateur, reduced to wet cloths for his skin and unsuitable food. As long as this cottage exists, magic exists inside it. The water pitcher refills itself. The fruit bowl, and the plate of bread and cheese, replenish themselves, but she has no medicine, no ingredients for soup.

Ever, in walking distance, is barricaded by a wall of snow. His damn phone is in his backpack, and his backpack is at the bookstore.

Love doesn't know what a fever feels like, but she holds out her hands to the flames in the hearth, getting as near as possible until it hurts and she has to snatch her hands back. How to describe it? Like the air is screaming.

She rests her palm against his soaked forehead, the way she has seen humans do to sick relatives, and compares his skin to the fire. They're similar. That's not good.

She has no inkling how to do this, to be mortal. If there are hints hidden beyond this house, in the woods or at the bottom of the pond, she is not there to find them. Everything but her and Andrew—the furniture, the embers from the fire—is motionless, looking on and watching her toil being something she is not.

⌒

One moment, he sinks into the mattress with a noise of contentment. The next, he's shivering and gripping the sheets.

It's hard to get him to drink water. It dribbles down his chin. Burning up and delirious, he slaps her. Her tears leak into his mouth, and his lips part. The taste calms him. She watches the shadows move across his face and turn it into a sundial.

The hours drag their feet. Her thoughts send her into a tailspin.

Marshmallows. Flat tires. Notebooks. Pillows.

Wonder's hands. Sorrow's frown. Envy's purr. Anger's love.

Andrew things. His coat. His backpack jostling against his hip. The stepfather's leathery face. Books and Miss Georgie. Andrew's arm sweeping through Love. Griffin's fist connecting with Andrew's cheek. His knee against Holly's.

His dead mother. If Andrew lives, Love will tell him to stop feeling guilty about the woman's death. She will insist that his mother understands why he survived.

Written words and ice skates. If he lives, Love will spoil him, do things for him, shower him with friendship and kisses and tokens of affection. She will treat him the way he's treated her, even when she gave nothing in return, nothing but a small and silly bouquet of winter stems.

Question marks. Love will paint the town with them, just like the ones painted on his bedroom wall, if only he'll wake up.

She'll buy him bookmarks and engrave them with clever advice—oh, she'll need to find a job in order to buy anything. She will, if only he'll wake up. *Just wake up!*

⌒

The farthest she ventures is the porch, granting herself a moment between flame-to-skin checks. She cannot reconcile the differences between indoors and outdoors. Hot and cold. How quickly these senses shift from soothing to intolerable. Treacherous elements.

The coat helps, though it would have been a good idea to wear her pajamas underneath. Ugly bumps race along her arms. Her teeth make tedious, clapping music.

What else will she discover about her new self? Will he discover the *else* with her?

Love pleads to the stars, but they're quiet. They don't belong to her anymore.

She grabs a handful of snow and crushes it into a ball. She wishes she could throw it at Andrew's face and laugh, and let him chase her. She flings the snowball to the ground and watches it break into powder.

⌒

When he dies, she will hold him. She will weep until her throat is fire and her heart is ice, and she will shrivel up on the porch and stare blankly at the landscape. She won't move until Anger returns, fights with her, and convinces her to let Andrew go.

When the snow melts, she will allow the god to carry the boy back through the woods into town. Anger will lay the boy on the front stoop of his house, and that's where the stepfather will find him, and the man will fall to his knees and blame himself for not keeping a closer eye on his son.

That's the last time Love will ever see Andrew. Anger will drag her away, and she'll spend her days hunting for shelter, mourning and mortal. She will lose her memory of being a goddess, but she will remember Andrew.

One day, Love will dust herself off. She'll step into the bookstore, where Miss Georgie will be sitting, still expecting the kiddo to walk through the door. The woman will notice Love standing there, and the woman will say, "Can I help you, honey?"

Love will say, "I'm Lily."

And Miss Georgie will cry and give Love a job. And Love will live.

That's what will happen.

⌒

Now she knows what heartbreak feels like.

His fever gets worse. There's not much time left, but he's stuck with her, a girl from an otherworldly place, a sad someone with no clue how to save him. Or how to lose him.

Even if she were to brush her knuckles across his cheek, he would still be dying. She finally understands—a touch between them isn't enough to fix this.

He's fading because of her. And she will miss the chance to say she's sorry. Sorry for this end. Sorry for betraying him in the first place.

She will miss everything: the inquisitive slant of his head, his storyteller's voice, and the way his hand would reach for hers, the very stubbornness of it. She will miss those tireless questions skipping from his lips. Especially the question he asked back when he discovered what she was.

Who takes care of you?

Silly human. For a little while, *he* did. But he shouldn't have. Oh, he shouldn't have.

⁓

"I love you."
"Don't leave me."
"Not like this."
"Please."

29

Some trickster tugs on her hair. She whines, and that trickster moves on to other endeavors like pinching her waist, pawing at her chin. What forest creature dares to bother her while she's resting?

She'd been dreaming, leaping from tree to tree. She fell and broke her leg. It was fascinating. Love wants to return to the dream and see how her injury changes the way she walks.

Another paw, gentle but insistent. She lifts her hand, fingers curled, ready to swipe back, then registers a pair of lips tickling her collarbone. Tamed, she arches her back for more.

Consciousness returns. She wakes with a jolt.

Andrew lifts his head from her chest and musters a drugged, lopsided grin. He looks exhausted, but he's no longer burning up. The temperature of his skin feels like hers.

"Hey," he breathes.

"My hand hurts," she says out of nowhere, blinking back tears.

He nods, not registering what she said. That's fine. He's barely recovered, and she's nonsensical from weariness and mortality.

"You're here," she whispers.

"Where else would I go?" he asks.

Somewhere far from this place. To the unknown where he can't see her.

Love throws herself on top of him, plastering kisses all over his face. He tries to reciprocate, but he's sluggish, and she's zealous. She veers back—he's too fatigued for this. His eyes are foggy, but he's with her. He didn't fade. She covers her mouth because the wounded sounds she's making are embarrassing.

"Hey, hey, hey," he repeats, rubbing her arms. "Don't do that."

"Am I crushing you?" she cries.

"I don't really care."

"You need water." She wriggles off his body, hurries to grab the pitcher, refills his cup, and dumps the contents down his throat. He guzzles, too dehydrated to object, then passes the cup to her before collapsing again, the pillows jostling beneath him.

Love soothes her own parched tongue. Outside, ribbons of midday sunlight sneak through the woods, through the branches, stretching across the landscape. There are no signs that a search party came looking for Andrew after she fell asleep, meaning the archers were right: Either the townspeople are also snowed in, or the forest is too buried for them to make it through. In an open area, they could push through with a large, noisy vehicle, however the woods are too dense for that—not that humans would see the cottage anyway. Still, the snow is melting, and with any luck, it should be clear by tomorrow night.

Then they can leave. Then, as Envy said, the cottage will vanish as if it never existed.

Andrew drags his thumbs over her cheeks to wipe them dry and pulls her down to him, cradling her in his arms, his heartbeat thumping with life, his embrace solid and warm.

Warm feels marvelous. She lets it sail down her body as her limbs braid with his.

"I'm tired," Andrew mumbles.

"Me, too," she says, her lids drooping. "We're snowed in."

"How romantic."

"You're a buffoon."

The last thing she hears is his sleepy chuckle before she floats into darkness.

⌣

It's morning again when she stirs beside him, waking him with her movements. Together, they unfurl from their locked position, spreading themselves across the bed like petals flapping open. They roll onto their sides and gaze at each other, stuck between peace and uncertainty.

"I saw them," he murmurs, the glint in his voice leaving no doubt he means the Fate Court. "They were beautiful." He pinches the bridge of his nose, thinking back. "And they shot me. Those beautiful fuckers shot me."

"Only one of them. He missed." Love gives his shin a kick. "It will teach you not to be a hero."

"I could give two shits about being a hero. What I wanted was you alive."

"That's why I'm going to kiss you in the near future."

Andrew pulls the blanket over their heads. "Tell me."

"You collapsed in the snow." Love slaps the mattress. "What were you thinking?!"

"That you'd just put an arrow through my chest—Jesus, I got shot at twice. You did it first."

She bows her head, her eyes stinging yet again. "I had to. It was wrong not to give you a choice. It's your life, and I should have let you decide between death and Holly—or at least when I would take aim—but I ran out of time, because there was a time limit, which I also didn't mention, and I'm selfish, but as I said, you would have died, and—"

"Look at me." When she does, his mouth quirks. "I would get more dramatic about this if I weren't such a forgiving guy. So there I was with my girlfriend-to-be, expecting sparks to fly, but all I felt was the wind knocked out of me. Holly felt the same when you nailed her in the chest. It was too stormy out, so Miss Georgie had to stop Holly from bolting to Griffin's house—she wouldn't quit blubbering about him. And you ran off into the worst blizzard known to man, wearing nothing but my coat and a half yard of fabric."

"You've seen me handle winter," Love berates.

"That's not how my instinct works. Love goes into a storm, I go after her, even though I should be love struck. What the . . ." Andrew seizes her bandaged hand. "Who did this to you?"

Love admires the way he traces the dressing, like he's making sure it was done correctly. Calmness settles over her as she speaks, watching Andrew's bent head, his fingers bringing her wounded hand to life. She tells him what happened in the bookshop and the forest, that none of the arrows worked on him, that she cut herself with her own weapon, that it didn't affect her. And that she's not going to be climbing trees as she used to.

She sees the moment it hits him. His touch stalls.

Andrew lifts his head, his reverent, wintry gaze coasting along her mortal skin, reaching her mortal eyes. "Really?" he asks. "You mean it? *Really*?"

"Yes," she says.

He gives her an impish smile, sits up, and gathers her onto his lap. "I guess I'll have to keep you around," he says, jubilant and leaning his forehead against hers.

"You're not disappointed?" she queries. "I've become a plain girl."

"You'll never be plain to me, Love. You stop my heart no matter what you do, what you are. Scale houses or don't, slip through my skin or not. As long as your voice is the same, I don't care about anything else. You're stunning holding a bow or holding my hand, but I'm not gonna lie. I'd rather just hold your hand. Look out, because I'm going to make your smile my life's work. We get to take care of each other."

Who takes care of you?

He does. She does.

Love gulps back tears. He's devoted. She wraps herself around that devotion, all muscles and bones, and relishes the privilege. As much as she would rather savor the feel of his bare shoulders, they're not finished talking yet. "About that. The reason I'm human. It's—it was—another *wee* lie."

He rears back. "You've got to be shitting me. Another one?"

The truth leaks out, about the stars, the lore of love and mortality, how their kiss on the pond changed them, that she ignored the possibility, refusing to believe in it.

Andrew shakes his head. "I should have told you how I felt a while ago. All of this would have been different."

"You don't really believe that would have been better," Love says with conviction.

If he had encouraged her earlier, made her realize that he had deeper feelings than awe or desire or friendship, she might have pursued him, taken a risk, tried to inspire a love that would have changed her life. Their time might have been less complicated, less painful, but they would have missed out on other things, too—moments, words.

Perhaps the stars hoped for this. When they advised her to

match Andrew, perhaps they had a greater plan. Did they want the Fates to lose Love? Possibly they knew this would happen. Or possibly they knew nothing.

Either way, she doesn't mind. Both sound good to her.

Andrew places her bandaged hand to his heart. "Right here. It's all you."

"I don't deserve it—"

She squeals when Andrew yanks her flush against him. Against her lips, he says, "Love. Shut up."

Very well. She kisses him back, giving him all of her mouth and taking all of his. They haven't loved as flawlessly as her matches, and they're not perfectly suited to each other, and she suspects they will fight often, with his questions and her impatience, his selflessness and her arrogance, but she likes their sweet, messy love.

They won't remember all that strengthened their bond, and that makes her ache, but this isn't the end. It's another beginning. She and Andrew have only just started, and something tells her more trials are forthcoming. They're not done yet. They were never done—is anyone, ever? Loving is endless learning, is it not?

There will be more for them ahead. They will make new mistakes, strive all over again, and grow stronger. She can learn to be good for him, and he for her. That's how they will find happiness.

"I dreamed about you while I was sick," he says, pulling away.

"Did I sneak into your room?"

"I was here, wreaking havoc with your sheets and sweating worse than Griffin on game day, when you said something spectacular."

His wintry gaze, made of pewter irises and goodness, searches her face. She knows what he wants to hear.

But not yet. There's more.

She forces the words out. "We're going to forget."

It's a hushed pronouncement. There and gone, lost to the air, as their memories will soon be, as this glass cottage and its view of the stars will be. It rinses the joy from Andrew's face.

Revealing the final kernel of their story frays the moment around its edges. For once, he doesn't ask questions or probe for solutions. He looks at her, rattled but not defeated—not him, not them.

Their arms wind and slip into a hug as they let the future simmer in their minds. Love is not alone. There's that. And there's him, with his scent, and his voice sounding like it comes from the pages of a book. And his friendship. And his affection. Those things aren't going anywhere.

Andrew speaks into her shoulder. "There are loopholes, you know. We could write the memories down."

"We could," she says, then hints, "Do you truly want to do that?"

Andrew's sigh acknowledges her point. Notes would recall the shadows of memories, not everything. And it's dangerous. It's better to forget the magical parts.

"Let's make new memories," he says. "It'll be fun."

"I have no place to go," she realizes with a fright. "I'm in danger of becoming a hobo." She points to herself, disgusted. "That could be me, the town hobo."

He pretends to consider this in earnest. "You'd look cute in rags."

"Andrew!"

"I'll buy you a cup to beg for change. Gotta start somewhere."

"Humph. I will learn to fend for myself," she says. "I will not shrivel up like an urchin—"

"Shake the chaos from your head. You're not gonna live on the street. We'll figure it out, tell them you're an orphan who was passing through Ever, hitchhiking to Nowheresville. Then you got lost in the forest, and that's when we met, and I set you up in the school basement while we decided what to do. It's not like a family is gonna to waltz into town and scoop you up. You're eighteen and suffering from memory loss, which'll be true soon anyway. People will buy it. I think we can spin a tale." He kisses her chin. "It'll be okay. It's you and me. We can make up anything, do anything."

Anything. Who will she be without a tree, the leafy throne from which she looked down upon the mortal world? No archers to spar with or Guides to lead her? What else might she do?

She said her peace to the archers. They will determine what to do with her words, what to make of her story. She can't fix the world, as much as she'd hoped to, because no one can on their own, and she doesn't have to in order to make a difference. She may not have changed things in the Peaks, but she has the chance to do good in her new world. When they leave this cottage, she will borrow a pen and paper from Andrew and write ideas to herself, to inspire her when she forgets. There won't be hints about who she used to be, only thoughts about what purpose she can serve, how she can help shape people's fates here, without robbing them of their choices.

She looks at Andrew, seeing the rest of the answer staring back at her. Above all, the greatest thing she can do is love someone as honestly as possible.

She can do it as a girl named Love. Or a girl named Lily. That much is for her to decide.

"Then we have only one more task," she says with a pang.

The Fates took away her blood-stained dress and her bow

and ... Wait. She owned a bow? What was she doing with a bow?

Love's thoughts mist, but she sets her teeth hard, then harder. She was matchmaking, that's what. She was a matchmaker. Andrew was her next victim.

Relief flows through her. Of course, she remembers her bow. She had good aim, and the arrows were made of ... of iron, she thinks. Like one of the other archers, she's certain.

Be that as it may, the bow and dress have been taken. Yet there's another memento that could trigger the past and must go, just to be careful.

She loathes the chore, and Andrew loathes it, but it has to happen. With reluctant fingers, she plucks Andrew's note from where she left it on the nightstand. The paper is still folded into an origami bird, their own little piece of magic inscribed with words from the hour they met. Words she ripped up and put back together.

They both know they'll have to destroy his notebook, too, all the things he wrote about her, but that will have to wait for later. One memory at a time.

They light the hearth. Andrew stands behind Love, encircling her waist, his chin propped on her shoulder, his bare skin against hers. Together, they toss the paper into the fire, watching a thread of orange blaze its edges until it splits and curls like fingers waving good-bye. Andrew hears her sniffle and wipes the stupid tears that have escaped from her eyes.

"So ...," she says.

"So ...," he echoes.

"If I say that spectacular thing now, do you think we'll remember it later?"

"I'd welcome the challenge."

With all the tenderness she feels, she whispers, "I love you,

you foolish mortal."

"Welcome to my world," he answers wistfully, his lips pecking her ear. "It loves you, too."

EPILOGUE

The stars are out. They're quiet in the darkness, blooming with light as though they have minds of their own.

Lily grins to herself. These kinds of strange thoughts tend to bustle in her head at the most unexpected times—not that it bothers her.

A pine-scented current of air rides through the woods. Standing at the bridge in the forest, she gazes up at the towering trees as the urge to scale a particular trunk grips her. She assesses the thickness of the branches, debating how much weight they can hold. She wouldn't make it that far up without scraping a knee or twisting an ankle—again. It happened to her before when she attempted to master those heights.

Her boyfriend calls her stubborn. She has the scars to prove it: marks on her elbow from when she threw a tremendous fit and swiped dishes off his stepfather's dining table, all because Andrew had accused her of "overreacting" to something—she cannot recall what. Oddly, the concept of overreacting had momentarily confused her.

For his part, Andrew matched her temper, grabbing the only surviving plate off the table and hurling it against a wall. Afterward, they ended up laughing hysterically.

Her other scar is a mystery. It's a slash across the inside of her palm, but she doesn't know where she got it. A vague image bubbles in Lily's mind of another girl with scarred hands, and another one with scarred arms. Maybe those girls lived in the orphanage where Lily came from—wherever that is, for the bubble pops a second later, the images gone. Something happened in the past to wipe her memory clean, like a snowplow pushing through slush. All she knows is that she was booted from the orphanage when she turned eighteen and hitchhiked into Ever twelve months ago, a place with old-fashioned streetlamps, quaint buildings, and cords of colorful winter lights hanging above the streets.

She's smart, too. Someone must have educated her. It's the sole explanation for why she has a polished vocabulary compared to the other kids here. Maybe she was born into a regal world, and as the black sheep, she was disowned by a grand family.

The past is a murky pit. Frustrating as it is, it's also a consolation.

Lily snuggles into her black coat and smoothes over the cobalt-blue beret that Miss Georgie insisted on buying her. When Andrew introduced them, the woman was flabbergasted.

She squinted. "You're Lily?"

It was like she expected a Lily, but not *this* Lily.

Miss Georgie recovered quickly, accepted some private assumption that she'd gotten wrong, and surveyed Lily. "Well, my kiddo has good taste," she said, slipping her arm through Lily's in a motherly fashion. "I hear you need a place to stay."

That's how Miss Georgie's house became Lily's home. Home, where they stay up late sipping tea by candlelight and talking about Lily's schooling and her blog, *Sweet Messy Love*.

She created the website eight months ago, after meeting a couple in the coffee house in town and falling into a conversation with them about how they met. The two men were eager to recap their courtship to a newcomer, Lily discovered a passion for real-life romances, and she came up with the idea to celebrate those romances after rereading a note she'd supposedly written to herself before she came to Ever: a curious list of ambitions for the future, all having to do with love itself.

She'd vaguely recalled debating the topic with Andrew, some time in the past, while they were lying in the snow. It was a heated debate, and she was riled up—to this day, Lily's still uncertain why she took a random subject so personally. They'd talked about whether or not fate existed, whether people controlled their destinies, their feelings, their passions.

Andrew had said to her, "A messy love is a real love."

Lily channeled that thought into a place where she collects teen love stories, interviews, articles, and videos. She's created pages for BFF confessions, love letters between admirers, and for summer flings to search for each other and reconnect. The blog has evolved into a place where visitors ask her for relationship advice. She talks about first kisses and sex and break-ups. She has a rather stout opinion, but what visitors do with her advice is up to them. Her little project has grown, with more followers than she ever imagined. It could become something big. Eventually, she'll quit being anonymous.

Anonymity used to be her salvation. In the very beginning, Lily cowered from the people in Ever, overwhelmed by their attention, inexplicably afraid of couples who seemed familiar but couldn't be. Her behavior was strange back then, so very strange.

The snow layering the forest shimmers beneath the moon and stars. The temperature drops, and Lily closes her lids to enjoy it.

Snow crunches beneath a pair of boots. Her lids flip open,

eyes focusing on the powdered branches above her. There's a distinct scent, young but masculine—and close.

How curious. She recognizes this moment as though she's reliving it, except on the ground instead of . . . Where?

A pair of arms slip around her waist from behind. Tepid puffs of breath caress her neck. The air smells of mint.

"I knew I'd find you here," he says.

"The trees are pretty at night," she says. "They don't look as tall in the dark."

"Huh. So you've been thinking about climbing one, have you?"

She never fools him. These woods, this bridge where they stand, are special places. The bridge being the second place they ever spoke.

The first time was in another part of the woods. He came upon her—or she came upon him, depending on which of them tells the story. Lily can't say what on earth she was doing out here, but the naughty side of her had decided to pick a fight with the pensive side of him, and she jumped out of nowhere to scare the poor boy.

Except he wasn't scared. He gave her his winter coat to keep her warm, such a selfless thing to do. Lily thinks she may have loved him immediately for that.

Andrew turns her around to face him and rubs his nose against hers. He looks tired from a day of Lit classes at the local college and then a shift at the bookstore. "What are you thinking about?"

"Always asking your questions," she huffs.

"You're my big, beautiful question mark," he teases. "I want to find you out."

"You already know me."

"I do."

Does he? When she doesn't know everything about herself? Well, that's fine. Their story still has a long way to go. They've had a little of *then*, but they have a lot more of *now*. There's plenty of time, and there's no rush to know everything, if it's even possible to know that much.

Whatever history they make, it will be real and mythical, fact and fiction. It will belong to them.

She winds her arms around his shoulders. She loves his shoulders, loves the word *love*, and loves attaching that word to him. She may be a simple girl who can't climb trees, but she can love.

"Hi, my only one," she says.

"Hey," he flirts, his eyes dancing. "Kiss me."

"Later. I was—"

"Screw later."

He swoops in, but she places a hand on his chest to stop him. She wants to finish her thought, and Andrew knows she doesn't like being interrupted. It's a constant thorn whenever they bicker.

"I was thinking about this bridge," she says, then holds up her palms. Andrew rests his own palms against hers and waits. "It could have been a secret place once, where people from different worlds met, crossed the threshold, and found a way to be together. Might that be possible?"

Andrew grins and laces their fingers tight. "Yeah, it's possible."

"Good," she says, pleased.

He tugs her forward. "Come with me. I have a surprise for you."

Lily is about to remind him of the kiss he wanted, but the air shifts. A wall of it moves, gets thicker, colder. The sensation comes from some distance behind her, and she wants to turn and look, but the hairs along her arms stand up, warning her not to.

When has she ever listened to reason? She cranes her head. Nothing. Just stars and trees and blue-white-silver snow.

Except it's not nothing. It's like being watched. Something with a heartbeat, a pulse that drums like a set of fingers, is watching them. Watching her.

The chill isn't dangerous. It's lonely. Lost.

Protective?

It strokes her cheek and makes her throat clog for whatever it is that yearns, that looks out for her. She wishes she could answer it, stroke it back with her fingers.

"Lily?" Andrew asks. "You okay?"

"I am now," she says to the forest, hoping the chill heard.

Or it's her imagination. It has to be.

Just in case, Lily raises her free hand toward the woods, not quite a wave but hopefully a comfort. With the other hand clasped in her boyfriend's, she lets herself be led away into town, aware she won't feel that rush again, and that soon enough she'll forget it.

⌒

Andrew covers Lily's eyes as he guides her into her bedroom. Her arms pitch out in front of her, grasping nothing but air.

She warns him, "Orphans don't fancy surprises."

"Whatever. You're not an orphan anymore. Keep walking."

Grudgingly, she stumbles forward, trying to wrestle his hands from her eyes. "Release me," she says.

"Behave yourself."

"Then talk. Talk to me."

"I'm going to surprise you with something you'll like. And after that . . ." He lets the sentence hang open for a moment, provoking an influx of wicked thoughts. "I'll touch—"

"Let me go. Let me go this instant!"

He removes his palms from her lids. She is about to spin around and attack him with her lips when she sees what he's done. Her bedroom in Miss Georgie's house—their house—is a treasure. Miss Georgie let Lily decorate it however she wanted, a privilege she's certain that she didn't have before she arrived in Ever. There's a bed tucked into a white wood alcove, with a recessed bookshelf behind her pillows. On the wall, there's a faint sketch of a girl wielding a bow—Lily has a thing for archery, even though she's never tried it in her life and can't afford lessons. A telescope, salvaged from Miss Georgie's attic, faces a window surrounded by a cord of white lights bursting to life.

Best of all, Andrew's surprise: Above the bed, five ornaments hang at different lengths from the ceiling. Snowflakes, silver and white, their shapes reminding her of starbursts. A constellation.

Homesickness rises from the ashes. It's a happy sort of pain. Although she can't remember where this feeling comes from, it proves that she did have something in the past worth remembering.

Lily crawls onto the bed, tapping each snowflake with her finger. She finds that special one dangling in the center. Aside from her coat, pajamas, and list of ambitions, this tiny scuffed ornament was all she had with her when Andrew brought her to his house.

The mattress caves under his weight. "Do you like it?"

She nods. "It's magical."

He shrugs. "Your bed is a magical place."

His hint casts a spell over her. Grinning at her expression, he stands and backs up.

She heads toward him. "Where do you think you're going?"

Andrew holds out his arms. "Come and get me."

She sprints after him. He darts into the living room, knocking over a stack of jazz records, but she leaps across the couch and cuts him off by the kitchen. Her feet smack the ground as she lands in front of him. Shrieking like a damsel, he averts her grasp and whips back around, taking refuge behind a desk. Laughing in shock at the high-pitched noise he made, Lily halts on the other side.

They flatten their hands on the surface. Andrew jerks to the left, but she matches him, blocking his escape.

He jerks to the right. So does she.

His lower lip puckers as he blows the bangs from his forehead. Her mirth vanishes.

Andrew lurches across the desk, grabs the back of her head, and kisses her. It's hard and swift. She blinks, dazed, then grunts when she realizes he's gotten away.

Her bedroom door slams shut behind him. Two seconds later, it blows open from the force of her shove. Her eyes scan the room, landing on the closet door.

Ahh.

Lily marches forward. The closet whips open and Andrew barrels out, once again dodging her grip. He knocks a reading chair in her path, which she pushes out of the way. The sound of it crashing to the floor causes him to turn in surprise.

She tackles him, the impact sending them tumbling onto the bed. The lights around the window blink, flickering off the walls, off the snowflakes, off her and Andrew, making their bodies flash.

"It's like the lights are serenading us," she says.

"So what do we do about it?"

"We humor them."

Which is why, two minutes later, they're naked and clutching each other beneath her sheets. They've discovered touch in its many facets. The wrong touches, like when they argue, and she's stewing or he's giving her the silent treatment, and a mere brush of clothing is annoying. Or when he plucks her chin and forces her to look at him, which makes her even madder than she already was. Or when they're out with their friends, Holly and Griffin, and Lily wipes a crumb off Andrew's mouth as though he's a "fucking infant," and he gets embarrassed.

And the right touches, like when he squeezes her hand to calm her down, or when she smoothes the bangs from his forehead to soothe him.

And kisses. The kind that sizzle. The kind that leave a sweet aftertaste. He's learned that goose bumps shimmy across her skin when he licks the seam of her lips. She's learned that sucking on his tongue will make him sigh into her mouth.

Their bodies have learned the pleasurable suffering of *slow* and the instant, delirious rush of *quick*. She knows that clasping his backside while he's above her will make his hips twitch. He knows the exact rhythm to render her helpless.

Tonight, it starts with his hands. He braves them between her thighs. His finger presses on that button of hers, and her head lolls back, straining for more, more, more of that ache. Her eyes fall shut and—*one*, then *two*, then *oh, yes, three*—his fingers pry her apart and sweep through. He picks up on the signs, on her noises and the circular motion of her waist.

She dwells on their first time. Most of the details are clear, while other parts of that night are blank. It happened days after they met, when she had no home. They barely knew each other then, yet they discovered so much, so fast, so deep. They were friends, and friendship wove itself into *that* night.

Lily can't recall all the details about those days with him. But that kiss on the frozen pond and the things they did afterward? She remembers, inside and out, how they gave themselves up in the woods.

They managed to stay warm despite the snow. Maybe they didn't notice it. Or she didn't.

Tonight, it ends with the rest of Andrew's body. The lights flare brighter as he covers Lily and slips into that soft, dark place inside her. He rocks forward, his fingers clutching the edge of the mattress for leverage. Love's spine bows off the bed, her legs quivering around his waist, drawing him deeper into her, her hips rolling with his in an exquisite pace.

This is it, she thinks. *This is a loving touch.*

It's their chests sliding, their heartbeats slamming, her fingers scraping through his hair, his precious smile as he bends to kiss her, hot and sweet and open. It's the sounds they make, gaining momentum and then hardening into cries—selfish and selfless, take and give. It's Lily's hand finding Andrew's on the pillow, holding tight while they let go.

It's them lying together, gazing at starry snowflakes hanging from the sky of her ceiling. It's him speaking into her hair. "You once said you wanted to sleep beneath them," Andrew explains.

"You listened," Lily whispers.

"Someone had to."

He does. He listens. He sees her.

And that's the nicest part. Because now she knows what that feels like.

Thank you for reading Love & Andrew's story!

Ready for Anger?
Get *Torn* (Selfish Myths #2)!

⌒

Join my mailing list to get exclusive content,
advanced updates, and details about new books at
www.nataliajaster.com/newsletter

ACKNOWLEDGMENTS

Where to begin. I cannot imagine a more fitting heroine for my first book than a girl named Love. I'm so stoked that I got to spend time with her. Hope you guys are, too.

Like her, this little tale was created with the help of a constellation of people. Thank you to my editor, Lindsey Alexander, for bringing sparkle to these pages. To my beautiful betas and friends, Court, El, Michelle, and Nicole. To Angela, Kerri, and Susan for their publishing advice.

To my rockstar parents for their patience, even when I didn't know what I was doing, or how long it would take.

To Roman, the brightest muse of all. I like being matched with you.

And to my readers, longtime and new, from the world of YA and from the fandom (you know which one). Thank you for your enthusiasm and support. You make this one stellar gig.

It was fun playing storyteller for you. And I can't wait to do it again!

ABOUT NATALIA

Natalia Jaster is the fantasy author of the Foolish Kingdoms and Selfish Myths series.

She loves to dream up settings that are realistic yet magical. She loves when raw angst collides with lyrical beauty, and when sweetness escalates to hotness. And she definitely loves treading the line between YA and NA.

She's also a total fool for first-kiss scenes, fanfiction, libraries, and starry nights.

COME SAY HI! ♥

Join Natalia's mailing list: nataliajaster.com/newsletter
Bookbub: bookbub.com/authors/natalia-jaster
Facebook: facebook.com/NataliaJasterAuthor
Goodreads: goodreads.com/nataliajaster
Instagram: instagram.com/nataliajaster
Tumblr: andshewaits.tumblr.com

See the boards for Natalia's novels on Pinterest:
pinterest.com/andshewaits

Made in United States
Troutdale, OR
05/13/2024